# THE EX BETWEEN US

## NICOLA MARSH

## BOOKS BY NICOLA MARSH

# THE EX BETWEEN US

## NICOLA MARSH

*bookouture*

Published by Bookouture in 2022

An imprint of Storyfire Ltd.
Carmelite House
50 Victoria Embankment
London EC4Y 0DZ

www.bookouture.com

ISBN: 978-1-80314-677-5
eBook ISBN: 978-1-80314-676-8

*For Jen, my oldest friend. You haven't changed a bit in the four-plus decades we've known each other. Still one of the sweetest people I know.*

# PROLOGUE

I value friendship.

My friends have seen me through the worst times of my life, and the best. Shared confidences breed closeness. Tragedies too.

People move in and out of my life in ebbs and flows, like the tide along the Californian coast not far from where I used to live. I take the changes in my stride. Welcome and embrace them.

But the thing with friendships is, how well do we really know those closest to us?

A smile can hide a multitude of sins. Envy. Resentment. Evil.

A hug can constrict rather than comfort. Tight. Binding. Claustrophobic.

A helping hand can support just as easily as shove you off the edge of a cliff.

I trust my friends.

I think they have my back.

Instead, they stick a knife in it.

But I'm resilient. I've bounced back from worse betrayals.

And when you know your friends are actually your adversaries, it's a whole new game.

I thought I'd seen it all.

Until this summer, when everything changed.

Time to level up.

Time to show my best buds I'm not going to tolerate their deception.

Time to get my revenge.

# ONE

## ABIGAIL

"I can't watch this."

I raise my hands to my eyes and cover them, which might've been effective if I hadn't heard Rob zip his suitcase, ramming home the fact my only child is heading off to college.

"Mom, stop being so melodramatic."

"I'm not. I'm hiding my eyes so you can't see my tears."

"Guilt trip, much?" Rob gently lowers my hands and presses a kiss to my forehead, like I used to do to him after every fall as a rambunctious four-year-old with perpetually scraped knees. "You can't expect me to live here forever."

"Yes, I can. It's a mother's prerogative." I fake a sniffle and he rolls his eyes, but his smile brings out the dimples I used to dip the tip of my finger into until he wouldn't let me anymore, around the age of eight. "I can't believe you're making me an empty nester."

"And I can't believe you're wasting my last hour at home by making me feel bad."

That snaps me out of my funk. Rob is my world. We've been a team for a long time. Even when Callan's around, Rob's closer to me than his dad, as if he senses Cal can't commit to anything or anyone. Smart kid, my boy.

"Sorry, honey." I press my hand to his cheek, the scrape of stubble against my palm a reminder he isn't a little boy any longer. "Jo should be here soon and we'll have your favorite charcuterie board and dessert before you head off."

"Sounds good." He hesitates, his gaze sliding away for a moment before refocusing on me. "At the risk of making you really bawl, I just want to say thanks, Mom, for everything. You've been amazing and I'm going to miss you."

"Oh heck," I mutter, pulling him in for a hug as the first tears trickle down my cheeks. "I love you so much, my beautiful boy."

Rather than squirm away as I expect, his arms tighten around me, infusing me with the strength I'm going to need to cope with his absence. Not that he's going far. UCLA is just over three hours from Fort Chester, but to me it feels like he's off to Mars.

We're close and I'm luckier than lots of moms who have to take a plane to visit their kids at college, but I know the minute he walks out the door shortly, everything changes. He'll meet new people, have new adventures, explore new horizons. I want that for him, but I'm also terrified I'll lose him to some faceless girl who'll break his heart.

Silly, I know, because I can't protect him forever. But he'll always be my baby so it feels like I'm losing a piece of myself.

I cling to him, not wanting to let go, but he releases me all too soon and at the glimpse of tears in his eyes, I glance away. We need time to pull ourselves together before Jo arrives. My best friend is too pragmatic for soppy goodbyes. She'll tell us to buck up and stop sniveling, which is exactly why I invited her to Rob's farewell.

Besides, she loves her godson as much as I do and would kill me if I hadn't asked her to spend time with him before he heads off. Jo is like the sister I never had and would tell me off in no uncertain terms. Her straight talking is one of the things I admire about her, but I wouldn't want to get on her bad side. She has this way of looking at a person that eviscerates and I'm glad I've only been on the receiving end once.

The day I blurted the truth about Rob's paternity.

"It's a shame Dad couldn't make it," Rob says, his sarcasm accompanied with a smirk. "Where is he anyway?"

"Doing a shoot down in New Mexico."

I don't tell Rob I called Cal three times and sent several texts to get him to come home to his son's send-off. I may have a low opinion of Cal but I don't want to disparage him to his son. I never have, no matter how many times Cal let us down over the years. His precious career has always come first. He missed Rob's first day at preschool because he'd been photographing some rare iguana festival in Florida. He missed Rob's first baseball game because he'd been deep in the Amazon snapping photos of pythons. He missed Rob's first high school football game while taking pics of snow bunnies frolicking in Aspen.

I could mentally recite every single time he hasn't been here for his son but that never ends well: usually in me taking a bottle of vodka out of the freezer.

"Typical," Rob says, sounding flippant rather than disappointed. "I'm not surprised he never married you, Mom. He's wedded to his camera."

"Poor camera."

We share a conspiratorial smile. I gave up expecting anything from Cal a long time ago and his son did too.

"It's a shame Tom couldn't make it either, but he sent me this goofy video." Rob slides his cell out of his pocket and swipes it open. "He's in New York at some swank new boutique hotel."

As Tom pops up on the screen, with the iconic Flatiron Building in the background, I can't help but smile. Tom is Cal's best friend and Rob's unofficial godfather. He's the first person we met after moving to Fort Chester eighteen years ago and he's been an integral part of our lives since.

Like Cal, he's rarely home, moving from place to place as a travel writer. But it doesn't go unnoticed that Tom took the time to send Rob this video when Cal hasn't even contacted his son.

We watch it together. It's brief, a few lame jokes about what not to do at college, but I see how much it means to Rob. "Tom is a good guy."

"He's the best," Rob says, sliding the cell back into his pocket. "I'll miss him."

It's a glaring omission that Rob doesn't say he'll miss his father. I don't blame him, but I want his final hour at home to be happy so I won't say anything about Cal's complete disregard for his son. "Jo should be here any minute. Let's head to the kitchen."

"Good, I'm starving." Rob slings his arm across my shoulders, and I resist the urge to snuggle into him again. If I do, I may not let him go.

There's a loud knock on the back door as we enter the kitchen and I glimpse Jo peering through the window. She has a key and usually lets herself in, so I know why she's knocking. She wants to make sure I'm not a blubbering mess and if I am, to give me time to compose myself.

She waves when she catches sight of us, her face lighting up as it usually does when she spies Rob. I'm lucky having a friend like her because if anything ever happens to me, I know I can rely on Jo to be a stand-in mom. Cal probably wouldn't put down his camera long enough to attend my funeral, let alone stick around to support his son.

I give a little shake. I'm not prone to maudlin thoughts, but as a single mom I like to think my son would be cared for if I wasn't around.

"Mom, are you sure you're okay?" Rob asks, his glance concerned as he crosses the kitchen to unlock the back door.

"Yeah." This time, I give an exaggerated shake. "Don't mind me. Just trying to cast off my funk."

Rob's smile is knowing as he opens the door. He's used to my crazy mom antics. While I'd never admit it to Jo, I think Rob's on equal par with her in the best friend stakes. Our bond is strong, better than I could've ever anticipated. He didn't go through a rebellious teen phase. Instead, he confides in me, and I know I'm blessed. I sometimes wonder if his consideration stems from having to step up and be the man of the house a few years ago when Cal and me officially split up.

I never put that burden on him, but Rob's always been an intuitive kid and when Cal's absences became more frequent, Rob became more considerate. Small things at first, like taking out the trash without being asked and mopping the floors, to cooking a home-made spaghetti bolognese for me despite having a heavy homework load and football practice.

I love him so much and want him to embrace everything college has to offer, but I also wish I could lock him in his room and throw away the key.

"Hey, Robbie." Jo embraces him, her blue eyes wide as they connect with mine over his shoulder. She's stoic, but I see this is emotional for her too. "I brought supplies."

She releases him and picks up a hessian bag from the doorstep. "There's a bunch of healthy stuff in here so you don't starve at college. Quinoa, hemp seeds, goji berries, pepitas, figs, white and black chia seeds."

Rob stares at her in shock. One thing my best friend and my son share is a love of junk food, the greasier the better. Any time

I've had to work late over the years, Jo would take Rob out for burgers and fries. It has become their thing.

I can see Jo's struggling to keep a straight face and I'm grateful to her for trying to lighten the mood.

"Uh, thanks, Jo," Rob says, sounding as confused as he looks, when Jo bursts out laughing and thrusts the bag at him.

"Why don't you take a look at what's really in there?"

She's still laughing as Rob peers in the bag and breaks into a grin.

"Let me guess," I say. "Crisps. Salted nuts. Chocolate chip cookies. Cupcakes. Cheese balls."

"All the good stuff." Rob pulls Jo in for another hug. "Thanks, Jo. This is great."

"You can never have too many snacks for the road, and for when you first get there and find your bearings."

I don't tell Jo that Rob and I already spent an evening online checking out all the nearest food joints around campus. She's trying to be upbeat, and I appreciate it. She knows I'm a mess inside.

"Are you all packed?" Jo wraps an arm around my son's waist and rests her head on his shoulder like I've seen her do countless times before. It warms my heart. "Any room in your suitcase for one overprotective godmother who's going to miss you like crazy?"

"I'm not that far away," Rob says, faking exasperation when I know he's as fond of Jo as she is of him. "Let me get settled, then you can come visit."

"Deal." Jo releases him and casts me a quick glance. "Is Mom doing okay?"

"Mom is trying to put on a brave face," I say, pretending to knuckle my eyes. "I'll wait until my baby has left before falling apart."

"Will you two quit it?" Rob shakes his head and opens the

fridge to pull out the charcuterie board I prepared earlier. It has all his favorites: salami, prosciutto, double smoked ham, goat's cheese, Camembert, Brie, fig paste, purple grapes, dried apricots, walnuts, and stuffed peppers. "You're ruining my appetite."

Jo and I snort in unison, then laugh. My son's love affair with food is well known in this household. The only way I knew he was sick growing up was when he didn't eat.

"There's a pitcher of Mojito mocktails in there too," I say, pointing at the fridge. "Unless Jo wants to add white rum to hers and turn it into a real cocktail?"

"Mocktail is fine for me." Jo sits next to Rob at the table and snaffles an apricot. "Are you sure there's nothing I can do, Robbie? Anything you need?"

"All good, thanks." He squeezes her arm. "I will miss you, though."

Jo holds up her hand. "Stop. I refuse to weep."

"We'll wait until he leaves, then add rum to our Mojitos, and blame our cry-fest on the alcohol." I fill three glasses and hand them around.

"Good idea." Jo raises her glass and we follow suit. "To Robert James McFee. May you slay it at college and make all your dreams come true."

"I'll drink to that," Rob says, clinking his glass against ours.

I don't add anything to Jo's toast, because I can't get a word past the lump of sorrow in my throat.

My baby is leaving.

While I'm happy for him, I can't help but imagine the lonely days ahead, when I should be excited for the future after recently landing a prized job as a fashion coordinator for a local film studio that supplies projects to an up-and-coming streaming service. My colleagues have told me that my new life will be filled with film sets, award ceremonies and glamorous launches, but coming home to an empty house will be tough.

It has always been Rob and me against the world. A dynamic duo. A team. I'm going to miss him like crazy.

When I find Rob and Jo staring at me quizzically, I raise my glass too and clink it against theirs, forcing a smile while I struggle not to bawl.

# TWO

## JO

Robbie left an hour ago and as expected, Abi's inconsolable. Not even two rum-filled Mojitos has snapped her out of it.

Not that I blame her. Robbie's her world and she must be gutted to watch him drive away, knowing he'll only come home for Thanksgiving, Christmas, and the other holidays. I love that kid like mad and I'll miss him, so I can only imagine how Abi's feeling. She needs a distraction, because if we stay here drinking, she'll end up either crying herself to sleep or pacing an empty house with insomnia.

"Go take a shower and get dressed." I pluck the third half-drunk cocktail out of her hand. "We're going out."

"Don't be ridiculous, Jo." She points to her puffy eyes. "Do I look like I want to go out?"

"That's why we're going. It's not a question of wanting to go, we have to." I pull a face. "I'm not having you sit around here all night, alternating between crying and drinking. Let me take you out and cheer you up."

"Nothing's going to achieve that," she mutters, but I glimpse gratitude in her eyes. "My baby has flown the nest and I'm not handling it very well."

"You're doing okay." I pull her in for a quick hug and it results in another crying jag as she clings to me, sobbing into my shoulder. "Actually, scratch that."

I hear a muffled laugh as intended and she eases away, her smile watery. "What would I do without you, Jo?"

"I have no idea."

Though I do. Abi has fallen on her feet her entire life. Having the perfect parents who doted on her and supported her even when she fell pregnant at seventeen. Parents who helped with Robbie after he was born, who didn't chastise her for not attending college, who accepted Callan into their family even when they saw he wasn't father material. Landing the best part-time jobs—online influencer, function center hostess, boutique manager—allowing her to be a present mom too. And having the most gorgeous guy in school tied to her for life because she got knocked up by him.

I like to think she needs me. Our friendship is strong, despite a few hiccups along the way. We've been through a lot together, and the day Rob was born and I took one look at his tiny squished-up face—and fell in love—I knew I wanted to be a valued member of their family. Having Abi ask me to be godmother, a role I take very seriously, means we're closer than some families. I've done the right thing relegating the past to the past, because Abi's friendship means the world to me.

"What are you thinking?" Abi touches my arm and I realize I've been silently mulling.

"About the first time I saw Robbie."

It's a half-truth, because my best friend doesn't need to know how I still think about the past on occasion and how it hasn't got any easier over the years that she has a baby and I never will.

I love Abi and Rob but as I've watched him grow from a cute baby to a gorgeous kid to the striking young man he is today, I've died a little on the inside.

What if I'd fallen pregnant as a teen? Before the endometriosis ruined my chances of conceiving. Would I be leading a charmed life instead of grooming dogs for a living, dating extensively but never finding the right guy, and wishing I had someone to share my life with?

No good comes of analyzing my life or wishing the past could've been different, so I force a smile. "But let's not talk about your amazing son right now, because we'll both end up crying, so go take that shower, put on something fabulous, and let's go out."

I expect her to refuse again but she surprises me. "Where?"

"How about your favorite retro bar?"

Her eyebrows shoot up. "You hate that place."

"Yeah, but you love it, and tonight's about cheering you up so I'm willing to make the sacrifice." I pat myself on the back. "Because that's the kind of friend I am. Willing to listen to corny eighties hits played in an era when we were just born, surrounded by kitschy movie memorabilia, all because you have bad taste and like that stuff."

Her eyes sparkle with amusement rather than tears for the first time in the last sixty minutes. "You know my folks played seventies and eighties stuff constantly when I was growing up and that's why I like it."

"Yeah, I know," I say softly, seeing the exact moment the tears return. Abi's parents died in a car accident three years ago, leaving her extremely well-off and able to afford to maintain this five-bedroom modern Spanish stucco, Rob's college tuition, and anything else her heart desires. She doesn't have to work but wants to, another thing I admire about her. "Okay, enough reminiscing. Go get ready."

She salutes. "Yes, ma'am," but I've done something right because she stands and heads for her bedroom rather than wallowing about being an empty nester and the loss of her folks.

I'm happy to do this for Abi. She's supported me through tough times over the years—breaking up with Dave, my long-term boyfriend of three years, losing my favorite job as a veterinarian assistant, and the worst, receiving the devastating news I'd never be a mom—and friends stick together through good and bad.

It's what we do. Abi and Jo against the world.

# THREE

## JO

THEN

I hear my ankle snap as I land awkwardly after attempting a mid-air pirouette. The pain is instant and overwhelming, so intense black spots dance before my eyes before coalescing, and I wake to find my sadistic ballet teacher tapping my cheek none too gently and a crowd of students looking down at me.

"Joelle! Are you okay?" She's staring at me in horror, probably petrified she'll get sued despite Mom having to sign a waiver before I could take this stupid class I have no interest in. "You blacked out for a moment."

"Excruciating pain will do that to you," I mutter, and some of the girls giggle. The rest, who take their ballet far too seriously, have already turned away to return to the barre and resume practice.

"Let me help you up." Madame Suzette takes hold of my shoulders and pulls too hard, making me yelp. "Sorry, *chérie*. I'll be gentler, *oui?*"

Another thing that annoys me about this class. Madame

Suzette was born in San Francisco, same as me, but fakes a French heritage for her ballet business. I know, because I overheard Mom talking to Dad once about researching her background and Madame's only link to France is a grandmother who'd migrated from Paris to the United States eons ago.

I grit my teeth as she assists me to standing, pain shooting from my ankle up my leg. "Give me a minute," I say, dragging in steadying breaths so I don't cry. The last place I want to shed tears is in front of a bunch of prima donnas who think they'll be dancing on stages around the world, when most of them shouldn't be wearing pointe shoes.

Madame Suzette makes a disapproving tsk-tsk sound. "Come sit, then I'll call your mother."

The pain in my ankle is nothing compared to the throb in my head at the thought of what Mom will say when she hears what I've done. She's relentless in pushing me to practice at home in the vain hope I'll land the lead in the school's upcoming recital. It never would've happened anyway but now I have no chance and if my ankle wasn't the size of a grapefruit already, I'd be dancing with joy.

With a little luck, this injury will end my ballet career.

Though "career" is laughable considering I was born with two left feet, something my famous dancer mom has never accepted. Mom thinks I'm lazy and unmotivated rather than accepting the truth: I'm talentless. If I had any promise I would've showed it by twelve, and at eight, my sister Talia is a prodigy compared to me.

It doesn't matter how many hours I spend practicing my *arabesque*, I can't get my back leg to straighten perfectly. When an *adagio* is called for, grace and fluidity desert me. And my supporting leg refuses to co-operate during a *battlement fondu*.

I loathe the barre in our basement, where Mom spends countless hours standing over me like a tyrannical choreographer. I'd barely grown out of toddlerhood when the torture started. She'd yell *"changement"* over and over, a classical term meaning jump, or *coupe*, where one foot undercuts the other, or *entrechat*, when I'd jump in the air and scissor my legs in a braiding action. It had been ridiculous to try and master these complicated steps as a child but Mom never backed down. When I wasn't practicing at home she'd be watching my every move here, lamenting Madame Suzette's lack of nous as a teacher after every class rather than admit the truth.

I'm a lousy dancer.

But I persist because I crave Mom's approval, which is why I let her drag me to these classes despite my reluctance. I'm biding my time, knowing she'll soon give up as Talia blossoms more. And despite the pain in my ankle, I'm hoping this unexpected but fortuitous accident will expedite my retirement from ballet.

Madame Suzette supports me on one side as I hobble to the nearest chair. I can take a little weight on my ankle so while the pain's bad, it's probably not broken. Madame lowers me into a chair and says, "You wait here, I'll call Dolly."

With a name like Dolly, could my mom have been anything but a dancer? She'd graced stages from Broadway to the West End in London, a natural at whatever style a show required, though ballet was her first love. My dad met her at an after-party in Manhattan, a hanger-on friend of a producer. They were mismatched, my mom tall and lithe with long strawberry-blonde hair and eyes the color of a lush lawn, and my dad an inch shorter than her, with curly black hair, brown eyes too close together and a perpetual upturn at the corners of his mouth that makes him look like he's smirking all the time.

Yet they're still madly in love and I sometimes wonder if the only reason they had me was in the vain hope I'd follow in Mom's footsteps. And because I'm such a letdown, they had

Talia. With every passing day I resent them more and more. My parents dote on Talia. She's the smarter, prettier, extroverted version of me. Talia inherited Mom's gorgeous strawberry-blonde hair, mine's orange, the kind that stands out and not in a good way. Talia got the green eyes, mine are a murky combination of my folk's green and brown so kind of like a swamp. Very unattractive. And I inherited Dad's vertically challenged genes whereas Talia's already an inch shorter than me and she's four years younger.

Despite all this, I try my best to fit into my family. To love them as I'm supposed to. To be a good daughter, despite being an obvious second best. To be a cool big sister to a precocious brat who knows she's the favorite and never lets me forget it. But some days it's tough and I know that with me out of action, a welcome reprieve from dancing, I'll be stuck at home for those ten hours a week when I'd usually be at dance class or practicing. That's a lot of extra time to put up with my family's disappointment in me.

There's a light tap on my shoulder and I look up to see Madame Suzette looking down on me with obvious pity. "I'm sorry, *chérie*, your mother can't make it, and your papa is busy also. You will need to go to the doctor in a taxi."

I bark out a laugh that startles Madame and she hurries away like she thinks my insanity is contagious. Of course my parents can't come to pick up their injured daughter. Their other, more important child had an audition after school today and that's where they'll be, cheering on the prodigy while the big fat disappointment has to drag her sorry ass to a doctor by herself.

I should be used to this by now but I'm not. It never gets easier, being second best.

# FOUR

## ABIGAIL

As I throw my hands up in the air and shimmy to an old Duran Duran hit, I smile at Jo, who must be feeling really sorry for me if she's dancing.

In the twenty-three years I've known her, Jo has never danced, an aversion born from being forced to as a kid. When we met on the first day of junior high, I admired her stance, tall and aloof as she stood by herself near the lockers and knew instantly she must do ballet. I'd been ballet mad as a young kid but could never emulate the graceful posture of my teacher and her best students.

That day, after I'd defended Jo against the bitchiest cheer-leader in school, we'd bonded, and our friendship hasn't waned —discounting the time she didn't speak to me for months in senior year. So for her to be on the dance floor now, swiveling her hips and waving her arms around, I know she's the best friend I could ever wish for.

"Want a drink?" she mouths and I shake my head. Dancing is good. It's the perfect distraction from dwelling on the empty house I'll be returning to later tonight and as long as I stay on the dance floor, I don't have to think. Besides, the music is so loud I can't think even if I want to.

She holds up a hand indicating she'll be back in five and I sigh, knowing I'll have to follow her rather than be left on the dance floor alone. However, as I take a few steps behind her, careful not to jostle anyone, a guy is pushed in front of me and would've stumbled if I didn't instinctively reach out to steady him.

"Thanks," he says. At least, I think that's what he said, as I can't hear and I'm too busy staring at his exceptionally handsome face to lip-read properly.

"No worries." I release him but he doesn't move, looking at me with blatant interest.

I have no idea how long we stand there, staring at each other like a couple of goofballs, people dancing in time to the bass pulsing around us. He's a head taller than me, with wavy hair the color of my favorite caramel latte and blue eyes that are just visible in the dim lighting. With defined cheekbones, a strong jaw, and the hint of a dimple in his right cheek, he's gorgeous and I can't look away.

It's been a long time since I've been with a guy. My relationship with Cal broke down a few years ago but he still stays with us when he's in Fort Chester and that invariably leads to us sleeping together. Not from any real attraction but more a familiarity, convenience thing. I don't have sex with anyone else because I haven't got the time or the inclination and Cal happens to be in town a few times a year. There's an easy affection between us and I like the casual arrangement. But with Rob gone, Cal won't be visiting for a long time and in this moment, I'm oddly interested in this stranger and the way his enigmatic stare makes me feel.

Like I'm beautiful. A woman to be desired. An interesting woman with a life story to tell. And for the first time in forever, a woman who doesn't have a child to go home to. It's heady stuff.

He mimes raising a glass to his lips and while I refused a drink when Jo offered a few moments ago, I find myself nodding. He stands back and lets me walk in front of him and I'm glad I wore my best black skirt, the one that's tight until it hits my knees, where it ends in a flirty flare. I hope he's looking and liking what he sees.

When we reach the bar, there's enough light that I can see him better and I get this weird feeling in my chest as he smiles, revealing perfectly straight white teeth, and holds out his hand.

"Hi, I'm Noah. Sorry for bumping into you back there. The least I can do is buy you a drink."

"I'm Abigail, but my friends call me Abi." I shake his hand, liking that it's firm and cool.

"So what should I call you?"

Considering the way my pulse is racing, I like to think we can start off as friends. "Abi is fine."

His smile widens and my heart pounds so loud I can barely hear myself think. What is wrong with me? Sure, I've been attracted to guys over the years, but I've been too busy being a mom and too confused by my ongoing relationship with Callan to do much about it. Maybe the slight buzz is my body's way of telling me I'm alone and single and to get with the program?

"What will you have to drink, Abi?"

I'm already a little tipsy from the three Mojitos consumed at home and the glass of Chardonnay I had here earlier before we hit the dance floor, so I say, "A soda with lemon, please."

"Coming right up."

As he places our order with the bartender, I look around for Jo but she's nowhere to be seen. Probably in the Ladies. I slip my cell out of my bag and text her.

*Where are you?*

The three little dots appear almost immediately.

*Met a guy. Look to your left.*

I glance over my shoulder to see my introverted friend waving at me from the dance floor in front of a guy about her height with a man bun. I can't see his face but she gives me a thumbs-up sign and I laugh, glad she's having fun.

I fire back with *I'm having a drink with a cute guy. Text me when you want to leave.*

She glances at her cell and I see her thumbs tapping a response.

*I fibbed when I said I was getting a drink. Talked to this guy earlier at the bar and he's been eyeing me off since and I really like him. We might leave soon. Do you mind?*

Jo has never ditched me before when we've gone out together but I'm happy she's having fun. She deserves to, as she's probably feeling as bummed as I am that Rob left tonight.

*Go for it. Just be safe, okay?*

I sense rather than see her eye-roll from this distance.

*Yes, Mom. You have fun too.*

I send her a lopsided grin emoji, she likes it, and I turn back to the bar. Noah is waiting patiently and his politeness impresses me as much as the rest of him.

"Texting a significant other?" he asks, his gaze guileless, like it wouldn't bother him if I was.

"No significant other." I slip my cell back in my bag, feeling more lighthearted than I have in years. I'm done with Cal breezing in and out of my life, and his booty calls. Time for me to move on. "And loving it."

He nods. "Here you go." He hands me a tall glass and he's even taken the time to wipe the condensation from it with a napkin. "Can I make a toast?"

"Sure."

He raises his glass, and I try not to think about another toast made hours earlier, during celebratory drinks for my baby boy who's all grown up.

"To the clumsy oaf who bumped me on the dance floor so I ended up in front of you."

I laugh. "I'll drink to that."

Our fingertips brush as we clink glasses and unexpected heat streaks through my body. I've never believed in insta-lust, the kind portrayed in romcoms, but my skin is tingling like a million ants are doing a tap dance.

"Are you here with friends?" he asks, and I'm instantly on guard. It would be foolish to admit my friend is about to ditch me and I'll be alone shortly.

I nod and point toward the dance floor. "Yes."

"Good. I had a friend who got into trouble with a guy in a bar after her buddies left her behind and I wouldn't want anyone to go through what she did."

He sounds genuine and I'm impressed by his caring attitude, but I don't know him and he could use this line to reel unsuspecting females in. I'm smarter than that.

"Sorry to hear that, and you're right, you can't be too careful these days." I give a mock shudder. "I hear some real horror stories from friends on dating apps."

"You don't need to be on apps to have those," he says with a grimace, and I can't help but laugh. "It's a jungle out there."

"I'm pretty sure a guy like you would have no trouble getting a date."

I regret saying the first thing that pops into my mind as soon as the words have left my mouth. Because of course he's going to ask the predictable "A guy like me?" and I'll have to bluster my way through it, trying not to articulate how hot he is.

To my surprise, he glances at his drink, embarrassed, and I like him even more for his bashfulness.

To fill the awkward silence, I rush on, "I don't date much. I have a kid... had a kid."

When his startled gaze locks on mine, I add, "He's off at college. Left today, actually."

"How are you feeling?"

"Awful but trying to hide it." I make a perky face complete with wide grin and he chuckles. "Is it working?"

"You look fine to me." His intent gaze roves over my face as if he's trying to memorize every line. "Better than fine," he murmurs, and I swear I feel that deep voice ripple over me like a physical caress.

"You're quite the charmer, Noah."

"On the contrary, I've been told my taste in retro bars and hits from the eighties and nineties makes me a boring date."

"You actually like this music?"

He squares his shoulders. "I do and I'm proud of it."

More than pleased we have an eclectic taste in music in common, I smile. "I like it too. This bar is my favorite."

"I haven't been in town long but the minute I saw it, I knew I had to visit." He reaches out to tuck a strand of hair behind my ears and I almost swoon. "I'm glad I did."

"Me too," I say, taking several gulps of my soda to cool down.

"Once we finish these drinks, would you like to dance?"

"I'd love to," I say, increasingly drawn to this guy I've only just met.

I know I won't be going home with him—I've never had a one-night stand in my life, discounting Cal back in high school, and look how that turned out—but I'm not averse to having a little fun tonight.

This is the distraction I need and as I glance over to the corner to find Jo and her man have vanished, I must remember to thank my bestie first thing in the morning.

# FIVE

## JO

I'm dying to hear how Abi's night went, but I know mornings at work are manic for her so I send her a brief text, asking her to meet me for a coffee at the studio around midday. I don't have a job booked until two this afternoon, a Cavalier Spaniel in dire need of a trim, so it's easier if I choose a place convenient for her.

I want to hear the lowdown from last night because when I left the bar I saw Abi standing close to a handsome stranger she couldn't take her eyes off. I've never seen her look at anyone that way, not even Cal. Then again, I know they only got together and stuck it out for as long as they did because of Robbie, and Abi hasn't dated anyone since things ended with Cal a few years ago.

I've always wondered if they still hook up when he returns home because he stays at the house, but Abi vehemently denied it the one and only time I asked so I didn't push the issue. The three of us are good friends and I see little sign of affection between them when we hang out together, so she's telling the truth.

Cal's a natural-born charmer and flirts with everyone, but I haven't seen him flirt with Abi in a long time. I think he gave up trying once he realized she only put up with him because of their son, and that's when his absences from home became more frequent. They have a strange relationship but I'm glad it's worked for Robbie's sake. He's an amazing kid and deserves the best.

Fort Chester isn't exactly a thriving metropolis, stuck almost halfway between LA and San Francisco, but one of the big LA movie studios secured a large tract of land here a few years ago and erected a studio recently, resulting in Abi landing the plum job of fashion coordinator on many of their productions.

She's always had amazing fashion sense and makes anything she wears look good. Even when pregnant she rocked any outfit, her bigger boobs making her even more attractive if that were possible. Cal hadn't been able to take his eyes off her all through the pregnancy, like he couldn't quite believe his luck despite being an eighteen-year-old father-to-be. Then again, as we all discovered, Cal didn't have the brains to back up his beauty.

Though that's harsh. He's always been nice to me. Our interactions in our senior year may have been few and far between, but I'll never forget when he stuck up for me, and the conversation we had after he became a father. He's genuine, when not many men are, and for that alone, I think he's wonderful. Our friendship has grown over the years and he's definitely one of the good guys.

The studio sits on the outskirts of town, like a modern afterthought amid the heritage buildings that make up the main square. I never thought I'd live in a town like this but when Abi and Cal told me they were moving here, I made an impulsive decision to tag along. I was smitten with Robbie and the thought of being a godmother, so it seemed like a logical choice. I had nothing tying me to home after I graduated high school—my folks made no secret of the fact they thought my grades were a big fat letdown—so being with my new makeshift family instead had been a no-brainer.

Moving to Fort Chester had an added bonus: I met Tom.

He's the nicest guy: smart, funny, articulate. Like Cal, but with greater depth. Being Cal's best friend meant Tom started hanging out with us all the time and I liked that too, because it didn't leave me feeling like a third wheel alongside Abi and Cal. The four of us enjoy an easy friendship to this day, though I can't help but wonder if Tom and I could be something more, given half a chance.

We've come close to taking the next step a few times—a drunken night fueled by one too many vodka shots when we'd almost kissed, another night when Abi and Cal had gone to bed early on a camping trip, leaving Tom and me lying side by side next to the bonfire, staring up at the stars—but he's never made a move and I wonder if something's holding him back. I could ask but I'm too scared to hear his answer. The last thing I need is another person in my life deeming me not good enough.

There's a café tacked onto the side of the monstrous building, and I spot Abi standing and waving at me from inside as I reach the door. Not that I could've missed her in a chartreuse sundress that's so bright it hurts my eyes. Or maybe those tequila shots I had when I got home last night are contributing to my vision problem.

I enter the café and the aroma of coffee brewing gives me the wake-up jolt I need. I don't drink a lot as a rule but last night warranted it. The hangover, I can do without.

"Hey, Abs." I hug her when I reach the table she's reserved for us near the window so we can look out on the forest rather than the expansive car park on the other side. "Can I get you anything?"

"I've already ordered our coffees so we're good." She points at a chair. "Sit and tell me all the goss from last night."

"I could ask you the same thing." I sit and resist the urge to rest my head on the table, I'm that hungover.

"You first." She rests her elbow on the table, chin in her hand. "How was he?"

"Forgettable."

So forgettable I ended up going home alone and drowning my sorrows in tequila. I'm destined to be single. Not that I don't try. I put myself out there. I date. I do my best. But I'm hung up on one guy and no one else comes close.

"Ouch." She winces. "I was expecting a tale of rampant lust so overwhelming you couldn't keep your hands off each other and that's why you left."

"The lust petered out pretty quick when I discovered Chuck Bradford kissed better in sixth grade compared to this guy."

Her eyebrows shoot up. "You kissed a boy in sixth grade? Wow, impressive. Wish I'd gone to school with you then. You're a badass."

"I only did it for a dare and trust me, it wasn't good, so I didn't repeat the experiment."

"Until junior high when I saw you locking lips with—"

"Don't remind me." I hold up my hand to ward off Abi's recounting of my embarrassing high-school exploits. I'd been a dork so did whatever I could to fit in, including taking on dares from cool kids. Dumb. "Where's that damn coffee?"

Abi laughs. "Okay, I can tell you want to change the subject, so I'll give you the lowdown on my evening."

"Please do. That guy I saw you with was super hot."

Abi gets this look in her eye when she really likes something, a glint that brings out the gold flecks amid the hazel. I've seen it when she looks at Robbie, mint choc chip ice cream, designer handbags, and cute puppies. I'm surprised I see it now. She must've really clicked with that guy.

"He's... incredible." She sighs, and to my astonishment, a blush colors her cheeks.

I hate the frisson of jealousy her words elicit. Only Abi could be pining for her son, then meet someone amazing the day he leaves for college. I should be happy for her. I am happy, but it's hard to play second fiddle to someone as dazzling as Abi, no matter how much I love my best friend.

When I don't answer, she casts me a quizzical glance, so I say, "Wow. Tell me more."

"You know I haven't dated since I had Rob."

"Yeah, and you know what I think about you being loyal to a guy who only breezes into town when he feels like it."

"You of all people know what I think about Cal." She makes a mock barf sound. "Please don't let Cal ruin my loved-up haze."

Shocked, I say, "Love?"

She waves her hand, as if shooing me. "Just an expression. Though I am in a haze, because I can't stop thinking about Noah."

"Ah, so the hottie has a name."

"Noah Powell. Six-two, light brown hair, blue eyes, recently moved to town because he's an historian researching Californian towns for a book, loves retro music as much as me, and is a complete gentleman."

"You had me interested until the last part. So you didn't hook up?"

"No." Her mock outrage makes me chuckle. "But damn, it's the first time ever I wanted to after barely knowing a guy."

That's not true and I refrain from pointing out she had sex with Cal in high school when she didn't really know him. I'm not a judgmental person but the fallout from that night affected us all and I sometimes wonder how different our lives would be if it hadn't happened.

There's a small, smug smile playing about her mouth, like she has a secret I'm not privy to. She's so wrapped up in daydreaming about her new man Noah she doesn't realize I've gone quiet. With so much evolving—Robbie leaving, Cal and Tom away, Abi meeting a new man—I'm a tad worried our friendship will change. I'm the one Abi has turned to for so long. I'm her confidante. And with Robbie gone, I thought our time together would increase. I'd been looking forward to it. It's nice to be needed, when not many people in my life notice my nurturing side. I'd envisaged Abi leaning on me more than ever. The two of us sharing a pizza at her place while watching corny sitcoms, girly weekends in LA, and movie nights followed by bar hopping because we're single. But if she throws herself headlong into a new relationship, where will that leave me?

It's something I haven't considered and I hate that my plans for the next few months may have been thwarted by some guy who could turn out to be a loser.

Quashing my resentment, I ask, "Are you going to see him again?"

"Hell, yeah." The faint pink staining her cheeks deepens and it makes her look cute rather than flushed like me after a workout. Pale redheads with freckles should never blush. "I'm actually seeing him tonight."

So it's begun. She's leaving me behind. "Wow, that's fast."

"I know, but I couldn't resist when he asked me out."

She's looking at me expectantly, like she's waiting for my approval, and I know I have to subdue my insecurities and show some enthusiasm.

"Good for you, girlfriend. Robbie leaves town and you're immediately putting yourself out there."

I don't mean to sound catty but she must hear something in

my tone because a small frown dents her brow. "I'm going on a date, Jo, not sleeping with the entire town."

"I didn't mean it like that." I hold my hands up in surrender, hating that I've put a dampener on her obvious excitement. "I think it's great. Last night I didn't want you wallowing and I'm happy you've found a distraction from your empty nest."

I placate her, but I see I've taken some of the sheen off her newfound happiness because her eyes have lost the glint, so I place a hand on her forearm. "I mean it, Abi. I'm happy for you. I'm just grouchy because you found a prince and I got a toad." I refrain from adding, "Again."

She smiles and places her hand over mine. "Thanks for looking out for me, especially last night when I was feeling so lousy. I owe you one."

I return her smile, thinking if we're keeping tabs, Abi owes me more than one.

# SIX

## JO

My ankle sprain is so bad I get to stay home from school for a week because the doc insists I keep it iced and elevated as much as possible in the first few days. Mom agrees but her disappointment in me is palpable, like she can't fathom how clumsy I am. I'm not sure what Madame Suzette said to her over the phone when neither of my parents picked me up after the injury, but it looks like Mom's finally come to the realization I'll never be a dancer because she hasn't mentioned returning to class once. I'd dance a jig if I could.

I love being home alone. With Talia at school and my folks at work, I can do anything I want, including sitting in the sun in the backyard for longer than a few minutes. Mom's always lecturing me about avoiding the sun, that pale redheads should avoid it at all costs, but I love the feeling of warmth on my skin. Besides, I'm not stupid. I don't want to burn and make sure I slather sunscreen on and wear a hat. But she's obsessed with skincare and maintaining one's youth so I never get to do this, just sit in the backyard basking.

The spy novel I'm reading is boring, so I close my eyes and tilt my face up to the sun, loving the warmth as much as the freedom to do this, when a shadow falls over me. I open my eyes and scream, before I realize it's the kid from next door. Mom warned me off fraternizing with our neighbors because "they're not our kind of people": translated, they're poor and not good enough for Mom's snobby tastes. Mom's all about appearances: wearing the right labels, taking exorbitant time with skincare, always using manners, speaking when educated on a subject so as not to appear ignorant. It's tiresome living up to her standards —and always falling short.

"Jumpy, much?" he drawls and I'm immediately captivated by his deep voice. He's about my age but all the boys at school haven't had their voices break yet so it intrigues me, hearing a voice like that from a boy who's wearing a kiddie dinosaur T-shirt.

He must see me staring at his top because he grimaces and gives a self-deprecating laugh. "It's my Gran's favorite. She's not feeling well so I wear it to cheer her up."

He's lying. I know, because I've seen him wear this same T-shirt for the last two weeks since they moved in. Not that he's spotted me spying on him from my upstairs window. The rundown cottage next door has been empty for years so it had been a big deal when a small van pulled into the driveway. Mom and Dad had been at work, so Talia and I had watched the people unload. Two oldies who looked to be about a hundred and the boy now looking at me with defiance, as if daring me not to believe him.

"How come you moved here?"

"Gramps owns the place."

"But it's been empty for years?"

"We've been living in Vegas."

"Where are your folks?"

"Dead."

"Sorry."

"Don't be. I like living with my grandparents much better."

I like how we're communicating: short and to the point, no messing around. I hate when my mom and dad use platitudes to drag out what they're really saying: that I'm not good enough and never will be.

*"Joelle, why don't you wear the black skirt? It's slimming."*

*"Joelle, don't you think water is a smarter choice than diet soda?"*

*"Joelle, no boy will ever date you with that slouching posture, pull your shoulders back."*

I could write a book with the judgmental crap I put up with, but why waste my time dwelling on stuff I can't change?

"What's your name?" he asks.

"Joelle."

He laughs and I roll my eyes. "My mom likes fancy names. I hate it, so everyone but her calls me Jo."

"Don't you want to know my name?"

"Nope, already know it."

His forehead crinkles in confusion and I say, "Nice to meet you, Rex."

He looks thoroughly bamboozled, and I point at his T-shirt and laugh. "Tyrannosaurus rex, get it?"

He laughs. "Gran and Gramps call me Jerome, but I think I prefer Rex."

"Rex it is."

We shake on it and I like that I've found a new friend. But Mom won't like me talking to Rex and I'm not sure how to tell him.

As if reading my mind, he says, "We don't have to hang out

at each other's houses. There's a spot near the wharves where no one goes. That can be our place."

*Our place.* I like the sound of that. I also like that Rex isn't looking at me like some of the boys at school, the ones I know are thinking about wanting to touch or kiss me. Not in a creepy way, but because we're almost teenagers and some are more curious about stuff like that than others.

I'd had my first kiss a few months ago, with Chuck Bradford, a giant of a kid with black hair and beady eyes. It had been a dare from a bully and I'd done it to prove a point, though a small part of me had been secretly thrilled to try it. Chuck never teased me like some of the other boys and he didn't have braces. But the kiss had been sloppy, all saliva-swapping and teeth clashing, beyond embarrassing.

But the other boys had started looking at me differently since, like they wanted to try it too, and while I wouldn't let them, it felt good to gain attention for something other than my orange hair.

Rex isn't gawking at me like those boys, he's looking at me like a friend and I can always do with more of those. I'm not popular or cool. Most kids at school are nice to me but they don't want to hang out with me, so the fact Rex wants to is pretty darn appealing.

"Sounds good. Though I'm home for the week with this,"—I point to my bandaged ankle propped on a footstool—"and my folks are at work, so you can hang here if you like."

Though Talia can't catch him here because she'll snitch to Mom and Dad, so I add, "For your sake, you'll need to leave around three because my little sister gets home around then and she's a pain in the butt."

If he recognizes I'm trying to fob him off, he doesn't show it. Rex has a calmness about him that's unusual for a boy, as if he's waiting and watching the world unfold around him. "Fine by me."

As he sits cross-legged on the grass next to my chair and starts telling me about a seagull fight he witnessed down at the wharf last week, I'm content in a way I haven't been in a long time.

# SEVEN

## ABIGAIL

I may not have been on many dates in my life—try two, both in the six weeks after I slept with Callan and before I knew I was pregnant—but I know romance when I see it and sitting next to Noah on the tailgate of his Ute next to the river, sharing an intimate picnic, is the most romantic thing I've ever done.

"Are you warm enough?" Rather than taking the opportunity to slide an arm around me and make a move, he hands me a blanket. I love his thoughtfulness and his lack of sleaze. I've heard enough of Jo's dating tales to know some guys don't like to take things slow. I'd hate that.

"I'm fine, thanks." I take the blanket anyway and shake it out, draping it over our legs because it feels cozier. "This is nice."

He winces. "Nice, huh? The dating kiss of death."

"No, nice because it is. All this?" I gesture at the padded picnic rug he's spread out in the back of his Ute, the basket filled with bread, cheese, strawberries and a bottle of Shiraz, and the lanterns casting a soft glow. "It's beyond nice and I appreciate the effort."

He shrugs, adorably bashful. "I like to keep things simple. We could've gone to a fancy restaurant for dinner, but I thought this is quieter and gives us more time to talk and really get to know each other."

"I agree."

I take a sip of wine, savoring the smoothness, watching the light from the lanterns shimmering and fragmenting on the river's surface. "Tell me more about your job."

"Well, historian is just another name for nerd stuck in the past." We share a laugh. "But I love it. The small family-run museum I worked for back in San Francisco likes to highlight California's past, so that's what got me interested in collating information for a book. I already write the articles for their website and yearly magazine, so it seemed like the next logical step." He shrugs. "For the sake of thorough research, I've been traveling ever since. I've been to San Jose, Fresno, Stockton, Modesto, Merced and Visalia over the last six months, now here I am."

His gaze locks on mine. "I saved the best for last."

He's not talking about the towns and I want to kiss him so badly I inadvertently lean toward him. But making out isn't conducive to getting to know him, so I take a gulp of wine instead. "Is it tough, living out of a suitcase?"

"Not really. I'm used to it. And I like the freedom, but there's a lot to be said for finding a home and putting down roots."

His eyes haven't left mine, like he's trying to convey a message. But I'm so bad at this I have no hope of interpreting it. Is he warning me off him, implying he's a wanderer like Cal, who'll never stay put long enough for a relationship? Or is he saying he's tired of moving around and wants to stay in Fort Chester?

"I have a lot of notes collected from the last six months, so I wouldn't mind staying in town long enough to start working on the book."

"How long's that?" I ask, aiming for casual, when I'm very interested in the answer.

"At least three months but who knows? Maybe this is the place I end up staying?"

I'm still no closer to figuring out if that means he's worth taking a chance on or not when the loud croak of a frog makes me jump. He smiles and takes hold of my hand, and I try not to melt.

"I've got you," he says, squeezing my hand, and I carefully place my glass on the overturned cooler lid so I can swivel toward him.

"Thanks," I say, but it's for more than the hand holding and we both know it.

I'm being silly, wondering if he'll stick around, picturing a possible long-term relationship, when this is our first date and I should be enjoying it, immersing myself in every moment rather than questioning a future that may never happen.

"Tell me the Abi Smith story," he says, intertwining his fingers with mine.

"It's boring, but here goes. Pregnant at seventeen to a guy every girl in our senior year lusted after, the bad boy new to our school. Lucky enough to have supportive parents."

My parents had already bought a home in Fort Chester for a peaceful retirement when I headed off to college. When that didn't happen because of my pregnancy, they offered to buy me a house too, so I followed them. Though Cal had stepped up when I got pregnant and wanted to be an active parent, I had him pegged as unreliable from the start, and I didn't want to be left alone as a clueless eighteen-year-old raising my son. It had been the best move I made, moving here, because my folks had been amazingly involved grandparents. I miss them every day.

He squeezes my hand. "Hey, are you okay?"

I nod. "Yeah, so the rest of the story goes like this. My folks retired early here from San Fran and I moved too. Lived with Cal, the father of my kid, and raised our son because it's the right thing to do, but Cal isn't keen on sticking around beyond the first few years so comes and goes at will. My folks died in a car crash three years ago and I miss them terribly. Landed a dream job recently. Love being a mom to the most gorgeous boy on the planet, who left for college yesterday, as you know. Now here I am."

He's staring at me like he's hanging on my every word and I like the attentiveness. Most of the guys I work with are more interested in talking about themselves—their cars, the sports they watch and play, their conquests—but Noah seems genuinely interested in learning more about me.

"Is it wrong that I'm happy it sounds like your son is the love of your life rather than the schmuck who didn't stick around?"

I laugh. "Not at all. Rob is the love of my life. He's a great kid and I'm missing him like crazy, but..." I brush my thumb across the back of his, glancing at our intertwined fingers, savoring the connection, "... being here with you, now, helps me forget."

His smile makes my heart flip. "I don't believe in fate. I'm too grounded in facts, most of them historical, to put my faith in anything nebulous. But I think it's fortuitous I met you now, in this town, at this time."

"Me too."

This time, I don't second-guess the impulse to kiss him and as I lean forward, and he meets me halfway so our lips graze, a fleeting brush before coming back for more, I feel like the luckiest woman alive.

# EIGHT

## JO

I apply a final slick of pink lip gloss and step back from the mirror.

Perfect.

I've gone to a lot of trouble to look good for the video call with Cal tonight. Somehow, seeing Abi so smitten with a new guy makes me feel less guilty for doing this.

I hate that my best friend doesn't know I regularly keep in touch with her ex. That Cal and I text all the time and video chat every few weeks. That I live for these calls. That I miss him more than she ever does every time he breezes into town then leaves again.

We're good friends, Cal and me, but that's not why I foster our friendship with these regular catch-ups.

I do it because Cal tells Tom everything and I want to make Tom jealous.

It's stupid and petty, but I haven't given up hope for Tom and me, and as the years tick by I feel the need to do something proactive. I tried bringing up the topic of him and me last year, tired of waiting around for him to make the first move. But he'd brushed it off and I'd known then he wasn't ready. Though from that moment, whenever Cal flirted with me, Tom would get this look in his eye, bordering on possessiveness, and I hatched a plan to make him jealous.

Do I feel bad for using Cal? A little, but he's a big boy and can take care of himself. Besides, I know it's a game to him and means little. He probably has women pining for him in every city he visits for work. That's the thing about being a photographer. The jobs are widespread across the country and beyond, and I doubt Cal's celibate. Not that he'd discuss his conquests with me but we share a lot and he's never mentioned another woman.

I'm a fool to contemplate I'll ever get what I want—me and Tom a couple—but on nights like this, when there's a warm breeze drifting through the open window in my bedroom, the chirrup of crickets punctuating the balmy night, and I'm lonely —I still like to dream.

Cal flirts with me—it's as natural to him as breathing—and it doesn't mean anything. But when Tom smiles at me in that way he has, with his eyes and his mouth implying I'm the only woman in the world, I can't help but hope.

My laptop emits a ringtone and I take a final glance in the mirror, hoping I look pretty in a subtle way—silky black singlet top, hair loose and casually curled, carefully applied make-up so it looks like I'm wearing none apart from the lip gloss. I don't usually preen for Cal because he's a means to an end, but tonight is different. If Abi has finally met someone she can move on with—and I'm making a giant leap because they're only on their first date tonight—she'll cut Cal free and what will that mean for our cozy foursome?

Ever since I hinted at a relationship last year, Tom has ensured we only hang out together when Abi and Cal are around. A great avoidance tactic if he doesn't feel the same way about me; or he's running scared. Considering how good we are together when we do catch up, I think it's the latter, so if Cal's out of the picture, is Tom too?

I can't let that happen.

So I need to reel Cal in a little more, play up to him, keep him interested long enough that Tom will finally figure out what he wants—me.

I sit on the bed, drag my laptop closer and hit the answer button. When Cal appears on the screen, my heart gives an annoying leap, the same way it's done since he strutted into my English class on the first day of senior year wearing faded ripped denim and a charcoal T-shirt that made him look like a bad boy and then some. Every girl in our class fell in love that day. It didn't help that Cal knew it and played up to each and every one of us. I hid my crush initially, but Abi found out. We laughed about it. Until it wasn't so funny anymore.

"Hey, JJ. Looking good."

He's the only person that calls me JJ. It makes me wish Tom had a nickname for me, something to make me feel special, something just the two of us share, a prelude to more.

"Good to see you too, Cal. Where are you?"

"Left New Mexico yesterday, in Seattle today. It's cold." He leans closer to the camera, bringing him into sharper focus: his sharp cheekbones, his stubble-peppered jaw, his mesmerizing eyes. "Wish you could warm me up."

I roll my eyes at his overt flirting. "With one of my signature hot chocolates?"

"That too." He winks and I laugh. Usually, if his flirting is too heavy-handed, I cut him down to size, chastise him, and change the subject, but tonight I'm throwing caution to the wind. If I make Cal want me, Tom will too. They've always been competitive. From baseball to football, poker to snooker, they love besting each other, so it stands to reason if I'm on Cal's romantic radar, Tom will see me in a new light. I hope.

"Did you get to see Rob before he left yesterday?"

I nod. "You have an incredible son and he's going to kill it at college."

"I have no doubt." He hesitates and I hate that I know what he's going to ask next. "How's Abi coping?"

Even when he's thousands of miles away, he asks about her. It's sweet. But if he truly cared about Abi, he wouldn't flirt with me, her best friend. It cheapens him in my eyes, and I don't like it. She deserves better. Of course, it's front and center in my mind what she'll think if she finds out I'm deliberately flirting with Cal in an attempt to make Tom jealous and how damn awkward it will be if that happens. The four of us have been a family for years, and I know that changing the dynamics may have far-reaching consequences. But I'm tired of waiting. As Mom used to say, one of the few things I agreed with, the heart wants what the heart wants.

"JJ, is Abi okay?"

Refocusing, I say, "She was maudlin last night but then she met someone and is out on a date as we speak."

He tries to act nonchalant, but I see the tightening of his jaw as he grits his teeth.

"What about you? Seeing anyone special?"

It's the first time I've ever asked and surprise widens his eyes before he grins. "Apart from the beautiful woman I'm talking with now? No way."

His trite response is cheesy but this is Cal and I'm used to it. "Good. Because I don't like sharing."

It sounds possessive so I temper it with an exaggerated batting of my eyelashes that makes him laugh. I enjoy this fun side of our friendship. I've been JJ his buddy for so long. Good old dependable JJ, always around to babysit or make a meal in a hurry or take Robbie to baseball. I did it because I thought making myself indispensable to Cal's family would ultimately bring me closer to Tom and in a way it has, but I want more now.

"I like a woman who knows what she wants." The corners of his mouth curve upward. "When are you going to make an honest man out of me, JJ, and take this flirting to the next level?"

I've spent countless hours of my life trying to stifle a blush. I'm too old to flash like a crimson beacon whenever I'm embarrassed or turned on. And I hope to hell all those hours I put in are working now, because when Cal mentions taking us to the next level I immediately envisage the two of us entwined on this bed, when it's Tom I want to make all my dreams come true.

"What do you mean by next level?"

I call him on it, because I'm confused. I know why I'm ramping up our flirting, so why is he? It disarms me, that by toying with him, he may misconstrue and think I want him.

"I mean you flying out to meet me wherever I am with a suitcase full of those triple-choc brownies you're so good at baking." He kisses his fingertips and makes a lip-smacking sound. "JJ, those brownies of yours are beyond next level."

Relieved, I smile. "In your dreams, buddy."

"And I have plenty of those." He winks again, and while I hate when other guys wink, coming from Cal it's endearing.

We chat for half an hour. More to the point, he talks endlessly about his latest photography gig in the parks around Seattle, and I listen, feigning interest, while I watch his lips move, his easy smiles, the flirtatious twinkle in his brown eyes, imagining all the while it's Tom chatting with me. Pathetic.

Because that's what most people would think of me, a sad case pining over one of my friends, and using his best friend to get to him.

The thing is, Tom's rarely around. He's like Cal; tying them to one place is like trying to contain a wild bird: they're happiest when allowed to fly. But I'm tired of waiting and hoping that one day he'll stick around.

I must've drifted off for a moment because Cal taps the screen. "Hey, gorgeous, am I boring you?"

"No, but I'm tired."

"In that case, why don't you slip into something more comfortable... while I watch, of course."

"Pervert."

"And you love me for it."

"On that delusional note, I'll say goodnight."

He raises a hand in farewell. "A pleasure talking to you as always, JJ. Take care."

"You too, Cal."

I hit the disconnect button, roll onto my back and stare at the ceiling, willing away the tears prickling my eyes.

This is stupid. I might've pushed the boundaries tonight and of course he responded in kind. It's what Cal does. But what am I doing? I'm not this type of woman, who toys with her best friend's ex to get the guy I want. And if Cal misinterprets my sudden overt interest and thinks I'm genuinely into him, how the hell will I tell Abi?

This is madness. I'm dallying with danger.

But this is for Tom... what if I can't help myself?

# NINE

## JO

It's Friday and Rex has come over every day this week after my folks and Talia leave in the morning. We play cards, gin rummy mostly, watch bad reality TV we poke fun at, and read. It's weird, sitting next to someone and reading, but it's comfortable, and Rex—I like that I have a nickname for him nobody else does —loves books. I lend him one every day and he returns it the next morning, keen to discuss the plot. He doesn't disparage the teen romances I favor, nor does he question my penchant for space opera fiction. He's so cool I can scarcely believe he's my friend.

The only downside is having to hide our friendship from my folks. If it bothers him, he doesn't show it, but I hate hiding him like a dirty little secret. He deserves better than that but I know what will happen if I broach the subject with Mom: she'll make up some excuse why I can't see him anymore or worse, forbid me completely. It's easier this way because I like Rex and I don't want anything to ruin the newness of our friendship.

"This book was interesting," he says, handing the dog-eared copy back to me. It's my all-time favorite paranormal fantasy *Scion of the Sun*, about a girl who discovers she can teleport to New York's inner world when the sun hits her forehead, only to find she's the chosen one—the scion—who can save that world from an ancient evil. "Though, of course, Holly had to be torn between Joss the warrior sworn to protect her and Quinn her best friend at boarding school." He rolls his eyes. "Give me a break."

I don't tell him the love triangle is my favorite part of the story. "Hey, I thought it was romantic."

"I guess." He grimaces. "Though if I discovered I had badass powers like teleportation and ruling a mythological Celtic world, I'd focus more on doing my job in saving that world rather than worrying about which boy likes me more."

"I like mushy stuff. Sue me."

We grin at each other, our teasing as easy as our friendship, and I value our camaraderie so much. I don't have many close friends at school and it's a shame he doesn't attend mine. Though I doubt he even goes to school. He said he's having some time off because his gran is sick, but if she's so bad why isn't he at home every day looking after her rather than spending all his time with me? Even weirder, I never see his grandparents. I haven't spotted them once, going out to get groceries or checking the mailbox, and they never get food delivered.

I know Rex is poor. He alternates between the dinosaur T-shirt and a black polo that's so threadbare I can see patches of skin through it, and the torn jeans he was wearing the first day I met him and a pair of khaki shorts that's miles too big.

If his poverty embarrasses him, he doesn't show it. And he's never greedy when I offer him snacks and lunch. But I see him eyeing the grilled cheese on toast I make for our lunches every day like it's his last meal and I'm determined to ask him about his living situation today.

Not that it's any of my business but he's a good guy and he's kept me company this week when he didn't have to. Most boys I know would rather be throwing a football around or glued to their cells, whereas Rex has been happy just to hang. I like him. Not in a crush sort of way, but as a nice person. My mom's always telling me to be on the lookout for 'nice' people but for her, I think that means people she can use or people with money. She's very judgmental and if she knew Rex visited daily, she'd freak.

"Can I ask you something?"

He closes the book and shrugs. "Sure."

"Do your grandparents look after you?"

His eyes narrow slightly. "What do you mean?"

"I never see them. Do they cook for you?"

"I can cook for myself." He squares his shoulders like I've insulted him, and scoots back a little from where we're sitting on the floor. "I can take care of myself."

"I'm not trying to be mean, Rex, it's just..." I trail off, unsure how to word what I want to ask—*are you poor and do you need anything?*—without insulting him.

"Just what?"

He crosses his arms and glares at me, and I know I should shut up but I want to help.

"I know we've only known each other a short time but you've been a good friend to me this week, and I look out for my friends."

His rigid posture relaxes a little. "What are you trying to say?"

"That if you ever need anything, food or whatever, let me know, okay?"

"I'm not a charity case," he mutters, but I glimpse gratitude in his eyes.

"I don't think you are, but if your gran's sick and your gramps is busy looking after her and can't get to the supermarket, I can give you stuff. Our pantry is overflowing. And Mom never lets us eat most of it anyway, she's such a health nut."

For an awful moment I think he's going to burst into tears. He leaps up from the floor and dusts off his butt. "Be back in a sec."

"Where are you going?"

But he's gone, bolting out the door like he has a dozen demons chasing him.

Great. I've overstepped. Mom always says I'm too curious for my own good, poking my nose into everything. The way I see it, there's nothing wrong with being curious. I like learning new things and if something doesn't make sense, I delve until I know why. It's the reason I'm a voracious reader. Books teach me new stuff, with the added bonus of transporting me away from here, where my folks scrutinize my every move and find me lacking.

I hear the back door slam a second before Rex is back, holding something behind his back.

"What you got there?"

He flushes red, from his neck to his forehead, as he thrusts a bunch of daisies at me. "These are for you. To say thanks for being my friend."

They're wilted and a few have petals fallen off, but when he hands them to me, I feel like I've been gifted the world.

"Thanks, Rex. You're nice."

"You are too," he says, backing away slowly. "Anyway, I gotta go. Gramps needs me."

"Okay."

I raise my hand to wave but he's gone and I clutch the daisies, feeling warm and fuzzy inside.

# TEN

## ABIGAIL

I float into work the next morning, unable to keep the grin off my face. My date with Noah last night was magical and I'm like a giddy schoolgirl with her first crush. I lay awake for hours after he dropped me home, rehashing our conversations, replaying that scintillating kiss.

I'm not this person. I'm a practical mom who hasn't got time for frivolity. But then I remember Rob isn't around any longer and apart from work, I'm at a loose end. Sure, Jo will hang out more if I want, but I don't want to monopolize my friend's time. She's single and has her life to lead without a pathetic empty nester clinging to her out of loneliness. Not that she'd ever complain. Jo has been my rock for many years and a second mom to Rob. I'm lucky to have her. Especially when I nearly screwed up our friendship.

I'll never forget that morning after the party Cal threw when his parents were away.

*I try to open my eyes but they won't co-operate. I poke at them tentatively but it hurts and I moan a little. What's wrong with me? I'm usually a morning person and love to wake before my folks so I can sit on the back porch by myself with a cup of illicit coffee that Mom hates me drinking—apparently seventeen is far too young to be imbibing too much caffeine—and listen to the birds chirping as the sun rises over the treetops.*

*There's movement behind me and a soft groan, and this time my eyes fly open. I wince as sunlight from the open plantation shutters streams into the room.*

*A room I don't recognize.*

*Baseball posters line one wall, football stars another. There's a study timetable above a messy desk covered in pens and textbooks and sheets of paper, with several empty beer bottles lying on their side. I hear a groan behind me again and I don't want to turn around.*

*Because even if I don't remember much of last night after Jo left to pick up some medicine for her mom who had a bad migraine, I'm not stupid. I've woken up in a strange room and there's someone behind me in bed.*

*Hell.*

*A hand brushes my hip and I jump, rolling over so quickly my head spins. Though that has more to do with the amount of alcohol I consumed last night rather than the fast movement.*

*When I see Callan McFee staring at me in bleary-eyed confusion, my heart stops.*

*I can't breathe.*

*This can't be happening.*

*"Hey," he mutters, before rolling over and pulling the blanket over his head.*

*I peek underneath the bedcovers to see we're naked, before I flop onto my back and press my fingertips to my eyes, willing my foggy brain to remember. Considering we're naked and I'm in Callan's bed, I can assume I gave my virginity to the most popular guy in school last night. The guy every girl wants.*

*Including my best friend Jo.*

*I open my eyes reluctantly to stare blindly at the ceiling. Regret makes my chest ache. If Jo finds out about this...*

*She can't. I scramble out of bed and do a frantic search for my clothes. My mini-skirt's hanging off a lava lamp—I love retro stuff so maybe that's why I'd lost my mind and had sex with Callan—my black ribbed singlet top and underwear are draped over the end of the bed, so after dressing in record time, I snag my shoes from under his desk and tiptoe to the door. Not that any noise I make would wake Callan anyway. He's snoring so loudly his side table is vibrating a little.*

*I'll need to talk to him when he wakes, to give him a heads-up not to say anything to Jo. Not that he's ever spoken to her from memory, but guys can be stupid about this kind of stuff. He'll brag to his buddies... that's when I realize someone at the party might've seen us go up to his room and they'll spread rumors about me and Callan.*

*Then again, kids hook up at parties all the time and one thing I do remember about last night is the amount of alcohol on offer. Most people would've been as drunk as me so it would be no biggie, me sneaking off with Callan.*

*But Jo can't know.*

*My best friend is... intense.*

*We tell each other everything so I know about her mad crush on Callan.*

*She'll think I deliberately betrayed her when nothing is further from the truth. I'd never hurt Jo. She's too fragile for that and doesn't have any other friends. So if she finds out I slept with Callan... she'll go nuts and our friendship will be over.*

*I hate lying but in this case it's warranted.*

*Jo can never find out about Callan and me.*

.   .   .

I blink as I reach my desk, dispelling the memory of waking up next to Cal after making the biggest mistake of my life. Getting pregnant at seventeen meant I missed out on following my college dream to study fashion design, meant I was so terrified of being a single mom I followed my parents when they retired to Fort Chester, meant I hurt Jo so badly she didn't speak to me for seven months after she found out I was pregnant and who the father was.

But that mistake also delivered me Rob and I'll never regret that.

"Abigail, can I see you in my office for a minute?"

Derek Fortuna, the head of the studio, waylays me when I've barely set foot in my office. I smile in greeting. He doesn't return it.

"Sure, Derek. Now?"

"Yes."

His short, sharp response is nothing like the usual way he speaks to me and when he stalks away without waiting, I know something's wrong. I do a quick mental check to make sure I've completed all allocated tasks by their deadlines and can't come up with a single reason why the head honcho would be mad at me.

As I reach his office to find him pacing, before he points at the door for me to close it, I'm worried. I love this job. It's a dream come true. Being able to combine my lifelong obsession with fashion and movies is incredible. I get to coordinate every costume, down to the tiniest detail, while being invited to glamorous launches and functions.

But I'm new here, still on trial, though it hasn't been spelled out that way, and I'm striving to be a valued member of staff. Until now, I thought I was. Everyone sings my praises and Derek, who's staring at me with a deep frown furrowing between his bushy brows, has been more than happy with my job performance.

"Take a seat, Abigail." He gestures at one of the leather chairs in front of his monstrous glass desk before sitting behind it. "We need to talk."

I bite back my first response, "Are you breaking up with me?", because I know it won't be appreciated. Derek may have a killer sense of humor, as demonstrated by his riotous impersonations of some of the studio's stars at our last Friday night drinks, but from his somber expression, he's not in a jovial mood.

"Is everything okay?"

"No, Abigail, it's not." He pinches the bridge of his nose before pinning me with a stare that has me struggling not to squirm like a kid hauled in before the principal. "Your mistake has cost us hundreds of thousands."

Dread coalesces like a lump in my gut. What have I done?

"I'm not sure what you're referring to, Derek."

"We've lost an entire day of filming because of the mix-up in wardrobe."

I want to ask "What mix-up?" but I'm already looking like an incompetent fool in his eyes so I wait for him to continue.

"We had a big day planned today. That action flick scheduled to start filming, the romcom's final scenes to complete, and the reshoot of the opening scenes of those two streaming dramas. But with the required wardrobe hanging on racks in our Burbank studio rather than here, we can't do a damn thing today."

His glare is formidable and I feel the heat creeping into my cheeks. "Derek, I can assure you I double-check the clothing orders personally and that's what I did yesterday."

"So how do you explain this screw-up?"

He doesn't believe me. His eyebrows are raised in

incredulity, the steely glint in his glare dubious. It's making me second-guess myself but I know I ran through my usual pre-filming routine yesterday, ensuring everything would be ready for today. I can't explain this.

But that's exactly what Derek wants, an explanation, so I need some time to look into this.

"I'm sorry, Derek, I have no idea how this happened, but I'm going to do everything I can to find out."

His nod is dismissive. "You do that, but it still doesn't change facts." He jabs a finger in my direction. "You cost us a lot of money today, Abigail. If it happens again, you're out."

To my horror, tears sting my eyes so I stand, mumble another apology, and leave his office as fast as I can.

Something isn't right.

I love working here and since I started a few months ago, I've gone from strength to strength. But recently, several things have gone wrong. Minor stuff mostly, like a coffee stain on a starlet's dress for a big scene, and seams coming apart during filming when they'd been double-checked, but nothing as catastrophic as this. I'd dismissed those other incidents as bad luck, but now... it looks like someone has it in for me.

It's a competitive industry and my job is sought-after—heck, I'd only landed this role by pure luck when one of Rob's friend's grandmother's, who had the job previously, retired and she recommended me. But I get on well with everyone. I'm a people person and always have been, so I can safely say I'm popular with staff, crew, and actors alike.

So why would anyone want to sabotage me?

I'm still at a loss when I get back to my office. To find Noah holding a cardboard takeout coffee holder with two cups in it.

It's a little off-putting that my first reaction is suspicion. We only had our first date last night and he's turning up at my work-place with coffee? But my distrust could be a result of my current mood and I don't want to sabotage us if there's a chance our connection can develop into something more.

He must sense my reticence because he grimaces and holds out a coffee to me. "Too much?"

"You just caught me off guard, that's all." I accept the coffee. "But thanks for this. I need it."

"Bad morning?"

"Yeah, you could say that." I open the door to my office and gesture him in. "I'm busy, but I've got a few minutes to chat."

I know it doesn't sound like the most generous of invitations, with my emphasis on "I'm busy", but I'm still reeling from basically being put on probation. One more screw-up and I'm out.

"It's okay, I've overstepped." He takes a step back. "I'm sorry."

There's nothing but genuine remorse in his eyes, like he's read the situation between us all wrong, and I feel awful.

"Please, come in for a minute. You're sweet for bringing me this and I'm the one who should be apologizing for being ungrateful."

He hesitates. "I've always been impulsive. Next time I'll text or call first."

"Come on." I place my free hand in the small of his back and propel him into my office. "You better come in or one of the casting directors around here will mistake you for an actor and whisk you off to a set."

He appears genuinely perplexed. "Why would they do that?"

Great, now I'll have to reveal how gorgeous I think he is. "Have you looked in the mirror lately?"

To my surprise and delight, he blushes. "If you're trying to sweet-talk me, it's working."

I laugh and he joins in. "You have no idea how much I

needed this." I raise my cup and tap it against his, but I'm talking about more than the caffeine hit. For someone I've just met, we're in sync in a way I hadn't anticipated. It's nice, to have a guy look after me for a change.

"Can I be completely honest?"

I nod. "Please." It'll make a refreshing change from the many lies Cal has told over the years.

"I guess I wanted to stop by to make sure last night wasn't a one-off. I mean, I know you agreed to go on a second date with me, but I had such a great time, and I didn't expect to meet anyone here, let alone click with them... ah hell, I'm rambling."

He runs a hand through his hair, spiking it in all directions, and I curl my fingers into my palms to stop from reaching out to smooth it. That's a girlfriend thing to do and we barely know each other. But what I know so far, I like.

"Say something, so I know I haven't blown this," he says, his expression hopeful but wary.

"You haven't. I had a great time last night too."

"Phew." He brushes his hand across his forehead in exaggerated relief. "So is it too much if I ask you to lunch?"

For a fleeting second, I think it is too much. Is he too eager? But I quash my doubts. I'm not jumping into anything. I'll give him a chance. Just not today.

"Actually, I can't. I'm having lunch with a friend today, but it looks like I need to deal with a major problem so I'll have to cancel on her too. Rain check?"

"Absolutely." He steps in close and my breath hitches in anticipation as he leans in to press his lips to mine in a soft kiss that ends too soon. "And for the record? I'm looking forward to that second date."

I am too, but first, I need to discover who's messing with my career.

# ELEVEN

## JO

Abi is late.

Punctuality has never been her strong suit but having to wait twenty minutes when her lunch break is short means she's caught up with work and hasn't texted.

A waiter stops by my table for the third time. "Can I get you anything?"

What he means is, *if you don't order soon I'll have to turf you out because it's the lunch rush and if you're not going to eat you can leave.*

My cell pings with an incoming text at that moment and I hold up a finger, asking for a moment. He doesn't wait around and when I glance at my cell, it's her. The message is short and sweet.

*Can't make it, so sorry. Major work drama. Back on probation! Talk later.*

I know Abi isn't deliberately dismissive but that's how her text comes across, like she hasn't got the decency or the time to call me and explain why she's left me sitting here when I didn't have to be. Though being back on probation at work means something big has gone down. They love her since she started so it must be a big screw-up she's dealing with. I'm still a tad annoyed though. I have a busy day scheduled. Three full grooms for a Collie, a Cocker Spaniel and a Shih Tzu respectively, that involve a complete body clip, a face and paw tidy up, nail clipping, ear cleaning, a shampoo and conditioner bath, towel and blow dry, and undercoat removal. My work may not be as glamorous as hers but my clients demand perfection—the owners, not the adorable dogs—and I had to carve out some time for this lunch. A lunch she requested.

I know why. She wants to spill details about how her date with Noah went last night. This is high school all over again, when Abi would regale me with tales of her interactions with guys and I would sit there at our cafeteria table being a good listener. One of my few talents, according to my mother. Abi rarely took a breath in those days. She'd go on and on, and while I liked listening to her and she made me laugh with the bubbly way she had of retelling a story, I often felt invisible. Didn't she want to hear about my crushes? My meager interactions with boys?

Then again, the one time I told her about my unrequited feelings for Cal, look what happened.

I'll never forget the day she told me she was pregnant with his child.

Things had been a bit off between us since Cal's party. I couldn't believe I had to leave early that night because my mom had a migraine and Dad had taken Talia to an audition so couldn't pick up Mom's meds. And while I may not be my mom's biggest fan, I knew how bad her migraines were and couldn't leave her alone, no matter how much I wanted to make a move on Cal.

Me, the introvert, had grand plans that night to have sex with Cal. My first. He may not notice me much at school but he would after that night. I'd read up on how to satisfy a man online, had even watched some icky porn. Once Cal knew how good I could make him feel, he'd never look at another girl again.

Delusional, I know, but I'd been so smitten with him I wasn't thinking rationally. Then fate had intervened, and I'd been called away from the party. Though she never admitted it, Abi secretly lusted over Cal like every other girl in our senior class, but I thought Mandy Corr would've been my biggest competition—that girl was crazy for Cal—so I never thought Abi would betray me like that. She avoided me for six weeks after the party. We hung out at school, but whenever I wanted to do anything afterward or on the weekend, she had an excuse. Until she turned up at my house one day and blurted the truth.

She was pregnant and the father of her baby was Cal.

I'm a pacifist but in that moment, I never wanted to kill someone more.

Abi's betrayal broke my heart. I couldn't eat. I couldn't sleep. The ache in my chest didn't subside no matter what I did to distract myself. Rex became my rock then. We'd maintained our friendship all through high school but in private. I liked the secrecy of our friendship. Rex was all mine, in a totally platonic way.

I thought I'd never forgive Abi but when Robbie was born and she asked me to be godmother, I couldn't say no. I could see Abi and Cal weren't a real couple and a small part of me hoped I had a shot. Turns out, I didn't, but here we are, eighteen years later, still friends and I'm glad I got over my resentment and left my teen crush in the past.

When I see the waiter giving me side-eye again, I stand and head for the door. I have forty minutes before I'm due to groom the Collie, my first job for the afternoon, so I'll grab a quick bite to eat at home. However, my plans to eat and run hit a snag when I arrive home to find someone has spray-painted LEAVE HIM ALONE on my back door.

I stare in disbelief at the wobbly black letters and glance around, like I expect to catch the vandal red-handed. Who could've done this?

The only "him" it could be referring to is Cal.

I shake my head, dismissing my first thought: that the one person who wouldn't like me hooking up with Cal is Abi.

It doesn't make sense. According to her, they haven't been a real couple in years. But what if she's lying and they're still sleeping together when he's around? I suspect they are, but she's sworn to me they're over.

Besides, I know Abi: she wouldn't do something like this.

That's when it occurs to me. Maybe the "him" is Tom?

But I haven't really told anyone about my long-standing crush. I think Abi suspects because she's mentioned it a few times over the years, how Tom and I would make a great couple, but she hasn't said anything for a while.

Unless Tom has a crazed ex and he's mentioned me to her? But if that's the case, it means I'm someone important enough to mention and I doubt that, considering our relationship is moving at a snail's pace.

It's baffling. I reach out and touch the paint. It's dry, which means it must've been done during the night and I hadn't seen it until now because I left from the front door this morning, something I rarely do, but one of my neighbors had taken a tumble on the sidewalk and when I'd glimpsed it from my front window I'd run out to make sure he was okay.

I contemplate popping in next door to ask if they saw anything but the Rostervilles are old and in bed by nine every night so I doubt they'd be of any help. And even if I did, I doubt whoever did this had brazenly strutted to my door without some kind of dark clothing or camouflage.

It's bizarre. I've lived in this small cottage for seventeen years, since I moved here not long after Abi, and have never had any trouble. I'm quiet, keep to myself, and maintain a polite but distant relationship with my neighbors. I don't have any enemies—that I know of—so whoever did this is someone close.

Which brings me back to Abi.

It's ludicrous to contemplate, but is my best friend as sweet as she likes everyone to believe? She's one of those annoyingly chipper people who is upbeat all the time. Everyone loves her. She's been popular ever since I've known her and that's why I worshipped her when we first met. How often does a popular girl stand up for a newbie being bullied? But she had and that cemented our unlikely friendship.

We're close. She's more like a sister to me than Talia has ever been. Which means I'd never accuse her of something like this but I will mention it and watch carefully for a reaction. That's another thing about my bestie. She's easy to read and always has been, which is why I knew something had happened at Cal's party before she told me about the pregnancy eight weeks later.

I stare at the sprayed-on message and try to fathom who did this and why. But I can't stand here looking at it all day and I'm no closer to an answer, so I open the door and head inside, tapping a reminder on my cell to stop by the hardware store on the way home to pick up some paint solvent.


I'm getting ready to head out to work when there's a knock on the door. I open it to find a delivery guy placing a basket of condiments on my step.

Hot on the heels of discovering the spray-painted message, I'm less than enthused to accept a gift.

"Who's that from?"

He checks an electronic tablet clipped to his belt. "Abigail Smith. Sign here."

Relieved, I sign for it, and he heads back to his van, leaving me staring at the gift basket filled with my favorite hot sauces and spices. Abi knows I like to play around in the kitchen, especially with Asian food, and she's been privy to my many experimental curries over the years. Though I'm careful with my garnishes, as Cal's allergic to cilantro and I almost gave him an anaphylactic reaction one day. If he hadn't seen it sprinkled liberally over the top, I hate to think what could've happened.

I may not be smitten with the guy like I was in high school, but he's important to me. I actually like our conversations. And he's helped me out more times than I can count: changing lightbulbs, hanging paintings, fixing leaky tap washers. He may not be around much but when he's in town, he always stops by to see if I need help with any handyman tasks and that means a lot.

He does the same at home, but Abi doesn't seem to appreciate him. She's too caught up in her anger because he isn't around enough for Robbie and while I understand, I think she takes Cal for granted. It must be tough to keep fronting up, knowing you're not entirely welcome and to Cal's credit, he keeps trying. I admire him for that.

I take the basket inside. It's huge, with six different chili sauces made from peppers of varying heat levels: Anaheim pepper, Fresno pepper, habanero, jalapeño, Padrón, and piquillo. The spice packets are plentiful: ground cumin, turmeric, cayenne, cloves, garam masala, as well as mustard seeds. The entire thing is wrapped in clear cellophane, tied with a peacock blue satin bow—it's perfect.

I slide the card from an envelope tied with the ribbon and read the message.

*Apologies again for missing lunch, Jo.*

*I was blindsided at work this morning, ended up running around to fix a problem, and texted you too late. Not good enough!*

*Hope that after an evening in the kitchen experimenting with this lot, you'll forgive me.*

*Love Abi xx*

It's sweet and the kind of thing she's known for. Abi always makes a big deal out of my birthdays, sending gift baskets like this one packed with things she knows I like: vanilla-scented bath-bombs, body oils, fancy hand soaps. And she often has my favorite local bookstore deliver latest releases because I'm such a bookworm, and for no other reason than she's thinking of me.

While this gift basket is totally unnecessary because I understand what it's like to get caught up at work, I appreciate her thoughtfulness. I want to call and thank her but one glance at my cell's screen shows I'm now running late and my first booking of the afternoon will wait for no one.

I'll call her later, and with one last glance at the basket and evidence of how considerate my best friend is, I head out the door.

# TWELVE

## JO

THEN

My summer has been better than expected. Rex and I hang out every chance we get, usually in our spot down by the wharves. It's a sandy nook, like our own private beach sheltered between pylons, and I love it. We can people-watch—families lazing on the beach, lovers strolling hand in hand, kids trying to outdo each other with who can build the biggest sandcastle. It's close to a snack truck too, and I'm thrilled to discover Rex shares my love of strawberry ice cream. I've never had a friend like him and I love sitting in our spot, listening to the waves, talking about books, and not feeling judged or inadequate in any way.

Mom and Dad still don't know about him being my best friend and I doubt I'll ever tell them. I see the way they glance at the dilapidated house next door and look away quickly, as if a peek may contaminate them somehow, like poverty is contagious.

I hate their snobbery. How they only approve of mixing with 'the right sort' of people and look down their judgmental noses at everyone else. Mom's always been a snob. Because she danced on Broadway, she thinks she's better than everybody. But Dad's a lot nicer than her and I expect better of him. Then again, he's like a mouse around her: Mom's overbearing and Dad just goes along with it.

That's another thing I like about Rex: he stands up to me. He has strong opinions and we often argue, but not in a nasty way. We spend a lot of time discussing the merits of various bands and foods and books. We talk about books most of the time. I've loaned him all my books so sometimes we go to the library now and he borrows more than me.

I've been to his house once or twice, but I know he's embarrassed and doesn't like us hanging out there. The place is surprisingly clean inside, at complete odds with how rundown it is on the outside. Though furniture is scarce. A rickety wooden table and four chairs in the kitchen and one three-seater threadbare sofa in the living room. No TV. And when he offered me a drink and opened the refrigerator, I glimpsed a carton of milk, a bag of carrots, a block of cheese, and some butter. That's it. Thankfully, he's not too proud to accept food from me sometimes, though I tell a fib so he doesn't feel bad accepting and say it's stuff I made in home-ec class at school.

I haven't met his grandparents, though the second time I visited, I heard his grandfather bellow "Jerome" several times and I teased him about it, calling him by his real name for a week. He hated it, said he liked Rex from me and had got used to it. It's our thing. Guess he values our friendship as much as I do.

But summer has gone and now it's my first day of junior high. A few kids from my old school are here but we've never been close and as I stand near my locker, fear making my fingers fumble as I fiddle with the lock, I wish more than ever that Rex was attending this school so I wouldn't feel so alone.

I finally get my lock to work, jam my bag and books in the locker, clutching what I need for the first few lessons and close it. I'm staring at a map of the school to locate the classroom where English is being held, when I'm jolted hard from the side and stumble. Expecting an apology, I glance to my right and lock eyes with a girl who's staring at me like I'm something nasty she stepped in.

"Watch where you're going, Red." Her dismissive glance flicks to my hair and she smirks. "Or should your nickname be Orange?"

I hear snickers from the girls with her and I know in an instant I'm being teased by a popular girl. Great. On my first day. I begged Mom over summer to do something with my hair: to soften the color, to put blonde streaks through it, anything, so it wouldn't make me stand out like a beacon. But she'd been too wrapped up in Talia's latest dance audition successes to take much notice of me and now I'll pay the price.

As the girls continue to stare at me and giggle, I remember what Rex once told me when I asked how he was so cool all the time, and he said, "Don't show fear. People feed off that. If you're brave and stand up to them, you'll be fine."

So I smile and say, "I'm Joelle, but everyone calls me Jo."

The girl takes a step forward and I inadvertently flinch, garnering more snickers. "Listen up, Red. I have no interest in who you are." She grins and I half expect to see pointy fangs, like the vampire queen in the latest paranormal book I'm reading. "And for the record, none of the boys will be interested in you either when you look like that."

She gestures at me from head to foot and that's when I feel the incriminating heat start in my chest and sweep upward, showing her how much she's hurt me.

"Hey, Mandy, look at that. Her face matches her hair now,"

one of the girls behind her shouts and the entire group bursts into laughter.

Worse than the blush, I feel tears prick my eyes and I half turn away, desperate to find the girls' toilets before my embarrassment is complete and I start bawling. But another girl is standing close by and this one shoots me a sympathetic smile before stepping in front of me so she's almost toe-to-toe with Mandy.

"Haven't you got anything better to do than pick on new students, Mandy?"

Mandy the bully's eyes narrow. "No one asked you, Little Miss Perfect Abigail."

"You're pathetic," she says, deliberately standing on Mandy's toes as she turns back to me and I bark out a laugh.

Whoever this Abigail is, she's my hero, and she winks at me when Mandy mutters "Bitch" and stalks away, her entourage of mean girls in tow.

"Ignore them," Abigail says. "They were like that all through grade school too." She points at my hair. "And for the record? Your color rocks."

I want to fling myself at her and give her the biggest, squishiest hug, but I settle for a grateful smile. "Thanks."

"Joelle, was it? I'm Abi."

"I prefer Jo."

To my surprise, she slings an arm across my shoulders. "Well, Jo, with our mutual loathing of Mandy, I think we're going to be the best of friends."

# THIRTEEN

## ABIGAIL

As if my day couldn't get any worse, I'm still trying to discover how that major screw-up with the costuming happened when I run into Mandy Corr in the staff cafeteria. Literally. She's carrying an iced coffee and I'm dashing in to grab an apple because I missed lunch with Jo thanks to Derek's lecture and subsequent warning, and we bump into each other.

I have no idea what Mandy's doing here. The last time I saw her had been back in San Francisco not long after I had Rob. Cal and I had been taking Rob for a walk in the park, Mandy had been jogging. She'd practically clambered all over Cal right there near the lake while I nursed Rob, oblivious to the fact he was a new dad and with me.

Then again, it wouldn't have mattered if we'd been married and sporting shiny new rings, Mandy had a serious obsession with Cal and didn't care if I witnessed it. Cal was a friendly guy but her overt flirting even made him uncomfortable so when I finished feeding Rob, I suggested we head home. The look Mandy gave me... I should've combusted on the spot. I'd teased Cal about it afterward and that's when he sheepishly revealed they'd kissed a few times before we hooked up and he might've given Mandy the wrong idea: that he wanted to date her. He also told me that when he set the record straight, telling her I was pregnant with his baby and he was in a relationship with me, she'd gone a little nuts: defaced his books, spread vicious rumors about him and me, thrown rocks at his window in the dead of night. She'd only stopped when Cal's dad had confronted her father and threatened reporting her to the police.

To see her here, now, after eighteen years, is surreal.

"Still in a hurry to get places, huh, Abigail?" Her high-pitched voice resembles the scrape of nails down a chalkboard.

"What are you doing here, Mandy?"

"I'm working. A role in the latest sci-fi thriller."

"You're an actress?"

Fitting, the way she paraded around the corridors of our high school, pretending to be saccharine sweet one minute, a psychotic stalker the next.

"Yes, I love it." Her eyes sweep me from head to toe and I see a spark of envy. Another bonus of my job, I get to keep the designer cast-offs once filming on a project is done. "What are you doing here?"

"I'm the fashion coordinator for the studio."

Her eyebrows rise. "For all the productions?"

"That's right, so we might be working together. Won't that be fun?"

My sarcasm scores a direct hit as she reddens. "Look, Abigail, high school was a long time ago. Let's forget about the past, okay?"

"Forget what?"

Not that I want her to spell it out or make her squirm, but I'll never forget how she belittled Jo on her first day of school.

Then again, maybe I should be thanking her, as Jo and I have been firm friends ever since.

She's confused and isn't sure whether I'm jibing at her or genuinely want her to recount her sins. But I haven't got time to stand around here all day—I have a problem to solve.

That's when I realize something.

Mandy had hated my guts for having Cal's baby and leaving San Francisco with him.

Could she be the one who sabotaged my work?

"How long have you been in town, Mandy?"

There's a flicker of something in her eyes before she blinks. "Two days. Why?"

"Is this your first day?"

She shakes her head. "I was on set yesterday."

I stare at her in disbelief. Surely her obsession hasn't festered for eighteen years?

"How's Cal? Does he pop in to have lunch with you?" She's trying to sound nonchalant but she leans forward slightly, like she's eagerly awaiting my response.

I'm stunned. Has she scored a role here so she can be close to Cal? Has she followed us here?

My mind spins with the outlandish possibility that she's still hung up over a high school obsession and while I shouldn't toy with her, I can't help myself.

"Cal's great. Amazing, actually. But he's out of town at the moment." I don't add, "But I guess you know that, you crazy stalker."

"Too bad. It'll be good to catch up, talk about old times."

Her response sounds genuine, but this is Mandy and after what she did to Cal back then I'd be a fool to let down my guard, so I force a smile, thinking Cal will stay away longer than usual if he knows Mean Mad Mandy has lobbed into town with the specific reason of seeing him.

"I have to run, Mandy. See you around."

As I walk away as fast as I can without breaking into a jog, I feel her stare stabbing like a knife in my back.

I'm rattled after my run-in with Mandy. Silly, really, because it's been almost two decades and she can't bully me now. Not that she ever tried with me, but Jo copped the brunt of her pettiness a few times. I hated girls like Mandy, who wielded their popularity like a weapon, so I avoided her. That might be difficult now with her working here.

Jo will get a laugh out of my suspicion that Mandy may have something to do with whoever sabotaged my work today, but when I pick up my cell to call her, I remember she has clients booked this afternoon. I'm about to slide my cell back in my pocket when my stomach rumbles, a reminder I haven't eaten—and that Noah asked me out to lunch earlier.

Is it too needy to text him? Will he think I'm prevaricating, blowing him off one minute, asking him out the next? I stare at my phone, second-guessing myself, before taking the plunge and texting him. He responds almost immediately and we agree to meet at a café near work in ten minutes.

I like his availability, something Cal never was. I lost count of the number of times Cal let me down over the years because of "assignments" he got called away on at the last minute. I didn't care so much for me, but Rob's disappointment irked. Then again, I'm being harsh. Cal provided for Rob through his photography and while he may have been an absentee father sometimes, he loved his son. We had good times when he was home and I know part of my empty nest fears revolve around not just losing Rob, but losing the camaraderie Cal, Tom, Jo and I shared all these years. Jo and I will be fine. Our friendship is solid, but the four of us had a lot of fun together and that'll change now.

When I reach the café, I spy Noah inside at a window table for two. The place is surprisingly deserted and I'm momentarily worried. What if there's a lull in the conversation and there aren't other patrons around so we can people-watch and pretend to interpret their body language? It's one of Jo's dating tips and something she's had to use many times apparently. But I haven't dated at all since high school and I hope my inexperience doesn't scare Noah off. I have a feeling he's someone I can grow to really like.

He stands as I approach the table and kisses me on the cheek. "Get that problem at work sorted out?"

"No, unfortunately, but I had to cancel lunch with my friend because I was dealing with it and I'm starving, then I remembered your invitation earlier."

His smile is warm as he pulls out my chair. "I'm glad you did. I was immersed in the agricultural history of this region when you texted and I've never been more happy to take a break."

"Is the subject matter too dry?"

"As arid as the landscape," he says, and I laugh. "They're about to close up here soon so I ordered two chicken salads for us. Hope that's okay?"

"Perfect."

He has no idea how much his consideration impresses me. I know I shouldn't keep comparing him to Cal, but he's my only yardstick, and Cal had been hard-pressed to buy takeout when I had a cold and was laid up in bed. The way Noah treats me when I barely know him rams home how much of a disservice I've done myself all these years. I should've ended things with Cal a lot sooner.

As a teen, I'd been scared to be alone to raise Rob and

grateful Cal had stepped up and taken responsibility. But falling into a romantic relationship of sorts for the sake of convenience hadn't been smart. I've been unhappy for a long time and trying to hide it. Noah couldn't have entered my life at a better time.

"What are you thinking about?" He reaches over to take hold of my hand and even that simple intuitive gesture has me sighing.

"You."

"Should I be worried?"

"No, it's all good." I smile and squeeze his hand. "*This* is good."

I wave my free hand between us and he instantly understands what I mean.

"Yeah, it's taken me by surprise too, how quickly we've gelled."

"So all the countless women in your past haven't been so lucky?" I'm fishing for information and am less than subtle about it, but he laughs.

"Countless? Hardly. I've dated over the years but nothing serious."

Considering he's kind and sweet and looks like he stepped off a movie screen, I find it hard to believe nobody special captured his heart. "Come on, there must've been at least one lucky woman."

His gaze slides away from me for a moment, before refocusing, and I know I'm onto something. "Childhood sweetheart. The usual story. Grew apart, fell for other people, moved on. It's why I'm not on social media. Can't stand the thought of people in my past looking me up, or the temptation to do it myself." He shakes his head. "Why cling to the past when the future's more exciting? Besides, I'm a historian who prefers old factual stuff with little time for posting my boring life online."

I must admit, the lack of social media presence is a red flag for me. I know he's not online because I checked the night we met, but I understand his explanation and appreciate his honesty.

"I'm glad you're not an online stalker."

He leans forward and wriggles his eyebrows so I'm laughing again. "Why? What deep dark secrets of yours would I find if I research you online?"

"Nothing nefarious here. I have one or two profiles, mostly with pics of my son in the early days, then life got too busy and I stopped posting."

But that doesn't prevent me checking out what other people are up to and it's a guilty pleasure, looking up colleagues to see the lives they lead outside of work. Maybe if I'd looked up old classmates, like Mandy, I wouldn't have been blindsided earlier.

Our food arrives and the conversation flows as easily as the delicious tahini dressing we drizzle over our salads. I know I need to get back to work and investigate the costuming drama, but for now, I'm content in a way I haven't been in a long time.

# FOURTEEN

## JO

Predictably, Abi brushed off my thanks for the gift basket when I called her between clients, but she sounded frazzled so I said I'd drop by her place later. I'm curious what's going on with her at work and want to see her, despite having a week's worth of invoicing to do. Then again, if it's a choice between boring bookwork or hanging out with my friend, I'll choose Abi every time. Besides, I want to talk about the vandalism at my house. It's bizarre to even consider she could've done it, but I want to watch her reaction when I mention it.

I arrive at her place with freshly baked choc-chip cookies and croissants from our favorite patisserie. She sounded like she could do with a chocolate and pastry hit. When I open the back door like I have a million times before, she jumps and whirls to stare at me, a hand pressed to her heart.

"You scared the living daylights out of me."

"Why? You were expecting me."

"I know, but..." She shakes her head and beckons me in. "It's been one hell of a day and I'm still processing it all."

She looks nervous rather than guilty but she's given me the

perfect opportunity to catch her off guard. "I've had an interesting day myself. Someone spray-painted a weird message on my back door."

Her eyes widen in surprise and either she's a damn good actress or she genuinely has no clue what's going on. "What did the message say?"

"Leave him alone." I slip my cell out of my pocket and open the photos section to show her. "Weird, huh?"

"Who's 'him'?"

She can't quite meet my gaze and my heart sinks. Surely Abi hasn't done this?

"That's just it, I have no idea. Unless it's some random guy I've dated recently who's married?"

Her brow crinkles and I can almost see the wheels turning as she thinks. "This may sound crazy, but I have something to tell you."

Dread creeps through me. Surely the person I trust most in this world, along with Rex, isn't going to confess to defacing my door?

"What is it?"

She gives a little shake, bracing to deliver the bad news. "I ran into Mandy Corr at work today."

My mouth drops open as I make the connection. The one person who hated my guts and was as obsessed with Cal as me back in high school was Mandy and she'd gone psycho when she discovered he'd knocked up Abi. The part of me that was hurting at the time relished some of the awful stuff she said about Abi but I never actively participated in maligning my friend. Mandy, on the other hand, had no such compunction.

But how would Mandy know about my connection with Cal now? Our calls are private. Unless he's told someone and it somehow got back to her? But that's so outlandish, it's laughable. The last thing Cal would want is word of our flirtation getting back to Abi so there's no way he'd risk talking about it to others. Except Tom, but I know he'd never say anything to Abi either. Tom's always been closer to me than Abi, almost as if he doesn't want to intrude on her relationship with Cal. If anything, he'd come to me first, and that's what I'm counting on. Because if Tom confronts me about flirting with Cal, it means he cares, and it gives me the perfect opening to tell him how I feel.

As for Mandy still knowing Cal, he's never mentioned staying in touch with people from school. And apart from Tom, he's not particularly close with anyone in town: he never sticks around long enough to build lasting friendships. So if Mandy has done this, how has she discovered my online relationship with Cal?

I try to stifle my curiosity and pretend like I'm not hanging on Abi's response. "What is she doing here?"

"She's an actress apparently." Abi rolls her eyes. "I looked into it at the studio after I ran into her and she's only got a small role. Has had nothing but bit parts over the years. The weird thing is, I get the impression she's here for Cal."

"No way."

She nods. "She specifically asked about him. You don't think she's still obsessed with Cal and came here for him, do you?"

"Considering her obsession in school, anything's possible." I shrug. "But eighteen years? That's too crazy even for a psycho like her."

"Well, it gets better. Someone sabotaged me at work." A frown crinkles her perfectly smooth brow. "The screw-up cost the studio hundreds of thousands in lost film time today and I got blamed for it."

I instantly understand what she's implying. "And you think Mandy had something to do with that?"

"She's been in town for a few days, I asked." She gnaws on her bottom lip. "It's too ridiculous to contemplate but she had access to my office and could've tampered with anything. I mean, what are the odds your place gets vandalized, and someone sabotages my work and there's no other explanation for it?"

I don't believe in coincidences but Mandy arriving in town and targeting us? She's a woman in her thirties now. Surely she's moved on?

"What should we do?"

Abi shrugs. "What can we do? We can't go around accusing her even if she's the only suspect. But I'll try to keep an eye on her."

"Good luck. She's a nutter."

Abi laughs at my dry response and I join in. But I'm uneasy. I have high hopes for Tom and me if my plan with Cal works, and the last thing I need is some crazy blast from the past butting in and ruining everything.

# FIFTEEN

## JO

THEN

I make a big mistake bringing Abi home.

I should've known my mom would love her more than me. Abi's pretty and vivacious and sweet, whereas I'm plain and quiet and withdrawn. Every time she comes over, Mom acts like royalty is visiting. She takes out the best china and buys expensive cupcakes and lets us have soda—a big no-no in our household. Mom regales her with dancing tales on Broadway and Abi's too polite to tell her to shut up. I sit at the table like a third wheel, watching them practically sparkle, they're that gushy and perky.

I think Dad knows how I feel. I see him casting concerned glances my way when he thinks I can't see. And he always makes an effort to include me in conversations at the dinner table, especially when Mom and Talia are chattering nonstop about some dance show.

Turns out, Mom got what she wanted: a brilliant dancer to follow in her footsteps. Talia has nailed every audition she's attended and has already had starring roles in a few recitals. I should be relieved because it means Mom focuses all her energy on my sister and leaves me alone, but I hate feeling second best all the time.

It's why I treasure my time with Abi and Rex. I have two good friends who like me for me, who don't make me feel like an afterthought. But that's the reason I can't introduce them. I've already seen my mom fall in love with Abi and prefer her over me, I couldn't stand it if Rex did the same. So I don't even tell Abi about Rex. And if he's seen her come in and out of my place, he hasn't mentioned it.

I haven't seen as much of Rex lately. Abi consumes all my time but I don't mind. I never expected to make such a good friend at school, and especially not such a popular girl. Mandy and her crew have left me alone since that first day and for that, I'm grateful. But our friendship isn't one-sided; Abi genuinely likes hanging out with me. We rollerblade on the weekends, spend time at the mall, and help each other with homework via video calls.

The only blip in our friendship is Lara. She went to grade school with Abi and is always hanging around, desperate to become part of our friendship circle. Abi's nice to everybody so Lara takes it as a sign she's part of our group when she's not. I know I shouldn't be jealous because Abi's known Lara longer than me but I can't help it. I keep expecting Abi to wake up, realize I'm boring, and ditch me. If my own mother ignores me, what hope do I have of keeping a friend like Abi?

But I don't say anything and today, Abi's invited Lara and me over to do our latest science experiment—mummification of a hot dog. I think it's lame but most of our class thought it was cool when we got to choose assignments, when I'd rather be doing spherification of food, which is a big trend in restaurants and more practical than seeing a hot dog shrivel over four weeks.

Lara's already at Abi's when I arrive and I'm annoyed, because I deliberately got here fifteen minutes early so Abi and me could have alone time before annoying Lara butts in. I hear their laughter coming from the backyard and I grit my teeth as I round the corner of the house. Abi has everything set up and they're waving the hotdogs around and giggling, their heads bent close together—Abi's blonde, Lara's a few shades darker— and in that moment I've never felt more like an outsider.

I want to ram a hot dog down Lara's throat but I paste a smile on my face and walk toward them. Abi spots me first. She leaps up and gives me a hug, but I see Lara's expression over Abi's shoulder: like she's just drunk sour milk. Interesting. Does that mean she doesn't like me or is jealous too and wants Abi all for herself?

Let her try. Abi's too nice to tell her to butt out but if she encroaches too far, I'm more than happy to give her a none-too-gentle nudge away from us. Though she'll probably tattle to Abi and that makes me look bad. I need to come up with a different strategy... maybe suggesting activities Lara doesn't like so she gets sick of us?

Yeah, like that's going to happen.

"I see you guys are all set up." I take a seat next to Abi and she hands me a hot dog and points to the container filled with baking soda in front of me.

"I thought it'd be cool for us to have a container each, that way we can compare results," Abi says, and Lara nods like she always does. She never disagrees with anything Abi says or does.

"We've already measured the length of ours and the circumference," Lara says, shooting me a pitying glance like I should've been here earlier but she's glad I wasn't. "So once you do yours, we'll roll them in the baking soda at the same time then seal the lids."

"Fun," I mutter. Abi laughs, thinking I'm being sarcastic about the experiment but Lara's eyes meet mine and she knows I'm referring to her being here and her compulsion to explain the experiment to me like I'm clueless.

I measure the hot dog, trying to tune out Lara's inane chatter about how cute her French teacher is and if the trendy skirt she saw at the mall yesterday after school will impress him. She's probably mentioning the mall visit because I hadn't been able to go with them yesterday. My English grades are bad and Mom threatened to ground me if I don't show a marked improvement over the next month, so I had to stay home and re-do an essay. I hated missing out and had ended up having to do the essay twice because I'd been so mad at the thought of Abi hanging out with Lara without me.

Lara starts prattling about another outfit at the mall and I'm over it.

"Ready," I say, interrupting her mid-sentence and she glares at me, while Abi gives me a thumbs up.

"Okay, we need to weigh them and record that too," Abi says, using the kitchen scales first before sliding them across to me and Lara's dour expression has returned since Abi chose me first. "Then pop the hot dog in your containers and cover them with an inch of baking soda."

"Wish all science experiments were this easy," I say, and Abi nods in agreement. "After this, we place the containers in a cool indoor spot and check the measurements weekly for a month until they're mummified?"

"Yep." Abi drenches her hot dog in baking soda, then seals the lid. "I'll keep them all here, if you like?"

"Thanks, Abi, but that makes the experiment too controlled. It'll be a better comparison if we each take ours home," I say, not wanting to keep them here for one reason: Lara will have to tag along every time we measure and that's the last thing I want.

Lara knows what I'm doing. I see the conflict in her stare, her inner nerd who agrees with me warring with her desire for friendship. She sighs and gives a little nod. "Jo's right, we should take them home."

"You two are dorky," Abi says with a laugh, and starts tidying up. "I'll take mine inside now and be back in a sec."

I almost yell "No, don't leave me alone with her" but I squeeze my lips together. Lara looks just as appalled as me, so I guess that answers the question of whether she likes me or not.

When Abi's out of earshot, I turn to Lara. "You seem really nice, but I think you should know Abi's tired of you hanging around all the time. She said you were like a puppy trailing after her in grade school and now you're doing the same in junior high. And Abi's such a good person she'd never say anything, but I think it's wrong to keep something like that from you."

Lara looks stricken and I fake sympathy, reaching out to pat her shoulder. "I wasn't sure if I should say anything but if it was me she was talking about, I'd want to know. Are you okay?"

She's tight-lipped and I see tears in her eyes. I know she won't call me out on my lie by asking Abi if she said those mean things. She won't want to get Abi offside and knows if Abi asks me if I said this stuff to Lara and I lie, Abi will choose me over her regardless.

I know I've let my jealousy get the better of me and done an awful thing, but better to get rid of Lara now than later if she's more invested in the friendship.

"Tell Abi I had to leave," Lara mutters, standing and grabbing her container.

"You sure you're okay?"

"Like you care," Lara sneers. "I'm not the only one trailing after Abi like a puppy, Jo, and everyone knows it."

Heat flushes my cheeks and I wait until she half-jogs away before pressing my palms to my face. I don't trail after Abi. We're friends. Good friends. And nobody, especially some lame nerd, is going to come between us.

# SIXTEEN

## ABIGAIL

A week goes by and thankfully, there are no more incidents at work. I go out of my way to avoid Mandy but I know we'll run into each other eventually. The sci-fi thriller she's acting in will take another six weeks to wrap and I've been commissioned to source more costumes for the final scenes, so that means I'll be on her set.

While nothing untoward has happened at work, I've noticed a few weird things at home. Two of Rob's garden gnomes—he collected them as a kid and I haven't had the heart to throw them out—have been decapitated, a rose bush has been pulled up, the lettuce in my prized veggie patch have been mangled, and one of the neighborhood dogs has taken a new liking to my lawn every night and has left daily reminders of how much.

The gnomes could be explained away by a freak accident, some animal bumping into them, and the dog poo is indicative of a lazy owner who can't be bothered picking it up on their midnight walks, but the ruined lettuce and rose bush, one of my favorites, have been physically torn from the ground, and I'm starting to wonder if they're all connected. Mandy's way of delivering subtle messages that while Cal's away, she's still watching and waiting?

I want to call him and ask if he's been in contact with Mandy, has he somehow precipitated this? But I'm still mad at him for not returning for Rob's farewell. He knew how important it was to me—for Rob's sake—but he'd blown us off regardless. What kind of selfish narcissist does that? Besides, as if he'll tell me if he's had a thing with Mandy behind my back. He hasn't told me about his dalliances in the past.

I know we have a weird relationship and most of that's on me. I've tolerated his coming and going over the years for Rob's sake, but I didn't need to welcome him into my bed. That has been my weakness, a thirst for affection, an easy way to satisfy my physical urges without going through the hassles of dating. So while I have no right to be jealous, and I'm not, I hope he's been more discerning and hasn't given Mandy false encouragement.

As if the last week hasn't been weird enough, when I check my cell at lunchtime there's a message from Lara. We've kept in touch sporadically since high school, but I've always been wary of her ever since she ditched me in junior high. One day, she was part of my friendship group with Jo, the next she avoided me. I tried asking her about it once but she gave me some lame excuse about her folks coming down hard on her for spending so much time with friends out of school and she really needed to focus on her grades, so I didn't bother after that. Besides, I was closer to Jo anyway and it didn't matter when Lara left our group.

She's a sales rep for a pharmaceutical company now, one of the big ones, and she's been through Fort Chester twice before. The first time about eight years ago we caught up for a quick coffee, the second a year later, a snatched lunch at a café before she had to hit the road again. Both times we slipped into easy conversation, talking about our jobs, our lives. She's still single, married to her career, and loving it. I'm looking forward to hearing what she's up to now. I glance at her social media profiles occasionally but not enough to know what's happening lately.

Lara's message says she has a spare hour between meetings at the various medical centers in town, so to make it easier on her I suggest a new Mexican restaurant near the hospital. She's early as usual and has snagged two stools by the bar. The place is packed for a lunchtime, and she stands and waves when I enter.

"Hey, Abi, good to see you." She hugs me. "The bar okay? They're fully booked."

"Bar's fine. We can always have a liquid lunch instead of food."

She laughs and we sit. "I would love a margarita, but I've got four appointments this afternoon about a drug, ironically, that is good for liver disease, so I'll stick with a soda."

We order our drinks and nachos to share. "So how are you, Lara? It's only been seven years since I've seen you."

"Time flies when you're having fun. Actually, I've been in and out of Fort Chester a lot over the last month but haven't had time to catch up until now." She shrugs. "I love my job, what can I say?"

"It suits you."

She looks fabulous. Her skin is flawless for mid-thirties, her hair artfully colored and cut, her taupe designer suit and matching shoes a sleek combination of professional and sexy. Makes my flamboyant taste in fashion—I'm wearing black and white striped flares, a crimson crop top, and a satin peacock-blue jacket—look gaudy.

"What about you? How's Robert?" She pauses for a moment. "Callan?"

I stifle a laugh. What is it about the women I went to high school with and their obsession with Cal? It's been eighteen years, get over it already.

"I have a new job as fashion coordinator for a film studio, which is fantastic. Rob left for college last week, and Callan's on location in Seattle."

"I see his photos everywhere."

Interesting that she doesn't ask more about my job or Rob, but focuses instantly on Cal. "Yeah, he's talented."

"He is." An inexplicable blush stains her cheeks pink. "Actually, I was hoping you could give me his number?"

I struggle to hide my surprise. Is this why she wanted to catch up? She has a thing for Cal and wants to call him? Presumptuous, considering she wouldn't know if we're still a couple or not. When Lara and I last caught up years ago, Cal and I had been together so this request is plain weird.

As if reading my mind, she says, "My company wants to do a massive shoot for their latest menopause drug, some kind of 'women dancing through a meadow in the prime of their life' thing, and I saw Callan did some great wilderness shots last year so I think he'll be perfect for this job. And I'd rather call because we knew each other in high school and it's more professional, rather than reaching out via his DMs, which are probably full of admiring fans."

It all sounds very plausible but why would a drug rep be interested in the organizational logistics of an ad campaign? And be keeping such a close eye on a photographer she knew in high school that she knows what kind of shots he's currently taking?

Cal plasters his work on social media. He has to, to keep the job requests flowing. He's good and I check out his photos regularly when he's away. I'm glad he's found his niche and earns a good living from it. For a while I hoped Rob would inherit his father's talent with a camera but Rob almost had an aversion to snapping pics and I wondered if that's because he didn't like the way his father treated us.

"I know this is out of the blue, Abi, but it'll really help if I can contact Cal."

I can't refuse her request without appearing churlish, so I say, "Sure, I'll give you his number."

"Thanks." She lights up like I've agreed to give her Chris Hemsworth's cell number and I know there's more behind her request. "Jo still skulking around?"

I instantly bristle. Nobody talks crap about my best friend. "Jo's fine. We see each other all the time."

"I bet," she mutters. "Is she still possessive of you?"

"Not at all."

I hate that Lara has put me in the position of defending Jo, when in reality I don't have a lot of close friends apart from her. Acquaintances, yes, but Jo's my go-to person when the going gets tough and I'm lucky to have her.

"Glad to hear it. You must have a large circle of mutual friends, living here so long?"

I don't. I've been so focused on raising Rob I haven't socialized a lot. It's been easy having Jo come around all the time, another member of our family, rather than me going out in search of new friends. Tom's great too, but he's more Cal's friend and they're so much alike that I can't adore him wholeheartedly. There's something about him that's a little off-putting, as if he says and does all the right things but has an ulterior motive. And I've caught him staring at me a few times, as if he'd like to be more than friends if Cal wasn't in the picture. It's unnerving so I do my best not to be alone with him. I think Jo has a thing for him too, despite trying to hide it, and

I'd never encroach on her territory: not again, no matter how inadvertently I'd ended up with Cal.

Though Tom's been a good friend too; we've known him since we moved here and he's fun to be around. These days, he's as absent as Cal is because of his job, and a small part of me is relieved. It would feel weird, Tom hanging around us with Cal away. But apart from Jo and Tom, I'm not close to anybody. I know a lot of people through my various jobs over the years, but they're more acquaintances than friends.

Not that I'll tell Lara that. I don't like what she's implying, that Jo monopolizes my time and deliberately keeps me away from other people. Jo's not like that. She hasn't got a jealous bone in her body; not anymore. If she moved past what she perceived as the ultimate betrayal when I got pregnant to Cal, she's not possessive. And I'm eternally grateful she's stuck by me all these years.

"At the risk of sounding like a boring stay-at-home mom, I don't get out much." I fake a grimace, when in reality I've loved every minute of being a homebody for my son. "So, yeah, I have other friends besides Jo, but I don't see them much by choice."

Her noncommittal "uh-huh" is an odd response, like she doesn't believe me, and I'm thankful when I see the waiter wending his way toward us.

When our drinks and nachos arrive, we make small talk as we eat, but by the end of the hour, I'm no closer to figuring out what's Lara's deal is with Cal.

And if she's been in and out of town over the last four weeks, does she have something to do with Jo's vandalism and the odd incidents around my house?

# SEVENTEEN

## JO

"How's life in backwater Hicksville treating you?"

I poke my tongue out at Rex. "It's almost eighteen years since I moved to Fort Chester. Are you ever going to build a bridge and get over it?"

"No. My abandonment issues run deep." He clutches his chest, his expression one of deliberate misery, and I laugh.

"We catch up here in San Fran often enough." I point to the view of the harbor outside the restaurant window. "Don't want you getting tired of me."

"That'll never happen and you know it." He picks up a fry from the share plate between us and swipes it through ketchup, the memory of him doing the same thing when we first came to this restaurant years ago bringing an unexpected lump to my throat.

I'm not big on reminiscing as a rule. The past kicked my butt and I prefer to focus on the future. But my friendship with Rex has stood the test of time and I always try to catch up with him in person every few months.

"How's the perfect princess doing?" He pops the fry into

his mouth and chews, and I know he's only asking about Abi out of politeness, because he knows how much she means to me, rather than any real interest.

"Abi's good. Coping surprisingly well now that Robbie's at college."

"Bet you're making it easier on her." He makes a disparaging snorting sound. "I hope she's not taking advantage of you."

He's said this often over the years and I usually play it down, but a small part of me likes the fact Rex isn't Abi's biggest fan when everyone else dotes on her. He's never forgiven her for being the reason I left San Francisco and moved to Fort Chester and isn't reticent in letting me know.

While I don't badmouth Abi, I don't exactly stop him from doing it—my one small rebellious act in our otherwise solid friendship.

"Will you stay in town now Robbie's moved away?"

His question comes out of left field but I know what he's implying. That I only moved to Fort Chester because of my godmother duties and my friendship with Abi isn't as solid as I'd like him to believe.

"Of course I'll stay. Fort Chester is home now." And as long as Tom keeps returning, I'm not moving.

His eyebrows rise a fraction, like he doesn't believe me for a second. "Jo, I worry about you sometimes. Your obsession isn't good for you."

He pushes the barely touched plate of fries away, an action almost as shocking as his declaration.

"What are you talking about?"

Surely he hasn't figured out why I've willingly stuck around Fort Chester all these years?

"Abi, you're obsessed with her." His mouth turns down at the corners as he shakes his head. "It's not healthy."

I almost laugh in relief but stifle it at the last moment. "It's not an obsession when it's a friendship." I wave my hand between the two of us. "Do you think I'm obsessed with you? Because our friendship is just as important to me."

"Not as important, considering you abandoned me to chase after the princess."

"Again with the abandonment issues, huh?"

Rex often jokes about me leaving him behind but I wonder if there's more to it. There's never been anything remotely sexual between us, yet could he be as good an actor as I am, hiding his feelings behind quips and banter?

"I don't like the way you gave up your life for hers, that's all." He shrugs, but I see the dislike in his eyes. "You deserve better than her."

"Like you?"

His answering smile is bashful. "I'll always have your back and you know it."

"Glad to hear it."

We pick up our beers and clink them together, taking a sip before launching into a detailed conversation about the latest spy thriller blockbuster everyone's reading at the moment. The familiarity of our book discussion soothes me, but I can't dismiss Rex's scathing assessment of Abi altogether. He's wrong about her. I don't deserve better.

But I do deserve to be happy like she is.

I plan on heading back to Fort Chester after lunch with Rex, but as I get in my car, my cell rings and my heart skips a beat.

I know that ringtone.

Tom.

Hating that my hands shake a tad as I answer, I make sure to sound carefree. "Hey, Tom, how are you?"

"Good, Jo. You?"

"Never better. I'm in San Fran for the day. Just had lunch with an old friend."

"Wow."

"You're surprised I have a friend apart from you, Cal, and Abi?"

He laughs as I intend. "No. I'm wowed because I'm in San Fran too." There's a long pause bordering on uncomfortable when he says, "Want to catch up?"

Elation expands in my chest. "Considering the odds of us being in the same city at the same time when I haven't seen you for months, we absolutely should catch up."

"Great. There's a new bar by Fisherman's Wharf. I'll text you the address and see you in thirty?"

"I'll be there."

He disconnects and I'm left staring at my cell in disbelief. Things like this don't happen to me. We text occasionally when he's on the road, but we don't chat often. So for him to call... this is big. Huge.

When my cell pings with the address, I plug it into my sat nav and I'm so eager I arrive ten minutes early. It's mid-afternoon, so the crowd is mostly tourists and I snag a table outside, giving us a good view of the pier and the bay beyond. I'm nervous, so I order a vodka shot and down it before he arrives. Crazy, because I'm not a big drinker but hope the alcohol will give me courage.

The last time Tom and I were alone was months ago, after one of Abi's games nights. She loves old classic board games and had invited 'the family'—me and Tom—to play with her, Cal, and Robbie. We'd laughed ourselves silly over Pictionary, invented words in Scrabble, and been bankrupted in Monopoly. Cal had drunk too much bourbon and gone to bed early, Robbie had gone to his room to play online games with his friends, and

Abi had fallen asleep on the couch, leaving Tom and me to clean up the pizza boxes and chat.

It had been a great night. He'd told me about some of the amazing hotels he'd stayed in recently, I told him about my misbehaving clients. We'd talked. We'd laughed. And for that all-too-brief hour when it had just been the two of us, I'd imagined the spark was real.

Predictably, he'd backpedaled after that night, retreating firmly into the friendship zone, and we haven't talked much since.

Until now.

The odds of us being in the city at the same time are minuscule, let alone him reaching out to me, so when I see him striding toward me—faded denim highlighting his long legs, white polo clinging to his chest, brown hair tousled, hazel eyes twinkling—I lose the plot a little and fling myself at him.

He laughs as he hugs me and I embrace him, tight. When we release each other, there's curiosity in his eyes, and something else; something I dare not label in case I get my hopes up.

"I've missed you, Jo," he says, pulling up a seat next to mine. "How's this for a coincidence, huh?"

"I know, it's crazy, but in a good way."

A waiter approaches and we order two beers. I could wait until the drinks arrive to ask the burning question, but this is Tom, and it seems I've spent years "waiting" around him.

"So why did you call?"

"I wanted to check in. See how you and Abi are doing after Rob left for college."

I ignore the prickle of annoyance that he includes Abi in his question. Why can't he just be checking in with me?

"I'm good, Abi too."

"I worry about her. Her whole life has been wrapped up in that boy."

I happen to agree but we haven't seen each other in ages and all he can talk about is Abi?

I've watched them over the years, to see if there's any sign Tom's attracted to her. It would gut me to lose out to her again. And while I know she wouldn't dally with Tom deliberately, she's so bubbly and gorgeous that guys can't help but be drawn to her.

Thankfully, I haven't noticed anything untoward. Abi treats Tom like a goofy friend and he's never remotely flirted with her. It gives me hope that I'm the one he likes hanging out with and his invitation today proves it.

"Don't worry about her. She's met someone so that'll be a good distraction."

He stiffens imperceptibly and his lips compress into an unimpressed line. "So soon?"

Annoyed that he doesn't seem pleased, I say, "About time, if you ask me. She's been hung up on Cal for too long."

He nods but there's a tenseness about him that wasn't there when he arrived. His shoulders are bunched, his fingers clenched. Surely he hasn't been waiting for Robbie to head off to college so that gives him an open shot at Abi?

The thought makes the vodka I consumed earlier toss in my stomach and I press my hand to my belly to settle it.

"Speaking of Cal, there's something else I want to talk to you about." He screws up his nose, like he's smelled something nasty. "I don't know how to say this, so I'm just going to come out with it."

My heart sinks. This isn't the emotional declaration I've been hoping for. It's something unpleasant and I brace.

"I spoke to Cal and... uh... he seems to think you have a thing for him."

I force a laugh when it's the last thing I feel like doing,

because Tom doesn't sound jealous as I hoped. He sounds...
disgusted.

"You know Cal. He thinks every woman in the world is in
love with him." I roll my eyes. "Give me a break. He's Abi's and
always has been. Do you seriously think I'd go after my best
friend's ex?"

"No." He doesn't sound convinced and he's looking at me
through slightly narrowed eyes. "I brought it up because I don't
want you getting hurt. Cal's a player. And he might be toying
with you to make Abi jealous."

This time my laughter is genuine, as that's exactly what I'm
doing with Cal, but in reverse. "Don't worry about me. I know
what Cal's like, we've flirted for years. It means nothing."

But as the beers arrive and we slip into comfortable territory, talking about his job and mine, laughing at a video message
Robbie sent him from UCLA, chatting about plans for Thanksgiving, I can't help but wonder if I'm playing with fire.

Is Cal getting the wrong idea?

Am I taking my plan too far?

# EIGHTEEN

## JO

My high school years are much better than expected, thanks to Abi.

We're a solid twosome, surviving everything from a wilderness camp that gave us both a bad case of poison ivy, to prom, which we attended with two quarterbacks, best buds like Abi and me, who made the night fun. I know I never would've got an invite unless Bradley didn't have a crush on Abi and was scared she might say no if his friend Sammy didn't ask me, but I didn't care because I got to go with Abi rather than being left out and that was enough for me.

Everything is good until our senior year.

Callan's arrival changes everything.

Not for her, but for me. I've never had a crush on a guy, not like my feelings for Callan. He's the most gorgeous guy I've ever seen and he's always smiling, like he knows a secret the world doesn't. He wears faded denim and black T-shirts, like some bad boy wannabe from the fifties, and he struts rather than walks the corridors of Lilydale High.

It's love at first sight.

Unfortunately, Callan has the same effect on every girl in our senior class, not just me, and his name is on every girl's lips during breaks, during gym, and after school. Abi doesn't seem particularly enamored but she's one of few; or maybe she's better at hiding it. I'll need to fight the rest of the girls to the death for Callan's attention.

Abi waves a hand in front of my face. "You're spaced out today. What are you thinking about?"

"Nothing," I mumble, and take a bite of my salad sandwich. I don't want to share the news of my crush with her just yet. I want to savor it, like an illicit secret. Then again, I blush every time I think about Callan and Abi's smart so she'll figure it out.

She pops a few crisps in her mouth and chews, studying me. "Don't tell me you've joined the masses."

"What do you mean?"

She rolls her eyes. "You're crushing on Callan."

I could deny it but what's the point? My cheeks are on fire and she sees it, pointing at my face with a big grin. "You don't have to say anything. The answer's right there."

"I hate being a redhead," I mutter, and she slings a sympathetic arm around my shoulders.

"It's okay to like a guy."

"I don't just like him," I blurt, wishing I could take the words back when her eyebrows shoot up.

"What does that mean?"

"It means I'm an idiot and I think I'm head over heels in love for the first time in my life."

I practically whisper the words, as if saying them out loud will mean everyone will know my embarrassing secret. How could I love someone I barely know? Someone who barely acknowledges I exist? It's crazy but I can't help it. My chest aches every time I see him, in the same way it does when I watch *Sleepless in Seattle* and want to bawl at the end but try not to.

"Wow." Abi's looking at me like she can't quite figure me out. Join the club. I'm not like other girls who've had crushes all through high school, so maybe that's why I've fallen particularly hard for Callan. "Just be careful, okay?"

"Of what?"

Abi's nose crinkles like it does when she's thinking. "He seems like a nice guy but I think he knows every girl's crushing on him and he might take advantage of that."

"By?"

"Dating. Sleeping around." She shrugs. "I just wouldn't want you to get hurt."

"Because you don't think a guy like him would be interested in a girl like me?"

Abi slugs me softly on the arm. "You know that's not what I mean. I'm just wary of guys like Callan, because they can have anyone they want and know it."

"As long as you don't set your sights on him, I'll be fine."

She laughs, thinking I'm joking, but I'm not. Abi attracts people to her wherever she goes. Everybody loves Abi, and I don't think I could cope if that extended to Callan. We've never competed over a boy before and I don't want to start now. Abi doesn't realize it because she's a nice person but I play second fiddle to her like I do to everyone else in my life: my mom, my dad, my sister. I'm an afterthought, never anyone's first choice. Even in gym, I'm chosen last. I pretend it doesn't affect me but it does. I'll be gutted if Callan chooses anyone over me, which he inevitably will, but I can't cope if it's Abi.

"Did you hear he's having a big party at his place this Saturday night?"

I haven't but it's been eight weeks since Callan started school here, fifty-six long days in which I've watched him from afar, planning how we can be together.

A party seems like the perfect place to make a move.

And what better way to get a guy to notice me than to sleep with him?

"Are we going?" I try to sound casual, but it's moot after I've just admitted being in love with the guy, and Abi smiles.

"Of course. Maybe I'll discover what all the fuss is about?"

I hope not, because come Saturday night, Callan's going to know who I am.


An hour later, I'm putting the finishing touches to my English literature project, confident I've nailed the brief. Being a book-worm, I watch anything online that fuels my passion so the moment this assignment landed, I knew what I was going to do to boost my grade. I've taken some of the classics—*Pride and Prejudice, Jane Eyre, Little Women, Wuthering Heights, Great Expectations* to name a few—and recreated them in miniature form. It's taken me hours but I'm thrilled with the final result.

I'm taking photos of them when a shadow falls over me.

"Well, well, well, look who's playing with books taken from her doll's house," Mandy sneers and I'm annoyed that it does little to detract from her beauty. She's the quintessential cheer-leader: long legs, big boobs, perfectly straight white teeth, big blue eyes, silky-straight blonde hair. We've had the occasional run-in over the last few years but for the most part, she looks straight through me.

I have no idea why she's targeting me now but I'm older and wiser—it's not my first day of junior high, the last time she tried to bully me—so I'm not putting up with her crap.

"I'm busy, Mandy."

"I can see that." She snickers. "Must be very time-consuming, playing with doll's stuff."

"Just as time-consuming as playing with shredded paper tied together to make pom-poms," I say, saccharine sweet, and my comeback has the desired effect when she flushes an angry crimson.

"You're pathetic," she mutters, picking up one of my miniature books and squashing it between her thumb and forefinger. "And everyone knows it too. The only reason anyone talks to you is because you're friends with Abi and she's popular." She leans in close, close enough that I can smell her cloying jasmine-scented body spray. "You'd be a nobody without her."

Fury floods every muscle in my body and I leap to my feet, but before I can physically harm her, Callan saunters into the classroom. He's behind Mandy's back and she hasn't seen him so it's the perfect opportunity for him to see her for what she truly is. They're usually close; she's always fawning all over him and he laps it up. Time for Callan to get a wake-up call regarding the company he keeps.

"That's harsh," I say, keeping my tone steady with effort. "I know Abi's popular, because she's a great person. Everybody loves her." My gaze deliberately takes in her black mini and tight tank top, before I raise an eyebrow, implying the opposite for her.

Anger sparks her eyes as she takes the bait. "I'm a hundred times more popular than her and always will be. But don't try sucking up to me because I wouldn't let you anywhere near me. You're a pathetic loser who's friendless and Abi only allows you to hang around her out of pity."

I bite back a triumphant grin as Callan approaches, a disapproving frown denting his brow. I expect him to say something to put Mandy in her place. I don't expect him to drape an arm across my shoulders and say, "Hey, babe. Your assignment looks awesome. It's turned out great."

Mandy's jaw drops and her stunned expression is so comical I can't help but laugh. It's a tad hysterical, because the most gorgeous guy in school has his arm around me and it feels so good.

"You're nasty, Mandy." He makes a shooing motion with his free hand. "Why don't you run along now and go play with your mean girls?"

For a second, I'm glad we're not in the science lab surrounded by beakers and test tubes and other potentially dangerous instruments, because Mandy looks like she could easily kill me.

With a shake of her head at Callan, and a last malevolent glare at me, she spins on her heel and stalks out of the classroom. I'm relieved, but disappointed when Callan removes his arm almost immediately.

"You okay?" he asks.

I nod, predictably tongue-tied now it's just him and me. It's the first time he's even looked at me, let alone spoken to me. As for the way he defended me, I'm beyond speechless. We don't know each other at all. He's surrounded by popular kids in every class, I'm usually down the back blending into the shadows, so him acknowledging me as a fellow classmate let alone standing up for me... I could hug him.

"Don't let Mandy get to you. She's jealous of the competition."

Before I can fathom what he means, he picks up a strand of my hair and rubs it between his fingertips, murmuring, "Gorgeous," before letting it fall and it happens so quickly I wonder if I imagined the whole thing.

"How do you even know who I am?" I blurt, mortified when he chuckles.

"Babe, with hair that beautiful, you stand out."

He thinks my flaming red hair is *beautiful*? He's noticed me because of it? My run-in with Mandy had been the pits and she ruined one of my books, but having Callan stand up for me and compliment my hair... could this day get any better?

I must be grinning like an imbecile because he chuckles. "Don't let girls like that get to you. It seems like every one of them is in competition since I got here," he says, with a wink, and my embarrassment is complete. Of course he knows all the girls like him and to Callan, I'm one of many. "But I won't tolerate bullying and I'll tell Mandy to lay off you, okay?"

I don't need him fighting my battles, but I know Mandy. If she thinks she has dibs on Callan, she won't want to get him offside again and will do as he says.

I shrug, as if his chivalry means little, when I'm swooning a little on the inside from him coming to my rescue. "Thanks for sticking up for me. I appreciate it."

"Anytime." He winks again and his lopsided smile makes my pulse race.

But before I can say anything else students start filtering in and my opportunity to wow him with my scintillating conversation is lost. It doesn't matter, because now Callan will remember me and come Saturday night at his party, I'll have an excuse to approach him.

I can see it clearly. We'll strike up a conversation, I'll flirt a little, maybe lay my hand on his arm, show him I'm into him, and then... he's so hot he would've definitely had sex before so he'll know what he's doing even if I don't. Apart from how much I like him, he's the perfect guy to give my virginity to.

I can't wait.

# NINETEEN

## ABIGAIL

I've been so busy at work trying to put in extra hours to make up for that major screw-up that wasn't my fault, I've hardly seen Noah. Since our lunch at the café he's visited me twice at the studio, once for a quick coffee, the other for a walk around the block one lunchtime. Both times an extra has mistaken him for Zac Efron and it's become our in-joke. It's like he has no idea of how good-looking he is—humble as well as gorgeous—and he's incredibly considerate, as demonstrated by the snacks and lunch he brought me both times. He's incredible and I'm glad I'm swamped with work otherwise I'd be at risk of seriously falling for him.

It's too soon and I'm wary in case I'm transferring my love onto him now Rob isn't around anymore. But he's sweet and kind and understanding, and I know the more time we spend together, the harder it will be not to throw caution to the wind and fall into a heady relationship with him.

Today's been another bad day. A uniform went missing from an ongoing police procedural drama, a consignment of cheerleader outfits hasn't arrived for a teen musical starting shooting tomorrow, and my favorite pen leaked ink all over my diary, so I'm not in the best of moods when I walk into the restaurant to meet Noah for an early dinner.

He stands when I reach the table and I'm struck anew by how good-looking he is. I've always gone for the clean-cut/strong jaw look, and tonight, his ivory button-down shirt highlights his tan and his chinos emphasize his long legs. And when he smiles, the trials of my day fade away.

"Hey, Abi, good to see you." He kisses me on the cheek and I inhale his aftershave, an intoxicating crisp citrus blend that makes me want to burrow into his neck and sniff some more.

"Good to see you too." I squeeze his upper arm to show my appreciation for him agreeing to a quick dinner and being so understanding; and it never hurts to cop a feel of a good bicep.

"So how long have we got?"

I grimace. "An hour at the most. Sorry, but I've got so much to do at work. Lately, it seems to be one mess after another I have to deal with."

"That's tough." He reaches across the table and snags my hand. "And don't apologize. I'm grateful to be able to spend any time with you."

"You say the sweetest things."

"It's easy with you."

He's right. I've never felt more at ease with a person I haven't known long than with Noah. He's comfortable to be around. Undemanding, laid-back, just what I need in comparison with my crazy job currently.

"Before we order, I've got something to tell you."

My heart sinks. Of course this has been too good to be true. If he has a girlfriend or wife, it'll top off my crappy day nicely and I may scream.

"What's up?"

He hesitates, and I know his news isn't good. "I may need to leave town sooner rather than later."

I clamp down on my first response, "Hell no," and ask, "Why?"

I try not to sound needy but I'm disappointed. I know his job is transient and he moves around a lot to research the towns for his book, but he mentioned sticking around for a while and implied it's because of me.

"I'm being kicked out of my accommodation." He shakes his head. "The rent was minimal so I could stay indefinitely. And with taking a year off to write this book, it's not economically viable to dip into my savings to stay at a motel long-term, and there's no trailer park in town for short-term rentals."

"So how soon will you leave?"

"By the end of the week."

I had no idea how much I like him until this moment, when the thought of him leaving town before we've had a chance to explore this thing between us leaves me cold.

There's an obvious solution but I'm crazy to contemplate it.

I have two spare rooms, the one Cal uses when he returns to town and Rob's room, but I'm not comfortable having a guy I've only just met move into my house. I may like Noah, but I'm not a complete idiot. Especially when he has no online presence. I believed his rationale when he told me why, but it's a blip I can't ignore. Everyone I know, except Jo, has at least one social media profile. Though even my introverted friend has a website for her dog grooming business.

I'd never invite a guy I barely know, no matter how cute and sweet, into my home, but there's a room over the garage I use to store stuff. Racks with favorite fashion trends I can't bear to part with. Boxes of Rob's old baseball trophies and books. Random memorabilia. I've always thought I should clear it and rent it out.

While my parents were more than generous in gifting me the house and paying for Rob's college tuition, I never took their support for granted and like to have a good nest egg. Their life insurance policies gave me financial security, a sizeable six figures, and I rarely dip into it. Jo teases me about my "just in case" fund but I want my son to have the security I did growing up in case anything happens to me.

"You've gone quiet," Noah says, squeezing my hand. "If it was up to me, Abi, I wouldn't leave. I'm enjoying getting to know you but I need to manage my savings carefully so I can take as much time off as I need to do this book justice, and that means I can't stay in Fort Chester."

He releases my hand and sits back. "I've already checked out cheap accommodation in the next town I'd planned on visiting so it's time I made a move."

Before I can second-guess the wisdom of offering a virtual stranger a room, I say, "What if you didn't have to leave Fort Chester?"

"I have so much more research to do here so that would be perfect, but I already told you, I can't afford—"

"I have a room over my garage. It's clean and functional, with a sofa bed and mini fridge, so once I clear out the stuff I store there, it'll be livable." I snap my fingers. "And more to the point, rent-free."

Gratitude makes the indigo flecks in his eyes pop. "That's an incredible offer. Are you sure?"

I nod. "Absolutely. Your work's important and…" I bite my lip, wondering if I should say too much too soon, before continuing, "I'm enjoying getting to know you too. I think we could have a good time together."

"Me too."

This time he captures both my hands and raises one to his

lips, pressing a kiss to the back of it. "Though I can't live there rent-free. Let me pay you something?"

I shake my head. "The more savings you have, the longer you can stay in town, yes?"

He nods, and I add, "I have a feeling I'm going to like having you around, Noah Powell, so let's say you can pay me back with the occasional dinner. How's that?"

"Great."

He smiles at me and my heart races. My offer may have been impulsive but I can't help but feel it's right. I never really loved Cal. We fell into a relationship because of Rob, playing house and trying our hand at a relationship because it was the right thing to do. I've never had the whole "starry-eyed, heart racing, infatuation" most women have had at least once in their lifetime by the time they're my age. At thirty-six, I deserve a little excitement in my life and I think Noah can provide it.

"I really appreciate your offer, Abi."

"You're welcome."

As the waiter approaches and I realize I haven't even looked at the menu since I arrived, I hope Noah and I get to have dinner dates like this a lot more often in the months ahead.

# TWENTY

## JO

I'm standing outside Abi's door with sweaty palms and a churning stomach. The fact I'm using her front door and not the back as I usually do already makes me feel out of sorts, but she's invited me to dinner to meet her new man and it feels weird entering her house through the back when I could stumble on the two of them in a passionate embrace or worse. Not that Abi's the type to have sex with a guy on her kitchen table if she's expecting company but better to be safe than sorry.

To say I'm surprised she asked Noah to move in is an understatement. Though technically they're not living together, but he's over the garage and that's close for a guy she barely knows. By her grand gesture I can see how smitten she is with him but this is a big step for her. Apart from Cal, I've never known her to date any other guy and while a small part of me resents she's found someone so fast—I envisaged the two of us going out a lot more once Rob left and she needed to fill the empty-nester void —I'm happy for her, as long as this Noah is nice and treats her right.

I raise my hand to knock as the door swings open and Abi grabs my hand and pulls me in.

"Hey, what's—"

"Do you think I'm nuts?"

"With the way you just hauled me through your front door, yes, I do."

She pulls a face and only then do I notice how much trouble she's gone to with her make-up: shimmery ice-mint shadow on her lids and kohl rimming her eyes, careful contouring, bronzed cheekbones and crimson glossed lips. "Please tell me you'll give me your honest opinion later."

"You know I will. Now, can I meet this perfect man?"

"Nobody's perfect," she says, but she's so excited she's practically bouncing. "I really like him, Jo, and I trust your judgment."

"It's only dinner, Abi, you're not marrying the guy." I point to the kitchen. "Is he here yet?"

"Yeah. He's stirring the marinara sauce for me."

My eyebrows rise. "You cooked your world-famous seafood? You *are* out to impress."

"I just want tonight to go well." She's so nervous she's wringing her hands. "You're my best friend, and I'm hoping he'll become someone important to me, so I want you guys to get along."

"You don't need my approval." I placate her by stilling her hands, secretly pleased she values my opinion so much. "If he makes you happy, that's all that matters."

But it's not that simple and we both know it. Our gazes lock and guilt shifts in hers as she remembers the last time she asked for my approval—when she told me she was expecting Cal's baby. That day had been the worst of my life and tonight will be easy compared to that. She may not want to hear it but I'm right: I don't need to approve of her new boyfriend. It's her life and how she chooses to live it moving forward, it's not my place to judge. Besides, I'm hoping she won't judge me if my relationship with Tom progresses as I want it to and she discovers what I've done—flirt with Cal—to hurry him along.

"I have no idea why I'm so nervous," she says, and smooths a hand over her already-perfect hair.

"He's the first guy you've dated since Cal, it's natural."

"Yeah, but this?" She points to her made-up face. "It's war paint to hide the quivering mess I am on the inside."

"You look gorgeous." I tap the side of my nose. "Your secret's safe with me, now come on." I hand her the bottle of wine I've brought and give her a gentle nudge. "Let's get this dinner underway."

As I enter the kitchen behind Abi, Noah's replacing a lid on a pot and drying off his hands on a dishcloth. In profile, he's tall and handsome in a clean-cut way. Dark denim, navy button-down shirt, loafers. Not my type. I prefer my men scruffier, a little rough around the edges, like Tom.

When he turns to face me, I see the appeal. He has an understated sexiness, and those eyes... the striking color of the Pacific on a perfect summer's day. Compared to most guys, he'd stand out in a crowd and Abi's like that too, able to turn heads. They make a good-looking couple.

"Noah, I'd like you to meet my best friend, Joelle," Abi says, her head swiveling between us like she's watching a tennis match.

"Call me Jo." I shake his hand, and Abi visibly relaxes. What did she expect, I'd throw him over my shoulder in a martial art move? She's wound way too tight and it's a dead give-away she's already halfway to falling for this guy.

"Hey, Jo. Nice to meet you."

Noah's eyes are clear, his expression guileless. On first

impressions, he appears genuine, but if anyone knows appearances can hide a multitude of sins, I do.

I'm indulging in a heavy flirtation with my best friend's ex to make his bestie jealous and regardless of how long ago their relationship ended, Abi won't like it. But having a new man in her life will go some way to soothing the blow when I tell her the truth: how I'm using Cal, leading him on, with no intention of following through. With a little luck, she'll be so enamored of Noah by then, she won't mind.

Yeah, right. Since when am I prone to delusions?

She may not love Cal but she'll hate that I used him in my stupid plan. I know it's not fair on him but I'm tired of wanting something I can't have. I'm too old to sit back and wait. I need to make things happen.

"Noah, if you uncork the wine please, I'll dish up," Abi says, bustling about the kitchen like her nerves haven't eased at all. She opens the fridge, stares into it, before closing it again, followed by a weird cupboard-and-drawer-opening routine that has me stifling a giggle.

If Noah notices, he doesn't say, and that elevates my opinion of him.

"Sure," he says, and I notice his deep voice has a rich timbre that's also attractive.

As he uncorks the wine, we make small talk about our jobs mostly, and I understand what Abi sees in him. He's quiet yet charming, exuding a strength that's appealing. Abi's always needed nurturing—first by her parents, then Cal, even Rob—and though she'd never admit it, in her mid-thirties I think she still hopes for the fabled knight in shining armor to rescue and protect her.

I have no such illusions. My longest relationship, with David Settleby, a pet food store owner in San Fran, had been three years of settling. We met at a dog expo, clicked over our mutual love for Labradors, and started dating. It had been comfortable rather than spectacular and long distance had suited me because I still had my freedom to secretly lust after Tom without a live-in guy cramping my style.

Dave had been sweet but boring, and when he started hinting at investing a sizable chunk of his savings in a diamond engagement ring, I broke it off. He was a good guy and it wouldn't have been fair to him. Besides, he'd already expanded his store and opened another two, so that would've meant me moving back to San Francisco and leaving Fort Chester behind, something I wasn't willing to do.

I know relationships implode and people move on, so I'm determined that when I get my chance with Tom I won't screw it up.

Our time is coming. Soon. I can't wait.

As we sit and serve ourselves to Abi's signature spaghetti marinara, with sides of aromatic garlic bread and a Greek salad peppered with plump olives and feta, I watch the interaction between the happy couple. For someone who's only just moved in—and technically not in the house—Noah is very comfortable.

The one thing Abi and I agree on when it comes to men is that if a guy seems too good to be true, he usually is, and Noah gives off that vibe, like he's perfect but there's more beneath the surface.

Abi must be lonely with Rob gone and I hope she's not latching onto the first guy to pay her attention, because that makes her ripe for the picking from a scammer. The fact he has no online presence is a major red flag for me. Then again, I keep a low profile online too so I can't judge. The last thing I want is a bunch of people who barely spoke to me in high school being privy to my current life. I've never understood the attraction. Doesn't mean I don't do my fair share of cyberstalking, particularly Tom, who's more than happy to broadcast his whereabouts and photos online. Thank goodness.

He's had so many wild adventures over the years: traveling across the Nullarbor in Australia, caravanning through New Zealand, taking luxury trains through Europe, exploring the starkness of Alaska. I love reading his articles and how he brings alive each place he visits. It's a gift and I'm slightly envious. He and Cal are incredibly talented in their respective fields, when the best I can do is the occasional lion's mane on a poodle when an eccentric client demands it.

The meal is enjoyable, with Noah regaling us with tales of various Californian towns, Abi talking about funny outtakes of shows filmed at the studio, and even I have witty anecdotes to share from my dog grooming. But as the meal winds down and we push away our empty dessert plates—Abi's tiramisu is her go-to dessert to impress—I start feeling like a third wheel.

It's nothing overt and they don't do anything to deliberately alienate me, it's just a feeling. With their shared glances and casual touching as they clean up, I'm increasingly uncomfortable, and I beg off coffee when Abi offers it.

"If you guys don't mind, I'll call it a night. Dinner's been great but I have an early start in the morning and picky Pomeranians don't wait for anybody."

Abi laughs but Noah shoots me an assessing look, like he's trying to figure out if I'm lying or not. I don't care. I need to get out of here before Abi sees what I'm trying to hide: plain, old-fashioned jealousy.

Abi has led a charmed life and even now, when many empty nesters are crying into their gin alone every night, she's lucked into a great guy. I should be happy for her, and I am, but I can't help the envy that's a constant burr.

"It was fun getting to know you, Jo," Noah says, shaking my

hand again, and I smile, hoping it doesn't come out a grimace, as I say, "Likewise."

"I'll walk you out," Abi says, but I hold up my hand.

"I'm fine. You stay here with Noah." I squeeze her arm. "We'll talk tomorrow."

I know she's dying to hear my opinion of Noah but I'm not in the mood to wax lyrical about him. I want to leave them to their cozy twosome—I hate feeling extraneous.

"Okay." She mouths, "Are you alright?" and I nod, before leaving as fast as I can so my best friend doesn't see how much I covet her life at times like this.

# TWENTY-ONE

## JO

THEN

The morning after Callan's party, I'm still sulking. I can't believe I had to leave to get Mom's migraine meds, then look after her. Dad made me promise I'd stay with her because a few times in the past he's had to take her to hospital to get really strong painkilling injections when the normal drugs don't work.

So I stewed the whole night, imagining one of the many girls who lust after Callan as much as I do making a move on him, meaning I've missed my chance. But I'm not going to back down like I usually do, and before I can second-guess my impulsive decision, I head over to Callan's.

It's ten a.m. and I can offer to help clean up, prove how useful I am to have around. Who knows, maybe I'll pluck up the courage to ask him out?

There's a vast difference between having a few drinks and dropping subtle hints I want to sleep with him at a party, and declaring how much I like him in daylight, but I'll see how I feel when I get there and how receptive he is. Callan's nice to everyone and if I'm finally on his radar, maybe he'll notice me as dating material?

Since he stood up for me against Mandy, he's smiled at me a few times in the corridors at school so it's not like he's completely oblivious that I exist. Whenever he acknowledges me, Abi nudges me and giggles like she's in preschool and I pretend it doesn't mean much when I rehash those smiles every time it happens, usually to the detriment of the lesson after, and my grades are suffering.

Not that Mom and Dad care. They're so focused on Talia these days it's like I'm invisible. I relished not having my every move scrutinized and found lacking when I quit ballet, but now Talia's proving to be a prodigy in every form of dance, I hate being on the outer.

The most ludicrous thing of all is our family dinners. It's like my folks want to maintain this stupid façade of a perfect family when nothing can be further from the truth. Mom's obsession with having a daughter follow in her footsteps is ruining all our lives. Even our meals have become portion-controlled down to the last calorie, so Talia doesn't gain an ounce of weight. Every meal is some variation on a salad, with a tiny serving of protein on the side. I miss Mom's mac'n'cheese and Dad's burgers on the grill. She freaked when she saw I bought hot dogs for that science experiment, thinking I was going to eat them. I'm over it.

I'm barely a block from home when I run into Lara. Bizarre, like thinking about our science experiment conjures her up. We haven't interacted much since then and I'm glad. There's something about her I don't trust. She has this way of looking at me like she sees all the way through to my soul and can pinpoint every one of my insecurities.

"Hey," she says, and I nod in acknowledgment. The less interaction the better. I have places to be—namely, Callan's house—and I don't want to waste time talking to someone I do my best to ignore most days. "You missed a great party last night."

I loathe her smirk. "I was there."

"For about two minutes." She rolls her eyes. "Too bad. Everyone got wasted and had a ball."

I have no interest in getting drunk or high. But I did have an agenda last night and Mom's migraine put paid to that. I'm still peeved about it.

"You did me a favor when you told me what Abi was saying behind my back, so maybe I should do the same for you?"

Her upper lip is curled in a slight sneer and there's a hint of malice in her narrowed eyes. Either she suspects I lied about Abi to get rid of her from our friendship group or she's genuinely heard something about me.

She shrugs. "I mean, like you said, if it was me, I'd want to know."

I don't want to give her the satisfaction of agreeing but I am curious. I'll play it down, though, not appear too eager. "I don't listen to gossip."

Her lip-glossed mouth curves into a smug grin. "According to Mandy, this is fact, not gossip."

Mandy? I can only imagine what that cow has been saying about me. If Callan warned her off me like he said he would, I'd be number one on her hit list.

"Since when are you two close?"

"Since my other *friends* didn't want me around anymore." She glares at me with genuine hatred. "Besides, Mandy's much more fun than you and Abi. You're lame."

"And you're picking up Mandy's winning ways in labeling people, I see."

She doesn't respond well to my droll response, an angry red staining her cheeks like blush applied wrong. "At least Mandy's popular, which is more than I can say for you." She pauses, her dismissive glance flicking over me. "And she's right, Abi only hangs out with you because she feels sorry for you."

I refuse to show how hurt I am. It's not true. Abi and I have built a strong friendship over the last six years and I won't let Lara's petty jealousy or Mandy's meanness ruin it.

"If that's the best gossip Mandy can spread about me and you believe it, I feel sorry for you both."

She barks out a laugh devoid of amusement. "That's not the gossip. Believe me, it's a lot juicier than that. Like what happened at the party and you didn't see." She snaps her fingers. "But never mind. I think I'll let you stew over not knowing instead, that's much more fun."

Not for me, because now I'm dying to know what happened at the party and what Mandy's telling people about me. Then again, maybe I'm better off not knowing? Unless Mandy's spreading lies about me to Callan... that's not good.

"And for the record? It doesn't matter who you hang out with or who takes pity on you, you'll always be a loser."

With a final smirk, Lara saunters away and I'm startled by the compulsion to run after her, shove her to the ground, and pummel her face. But I have more important things to do— namely see Callan—so I close my eyes and imagine I'm in my favorite chair at home with a new book until my anger subsides, and continue walking.

As I reach Callan's house, I scan the yard for signs of... what? That I missed the best party ever? That everyone had been busy having such an amazing time they'd forgotten to clean up? But all I spy are a few big red cups some of the guys had used to play beer pong in the first few minutes I'd arrived, stacked in a row at the end of the porch.

Now that I'm here my earlier courage has deserted me and I'm starting to feel a little lightheaded. I take a few deep breaths, in and out, practicing the yoga breathing we'd learned in gym class last year. It doesn't help, but I'm calmer and about to stride up the driveway to knock on the front door when I see something that's so shocking I clutch at the picket fence to stop from collapsing.

Abi's strolling around the back corner of the house, wearing one shoe and holding the other in her hand, doing a weird hop, trying to squeeze into it.

What is she doing here?

Surely she hasn't...? I shake my head. I can't contemplate that Abi's spent the night with Callan. She'd never do that to me. I'm about to skulk away when I realize if I do, I'll be left wondering what happened between them and I can't do that to myself. I won't sleep, I won't be able to do anything; the curiosity will eat away at me.

So rather than running away as I want to, I take a step forward as she reaches the end of the driveway. If she's surprised to see me she doesn't show it and I should know, I watch carefully for her reaction. Apart from a flicked glance in the direction of the house, there's nothing but a smile on her face.

"Hey, Jo. What are you doing here?"

"I could ask you the same thing."

My retort is sharp and laced with suspicion, but she shrugs.

"I was pretty out of it last night. Got absolutely wasted and woke up in the tree house out the back." She presses a finger to her lips. "Don't tell anyone, okay? I've never drunk that much and I think I puked at some stage."

"You slept outside all night?"

She squints at her watch. "Well, there hasn't been much sleep involved. It feels like the party only wound down a few hours ago."

I want to ask how's Callan and where is he, but she's

turning a nasty shade of green and before I can say anything she's hunched over and vomiting in the gutter.

"Gross," I mutter, but hold back her hair regardless.

"Sorry," she says when she straightens and swipes the back of her hand over her mouth. "Remind me to never drink again."

"You don't usually. What got into you?"

"I have no idea," she says, sounding evasive. "But I missed you."

Somewhat mollified, I say, "Do you need help getting home?"

Bashful, she nods. "My folks should be at church so they won't see me wearing the same clothes. I said I might spend the night at your place if the party went late, and they were okay with that, but they'll be suspicious if you didn't lend me a clean set of clothes this morning."

"I'm not lying for you, Abi."

We have a strict code about that. As best friends, we don't lie to each other. About anything.

"I'm not asking you to, but they won't ask anyway, and if they do I'll deflect." Her smile is wobbly. "Thanks for being so great, Jo."

"Right back at you."

But as I lament another lost opportunity with Callan and walk her home, I can't help but shake the feeling I'm being too trusting and my best friend has lied to me after all.

# TWENTY-TWO

## ABIGAIL

"Did I pass the test?"

I'm snuggled into the crook of Noah's shoulder and we're listening to a relaxation playlist when he asks me this.

"Tonight wasn't a test," I say, and he chuckles softly.

"Sure it was. Jo's your best friend, you value her opinion. So, did I pass?"

"No idea, haven't had a chance to speak to her about you yet." I glance up at him and he's smiling down on me. "But that'll come and if she doesn't like you, you're in trouble, mister."

"You two are that close?"

I elbow him. "I'm joking. But yeah, we're close. We've been best friends since the first day of junior high."

"You're lucky, to have someone you can depend on that much."

"You don't?"

He shrugs, but I see the oddest expression on his face, a mix of wistfulness and regret. "I have a few good friends at the museum."

"No old school friends?"

He shakes his head and his lips compress into a thin line. "I hated school. What about you?"

"Jo made it bearable. Until I screwed up everything in senior year and got pregnant to a guy I barely knew."

"That must've been tough."

"You have no idea."

After I told Jo about what happened and who had fathered my baby, she ignored me. When I saw her at school, she walked the other way. She ignored all my texts and calls, and when I dropped in at her house she wouldn't answer the door. I understood why she hated me—she thought I betrayed her when I hadn't because I remembered little of that night with Cal—but I missed her so much during my pregnancy. I wanted to share every wondrous thing with her: when my belly started to bulge, when the baby kicked for the first time, when I discovered the sex.

I left her alone after a while but I didn't give up on us and when the baby was born, I got Cal to act as a go-between. Underhanded, I know, but I hoped she still had feelings for him and I could play on those. He visited her and I don't know what he said but Jo arrived at the hospital, took one look at Rob, and fell in love like I had.

It took a while to resume our friendship but seeing her dote on the baby like I did, and how comfortable she seemed around Cal despite her previous crush, made me want to include her in our lives, and we've been inseparable since. Heck, I never expected her to move here but she did, and I treasure our friendship.

"What are you thinking about?" He brushes my brow with a fingertip, a soft caress that makes me sigh.

"I owe Jo a lot. She's the one person who's stood by me."

"What about your son's father?"

"Cal isn't dependable. He's a wanderer and has been for years."

"So he's not your soulmate?"

"Hell no. I don't believe in them."

"Really?" He tips my chin up to stare into my eyes and I swear I could drown in all that endless blue.

"Attraction is chemical, the rest develops over time."

"What if I told you the moment I saw you in that bar I knew I wanted to be with you?"

"Are you saying you bumped into me on purpose?"

He chuckles. "No, but if that guy hadn't pushed me, maybe I would've."

"I guess I should be thankful, because look at us now." I gesture at the living room, illuminated by a single lamp, and the two of us curled up on the sofa like an old married couple.

"I want you to know, Abi, that I've never felt this way before. You and me? I think we're in it for the long haul."

His sincerity surprises me. "What are you saying?"

"That I'm falling for you and if I'm not careful, I'll be writing the rest of my book right here and ditching the first-hand research."

I think he's too impulsive and it's way too early to be thinking that far ahead, but as he pulls me closer and sets about showing me how much he's into me, I can't help but wish this works out.

With every caress, with every kiss, with every touch of his hands and mouth, I come alive. He lavishes me with the attention I crave and pleasures me in ways I never anticipated. And when we're sated and lying in each other's arms, I know I'm halfway to falling for him too.

.   .   .

Noah's snoring softly beside me and I spend a few illicit moments studying him. Soft moonlight is filtering through the blinds above my bed and casting shadows on his cheekbones, his jaw. His lips are curved at the corners, like he's having a pleasant dream, and I hope he's thinking about me.

I'm not envisioning too far ahead—I'm way too practical for that—but I'm enjoying getting to know him. For the first time in a long time, I feel... free. Free to explore what makes me happy, free to do what's right for me, rather than always putting Rob first. My son has been my priority for so long I know I've sacrificed a part of myself and I want to reclaim it. Noah's helping me do that.

He stirs, murmurs something, and rolls over, leaving me with an impressive view of his back. I'm tempted to reach out and trace the clearly delineated muscles, but that would be too creepy, so I carefully slide out of bed instead. I'm thirsty, so I'll grab a glass of water and place one next to him on the bedside table for when he wakes.

I pad to the kitchen, savoring and dreading the silence of the house simultaneously. When Rob was around, there would always be noise even in the dead of night. His computer left on because he was downloading a game, the occasional beep of his cell when he forgot to turn off notifications for apps, which was often. I liked knowing he was safe in his bed, even on those nights when he got home late and missed curfew.

But the silence is welcome too, because I know he's where he needs to be, making his mark in the world, exploring his options, becoming the man he's destined to be.

I fill two glasses with tap water and am heading back along the hallway when I hear it.

The faintest creak of the front porch.

I freeze, fear shimmying through me, before I realize this is my opportunity to catch whoever's been targeting me. I carefully place the glasses on the hallway table, but one of them slips out of my hand and crashes to the floor. It doesn't smash but it makes a noise loud enough to scare off whoever's outside because I hear the thud of footsteps sprinting away.

Cursing, I run to the front door, but by the time I unlock it, whoever was on my front porch is already in a car parked opposite.

"Hey!" I call out, but it's futile, because they gun the engine and screech away.

It's too dark to see the make or model of the car—the fickle moonlight that illuminated Noah so beautifully earlier has slid behind clouds—but it could be a sedan.

As for identifying the potential vandal, they were dressed in black, with a hoodie pulled over their head. So much for catching them red-handed.

"Hey, what was that noise?" Noah lays his hands on my shoulders, his soothing touch instantly calming. "Are you okay?"

"Dropped a glass, sorry for waking you."

"You're shaking," he says. "What's wrong?"

"I heard a noise outside and was going to investigate when I dropped the glass, and they took off."

His eyebrows rise. "You saw them?"

"I saw someone in a hoodie in a car, that's about it."

He shakes his head. "You should report it to the police."

And tell them what? A few gnomes have been decapitated, my rose bush vandalized, and my lettuce uprooted? They'll dismiss it as a kid's prank and I don't blame them. If I'd caught a look at the build of the person in that hoodie, I may have something to go on, but I've got nothing.

"Thanks for being here," I murmur, sliding my arms around his waist and leaning into him.

"Anytime."

As he holds me close, I realize I haven't felt this safe in a long time. Cal had been away a lot and when Robbie had been younger, I often worried about us being alone at night. Turns out watching one too many horror movies in my teens hadn't been helpful.

I've never depended on anyone but it's nice to have Noah here. It's early days for us and he's going to leave eventually, but for now, I intend on making the most of it.

# TWENTY-THREE

## JO

While I used an early start as an excuse to leave Abi's dinner party early last night, I hadn't been lying about it, so when I open my back door just after six thirty I'm shocked to find another spray-painted message, this time on the porch:

### HE'S MINE

A shiver runs down my spine and I give a little shake. I look around, unable to ditch the feeling I'm being watched, like someone is doing this to get a reaction. But the yard is quiet as usual and there's no one peeking over the fences.

I painted over the back-door message because the solvent left a nasty stain, but this one will be harder to remove as solvents don't always work on concrete. Regardless, I haven't got time to do much about it now but I wonder if I should pay Mandy a visit. Though what would I say? *"Hey, are you warning me off Cal even though you haven't seen him in almost two decades? Are you still that obsessed?"* Mandy was always a loose cannon and her behavior after she discovered Rob's paternity proved it.

I don't think Lara's a threat despite Abi mentioning her asking about Cal. My little white lie about Abi hating her trailing after her like a puppy definitely scared her off in high school, though she had appeared a tad unhinged when she confronted me the morning after Cal's party. Besides, as far as I know, she wasn't as crazy about Cal as the rest of us.

Then again, Cal could've slept with the entire senior class that year and I wouldn't have known. After Abi's betrayal I kept my head down and ignored everyone. When I attended class, that is. I spent a lot of that year with Rex—he'd been my rock and I wished I felt the same way about him as I did about Cal. He never made a pass at me but sometimes I'd catch him looking at me like he wanted to, but I always deflected because I didn't want to ruin our friendship. I'd already lost one friend; I couldn't afford to lose another.

Ironic, that Mom never noticed how upset I was that year: how I lost weight, how I barely ate, but she mentioned Abi not coming around anymore several times. How she missed seeing Abi's lovely face and listening to her fun stories. And though she didn't spell it out, Mom missed the bubbly, extroverted daughter she never had, though Talia was well on her way to filling that void by then.

Rex had supported me through it all and as I stare at that message on my back porch, it hits me: I miss him. He'd tell me not to worry about it. He'd make a joke, leaving me no option but to laugh at whoever's doing this. These days, we talk more often than we see each other, and it's not the same as sharing a soda like we used to down by the wharf.

Snatching lunch with him last week had been too brief. I'd planned on driving back for a job late afternoon, but Tom reaching out put paid to that. When he warned me about Cal having a thing for me, I'd been ecstatic. My plan was working. Tom was jealous. But once we got past the awkwardness of discussing Cal, Tom reverted to type, treating me as a friend. No loaded glances, no subtle flirting. I need to up the ante.

It's a shame I can't talk to Rex about any of this—he'd flip and tell me to grow the hell up—but I know he'll get a good laugh out of Mandy still pining after Cal, so as I get in the car, I call him. He always picks up on the second ring but this time it's the ninth.

"Hey, are you avoiding me?"

He chuckles. "Do you have any idea what time it is?"

Oops, I'd been so distracted by the graffiti I forgot how early it is. "Sorry. Got caught up in a few things and didn't realize."

"You're forgiven. How are you?"

"Okay."

"Just okay?"

The concern in his voice warms my heart. Abi and I are solid these days but I'll never forget what she did by sleeping with Cal. I may have forgiven her but I can't forget. Rex, on the other hand, is the one friend who's never disappointed me. He's reliable and steady and I love him. It's annoying that I never fell for him. My life would've been so much easier.

"Can I ask you something totally from left field?"

"You didn't answer my question about why you're just okay, but sure," he says.

"Why didn't you ever make a pass at me?"

He snorts. "You call me at this ungodly hour to ask me that?"

"No, I called to hear your voice, doofus, because I miss you. But it's something I think about occasionally."

I hear a faint sigh. "You're attractive, babe, and any guy would be a fool not to want you, but you're the one person in this world I can depend on and I didn't want to mess with our friendship." He pauses. "Still don't, if you're harboring ideas to come and jump my bones."

"You wish."

We laugh and there's a physical ache in my chest because I miss him so much. "So how's life treating you?"

"Since I saw you last week and you couldn't get away fast enough? Couldn't be better."

"Smart-ass."

He chuckles. "Though I'd be even better if I got to hang out with you more often."

"Soon, okay? And this time I promise to spend a whole day, not just a quickie lunch."

"I'll hold you to that. Are you sure you're okay?"

"Yeah, just some weird stuff I'm dealing with here, but it's nothing to worry about. Maybe I'll drive up to San Fran again one of these days and we can spend a weekend together?"

"Sounds good. And, Jo?"

"Yeah."

"I'm always here for you. I've got your back."

Tears prickle my eyes and I blink them away. I inject perkiness into my voice so he won't hear how much he means to me. "Right back at you. See you soon."

I hit the disconnect button so he doesn't hear how quivery my voice is. Maybe it's the new vandalism on my porch, maybe it's seeing Abi so happy with Noah last night, maybe it's Tom taking forever to see what's right in front of him, but whatever has me feeling like this, I don't like it.

I'm strong. I'm in control. I like my life.

But sometimes, I can't help but wish for more.

# TWENTY-FOUR

## JO

THEN

I'm reading in my room when there's a knock at the door and a few moments later I hear my mom's gushy voice. Must be one of her friends who are as fake as her, so I'm surprised when she raps once on my bedroom door and opens it.

"Joelle, you have a visitor."

For one insane moment my heart leaps in the vain hope it's Callan. As if. He still doesn't know I exist because I never got to make my move the morning after the party, thanks to Abi.

"Who is it?"

Mom flings the door open wider, theatrical in everything she does. "The delightful Abigail, of course."

She makes the "of course" sound like "who else visits you and wants to spend any time with you?"

Abi's hovering behind her and for the first time since we met way back in junior high, she looks terrible. Pale skin with a breakout of pimples on her chin, baggy gray sweatshirt, and leggings. I'm shocked because even when we hang out at each other's houses she always looks trendy. Dressing down for Abi is artfully torn jeans and a nice T-shirt.

"Hey," she says, raising her hand in a half-hearted wave, as Dolly blathers on, "Do you girls want a snack? I'm baking some oatmeal cookies."

Abi and I exchange a look and I struggle to keep a straight face. Dolly's fanaticism with weight and minimalist healthy eating means she hasn't baked a single thing over the last few years, ever since Talia started showing real talent. Everyone in the household knows she keeps an emergency stash of store-bought cookies on the top shelf in the pantry, behind the canisters of protein powder and chia seeds, in case our visitors don't share her starvation philosophy when it comes to food.

"We're fine, Mom, but thanks."

She flashes me a tight smile that broadens when she looks at Abi. "We haven't seen much of you, Abigail." Mom squeezes her arm. "You've been missed."

Mom's not a touchy-feely person. I can't remember the last time she hugged me or squeezed my arm for that matter. It strikes me yet again how much of a disappointment I must be for her to gush over my friend when she pops in for the first time in weeks, yet Dolly barely acknowledges I exist most days.

"I've been busy with homework. My folks are really cracking down on me in this final year," Abi says, but she's lying. I know because she can't meet my eyes and is looking at the poster over my bed, depicting my favorite fantasy author's latest release.

"Good for you, honey." Dolly flashes me a look that says, "See how amazing your friend is? Why can't you be more like her?" despite my grades being okay. Though that's going to change considering how little I've worked the last eight weeks. "I'll leave you girls to it."

I roll my eyes as Dolly tugs on Abi's ponytail as she leaves.

Abi knows I have a fraught relationship with my mom and she's always supportive so when Mom leaves Abi makes circles with her finger at her temple.

"Yeah, don't mind my mother, she thinks she's on the stage every day of her life and acts accordingly," I say, and Abi laughs at my drollness. "But Mom's right. I've hardly seen you apart from school. Is that true what you said about your folks?"

She nods, but she's chewing her bottom lip, her gaze evasive. "Listen, Jo—" she murmurs at the same time I say, "What's going on with you?"

She blows out a long breath and remains standing when I pat a spot on the bed next to me. "I have something to tell you."

This is about college, I know it. We've avoided the topic whenever it's come up over the last year because I know Abi's grades are much better than mine and her folks will want her to attend some fancy college, meaning we'll be split up. She's considerate of my feelings and knows I have no hope of attending anything other than a community college and that's why we don't talk about it. Whenever I hear Stanford or Harvard or Berkeley mentioned at school I freeze, because I know that next year I'll be back to square one, alone and having to make new friends wherever I attend. And I hate that Abi will be making a bunch of new friends easily and she might forget about me. She'll be mixing with highbrow types, popular people like her, and I'll be left far behind, a blip on her friendship radar—that dorky girl she took pity on the first day of junior high.

"What's up?" I try to sound casual but my voice comes out high and squeaky.

She's pale and what little color she has drains from her face. "You're not going to like it, Jo, but you have to believe me when I say this is the biggest mistake of my life and I never meant it to happen."

Stupidly, I say, "So this isn't about college?" when inside, I'm dying.

I'm not a complete idiot. If she regrets something that happened and looks so panicked telling me, this has something to do with Callan.

"Did you kiss Callan?"

She blanches, if that's possible considering her pallor. "It's worse."

My blood turns to ice. I swear I can actually feel it struggling to move through my arteries and veins, sluggish, depriving me of much-needed oxygen.

Because in that instant I know what's worse than kissing Callan.

I remember how she left his house the morning after the party, casual as you like, one shoe in her hand. How I couldn't believe she'd slept in a tree house overnight. How she'd blatantly lied to my face if she's about to confess to what I think she is.

"You had sex with Callan."

It's a statement, not a question, because I already know the answer before she nods, guilty tears seeping from her eyes.

"I'm sorry I didn't tell you, Jo, especially as we tell each other everything—"

"Not everything, apparently."

I can't bear to look at her, betrayal burning my gut, and I wrap my arms around my middle to ward off the pain. Tears sting my eyes and I stare at my dresser until they ease, not wanting to give her the satisfaction of seeing me bawl, wishing I didn't have to look at her, wishing she never existed.

The pain in my chest is awful, like a hacksaw has cleaved me in two, and I hug myself tighter. It doesn't help. Nothing will.

My best friend slept with my soon-to-be boyfriend.

"I didn't mean for it to happen. I got so drunk I can barely remember any of that night after you left, and I would never go after a guy you like deliberately. But it happened and I can't take it back. I'm sorry."

"Stop apologizing," I snap, my devastation giving way to pure, unadulterated rage. "As if that makes it better."

"Jo, I never meant any of this to happen—"

"Of course you didn't, Little Miss Perfect." I leap off the bed and stalk to the window, needing to keep my distance from her so I don't wring her neck. "You're one of those annoying people who swan through life without anything bad happening so you have no thought for your actions and their consequences."

I'm yelling and gesticulating wildly. "What? I don't have a right to be furious?"

She gapes at me, before murmuring, "I know you're hurt, Jo, but technically, I haven't done anything wrong. You weren't dating Callan and every girl in our class has a crush on him."

Her gall astounds me and red spots of rage dance before my eyes. I blink several times to eradicate them before speaking. "Yes, but not every girl is best friends with you, and best friends don't sleep with each other's crushes. I would've thought that's obvious and doesn't need to be spelled out."

Her shoulders slump as she visibly sags. "You're right. I'm awful."

I refuse to feel pity and grit my teeth so hard I'm surprised I don't hear one of them crack.

"Can you forgive me?"

"No."

My refusal is instant and I mean it. I'll never forgive her for this.

An awkward silence stretches between us and I know

there's worse to come when I see her face crumple. She starts sobbing and I clamp down on my first instinct to hug her.

Instead, I brace for the words that will detonate my life completely.

She can't look at me as she murmurs, "I'm pregnant."

# TWENTY-FIVE

## ABIGAIL

After I disturbed my masked assailant last night, Noah had searched for clues on the front porch and came up with nothing. He'd been concerned and had taken me back to bed, holding me close, before slipping out in the early hours. I'm not really scared by someone who's beheading gnomes and tampering with my vegetable patch, but it had been comforting nonetheless.

Now, eight hours later at work, I alternate between picking up my cell to call Jo and Noah. Jo, because I can't wait to hear her opinion of Noah—though it's kind of moot because we slept together last night and it was phenomenal and even if she hates him, which I doubt, I'm not giving up the best thing to happen to me in a long time—and Noah, just to hear his voice.

Instead, I try to focus on work, waiting until lunchtime to text Jo.

*What did you think?*

I see the three moving circles appear and a second later, a flame emoji.

I laugh and fire back.

*Got time for a chat?*

She responds with *Work busy. Will call you later.*

I like her comment and head for the cafeteria. There's yet another problem I have to deal with, this time a leading lady's wardrobe malfunction that needs fixing pronto, so I barely have time for a snatched sandwich.

There's a long line at the checkout—one of the thriller movies wrapped up filming today and looks like everyone's ravenous and needs food before they hit the celebratory alcohol later—and I'm dithering over a boiled egg, lettuce and mayo on sourdough or a roast beef on wholegrain, when I hear a familiar laugh.

I glance over my shoulder to see where Mandy is so I can avoid her, but I needn't have worried. She's deep in conversation with her lunch companion.

Lara.

Mandy hardly spoke to anyone in high school apart from her close-knit bunch of fellow mean girls and Lara had only been on the periphery of her group, so to see the two of them chatting and laughing like best buds is weird. They probably ran into each other in town but to agree to have lunch together... It's probably nothing, two women who attended the same high school catching up on old times, but my late-night visitor and the odd incidents lately are making me suspicious. Maybe Mandy and Lara have formed an "I HEART CAL" club and are plotting ways to undermine me?

Crazy, I know, but I'm good at my job and I've slotted seamlessly into the team, so to have one problem after another at the studio in two weeks is bizarre. I can't get Derek's warning out of my head, that I'm basically on probation and if I screw up one more time I'm out, so I'm particularly angsty and that's probably leading to my wild suppositions that these two women I went to high school with may have something to do with me being undermined.

Jo will laugh at my conspiracy theories and while I know she's busy, I fire off another text.

*You won't believe it. Mandy and Lara are lunching together.*

There's a long pause before Jo responds with *WTF? I got another message spray-painted during the night, on my back porch this time. Coincidence?*

Heck. Maybe my outlandish conspiracy theories aren't so far off.

*What did it say?*

The dots appear. *HE'S MINE.*

My gaze is drawn to the women again, chatting like they don't have a care in the world. It's been eighteen years since we finished school and a lot has happened since then. But I don't believe in coincidences and the appearance of these two women at the same time Jo and I are being targeted...

But if they're still hung up on Cal—ludicrous for women in their mid-thirties—why wouldn't they target me with the painted messages? None of this makes sense and I hope Jo has a logical explanation when we talk later.

I type *Bizarre. Call me when you can.*

She sends a thumbs-up emoji and I slip my cell into my pocket. I choose the egg sandwich and a small tub of blueberry yoghurt and contemplate going over to Mandy and Lara's table.

But what's the point in exchanging false pleasantries with Mandy while wanting to ask Lara, "Why are you hanging out with this loony?"

I duck behind a six-five guy in the queue, willing the line to the checkout to move faster. I almost make it when I hear my name being called and I look over my shoulder to see Lara waving me over. Great. Now I have to say hello so I don't appear rude, but at least I have a genuine excuse not to linger.

After paying for my sandwich and yoghurt, I wend my way between the tables. Lara's already grabbed another seat for me and I feel bad, because she's genuinely nice the few times we've caught up over the years. Which makes me wonder, why is it this visit that she seems so interested in Cal? She's asked about him the previous two times we've caught up, but it's been blasé and in passing, not the obsessive way she asked me for his phone number this time.

"Hi, ladies," I say, when I reach their table. "Having a nice lunch?"

Mandy manages a tight smile as Lara gestures at the chair. "Please join us."

"I'd love to, but I've got a costuming problem to attend to that won't wait."

"You seem to have an awful lot of problems at work lately," Mandy says, her eyes glittering with malice. "Maybe if you spent more time focusing on your job rather than matters at home, it'd be smooth sailing?"

I'm about to ask, "What are you talking about?" when Lara intervenes for me. "That's a tad rude, Mandy." She smiles, trying to defuse the tension. "Besides, if I had Cal waiting for me at home every night, I'd be distracted too."

While I'm still trying to process Lara's comment, Mandy says, "Oh, it's not Cal warming Abigail's bed these days."

Lara and I must look like matching sideshow clowns as our mouths drop open in unison.

Mandy's been spying on me. Which means she's responsible for the decapitated gnomes, dog poo, mushed lettuce, and uprooted rose bush. And she's probably my unwelcome visitor in the dead of night too. She's a lunatic and I have to warn Noah to be on guard.

Thankfully, I recover first and say, "My personal life is no concern of yours, Mandy. And I'd appreciate it if you leave me the hell alone."

I spin on my heel and walk away, silently fuming that Cal once again has ruined my life. Not that it's totally his fault for attracting crazy women, but I suspect the only reason these women are in town is because of him.

What I want to know is why.

# TWENTY-SIX

## JO

I want to get off the phone fast. Usually, I like chatting with Abi but not today—I have more important calls to make.

Abi told me about her unexpected visitor last night and she rehashed what happened when she saw Mandy and Lara at lunch this afternoon, then we gossiped about what it means, but I ended the call a few minutes ago because Cal sent me a message earlier saying he'd love to talk tonight at seven and I don't have long to get ready. I had back-to-back jobs all day and have only just got home and I want tonight to be special.

Time to up the ante.

It's crazy, but after meeting with Tom recently and hearing him warn me off Cal, it's time I find out one way or the other if there's any future for us. And the only way to do that is to get Cal to want me so badly, Tom has no other option than to step up and declare his feelings.

It's a dangerous game I'm playing and the whole thing can backfire, but I'm done waiting. Seeing Abi so happy with Noah, after she already led a charmed life with Cal, has made my latent jealousy flare. Not that I'm envious of Abi, per se, but more the ease with which everything comes to her. For me, I have to make things happen, and if Tom is genuinely interested in me romantically, I need to know.

I know it doesn't make sense, how much I still want him after all this time. But being part of his life for so long, spending time with him as a friend, has only served to stoke my desire for him.

I've had to be careful over the years, hiding it from Cal, Tom, and especially Abi, but I often wonder how she didn't realize. Is she that self-absorbed? Then again, when the four of us had been together with Robbie, our focus had been on him and as a new mother she doted on him. I admire her focus on raising him. She gave up her dream of college and hadn't let it bother her. I asked her about it once, if she regretted keeping the baby and not having the life she planned. She'd been affronted and continued packing Robbie's lunch for school the next day. He'd been about seven at the time, and we'd been mid-twenties, and I envied her self-confidence and contentment, when I was still trying to figure out what to do with my life.

Turns out, I hadn't even ended up going to community college. Instead, when Abi and Cal asked me to be godmother to Robbie, and told me they were moving to Fort Chester, I tagged along too. I had zero interest in studying accounting, which is what my careers teacher at school recommended. Mom and Dad hadn't cared, as Talia had made nationals in a dance contest by then and prestigious ballet schools in New York were sniffing around, so my future plans were of little consequence. They gave me ten grand and wished me luck.

The money came in handy. It allowed me to rent my own place until I found a job and some security. I took on odd jobs—window washer, office cleaner, nanny, vet assistant—until lucking into the dog grooming gig. I always loved animals and wanted a dog, but while Dad had been amenable to the idea,

Mom had been vehemently against it. Grooming dogs calms me, centers me, and I like the quiet of not having to make small talk with people. Dogs don't demand anything of me. Dogs love me unconditionally, when not many humans do.

I have fifteen minutes to get ready so I have a quick shower, apply a little foundation so it looks like I'm not wearing any, and slip into a sexy black teddy. I've never been this bold with Cal before but I want to push him into telling Tom how fast our relationship is progressing and with a little luck, it'll drive Tom straight into my arms.

Cal will fall for my act. He's been a charmer from the first day he strutted into Lilydale High. I watched girls simper all through our senior year and he took it in his stride, smiling and chatting with them all. The other guys should've hated him, but even the jocks warmed quickly to the new kid because Cal had a way about him that snuck under people's defenses.

The thing is, I could've seen Abi and Cal becoming a couple back then. Both were popular and liked by everyone; they made an attractive pair. But Abi had shown little interest: until the night she slept with him and got knocked up.

Rehashing the past, even in my head, isn't good—I can't change it. Besides, I want to make new memories with Tom and that means when Cal calls in a few minutes, it's time to give him a plain message when he sees what I'm wearing.

There's a knock at the door at six fifty-seven and I contemplate ignoring it. Cal's about to call any minute and I'm not dressed for visitors. I peek through the blinds from the living room, giving me a clear view of who's at the front door. When I see who it is, my legs buckle a little and I sag against the sofa.

Cal's *here?*

Going through with my plan is a lot easier via a screen than having the guy I'm using show up on my doorstep.

He knocks again and I shake my head to clear it. I can do

this. No need to freak out. I can still toy with him a little then send him on his way. With a little luck, he'll call Tom and tell him about our in-person meeting and that'll send Tom directly to my door.

Taking a few steadying breaths, I pad to the door and open it.

"Hey, JJ..." His greeting trails off when he catches sight of what I'm wearing. "Wow. You look..." His hungry gaze roves over me and my skin pebbles beneath his scrutiny. "Incredible. Were you expecting company?"

"No."

It takes a second for realization to dawn and his eyes widen imperceptibly. "You wore that for me, for our call?"

I nod, my heart hammering as I open the door wider. "Come in."

He walks past me, stopping to place a kiss on my cheek. It's our usual greeting when he's been away and returns home, a brief, impersonal hello in front of Abi.

"What are you doing here?"

"I felt like seeing you," he said, with a casual shrug, but I see the glint in his eyes, the one that implies he wants me. I should be pleased my plan is working, but I'm nervous. There's a vast difference between playing a game via a screen and having the guy I'm using in my house.

"You haven't seen Abi yet?"

I know he hasn't because I got off the phone from her fifteen minutes ago and she hadn't mentioned Cal being back in town. But I want him to clarify what this visit is about before I jump to conclusions and ruin this before it's begun.

"I'm here to see you."

He takes a step closer and it takes every ounce of my willpower not to hold up my hands to ward him off. If Cal's turned up here and hasn't told Abi, it means he's taken the bait.

But I need him to tell Tom about it, not want to take our relationship to the next level.

"We've been friends for a long time, Cal. I'm your son's godmother. I'm Abi's best friend." Hopefully, mentioning her will put him off. "What do you see happening here?"

He's flummoxed for a moment, confusion creasing his brow. "I don't know, Jo. I'm not the one dressed like you're expecting a lover rather than a chat with a friend. You tell me."

Typical Cal, putting the onus back on me, not wanting to take responsibility. Though that's harsh, considering he stepped up for Abi when she discovered she was carrying his child. She's not the only one whose college plans got ruined. Cal gave up a lot too, though I guess it's easy when you have supportive parents willing to back you up, no matter how big the mistake.

"Are you sure you want to hear the truth, Cal?"

"I wouldn't have asked if I didn't."

But he's nervous; I see it in his fingers fiddling with his belt before he thrusts his hands into his pockets.

I want to be honest; tell him how long I've liked Tom, how I've been trying to make him jealous. But I'm scared how he'll take it. Not that I'm afraid he'll physically harm me, but I know Cal and the first thing he'll do is run to Abi and tell her the whole sordid story. And if that happens, I know he'll doctor the truth so he comes out looking fine and I'll be the trampy best friend who's been leading him on for ages.

Damn it, I've really screwed this up.

"Look, if it's Abi you're worried about, don't be. The last time I was here we decided we wouldn't sleep together anymore. So I don't owe her anything."

I clench my jaw so I don't gape at him like a fool. They've been sleeping together all this time? So every visit when he came home on the pretext of spending time with Robbie, every time he stayed in that house, they shared a bed. I'd asked Abi and she lied to me. Again. Why doesn't she trust me enough to confide in me? I thought we told each other everything.

He's looking at me expectantly, and I need to buy some time to think of a polite way to get rid of him, so I say, "I like you, Cal. But we can't do this. It's too complicated."

"It doesn't have to be."

In that moment, I know Cal's as selfish as Abi has always labeled him. He takes what he wants with no thought for the consequences. Does he seriously think my relationship with Abi won't change if I was crazy enough to sleep with him?

It has all been hypothetical until now, because I never had any intention to, but having him stare at me with genuine desire is unnerving. I fold my arms over my chest, wishing I'd had the sense to slip on a robe before I answered the door.

"You can't be that naïve, Cal. We're one giant complication just waiting to happen."

He scrubs a hand over his face. It does little to ease the tension, deep grooves bracketing his mouth. "Considering what Tom and Abi have going on, I think our little foursome is complicated enough, but who the hell cares? If I've put up with him loving Abi all these years, constantly dropping in when I'm not around, making himself indispensable to her, all their cozy catch ups, her treating him like a plaything... like I said, I don't owe Abi anything, JJ, and I want you. Screw them."

A loud buzzing fills my head and confused, I glance around to see if someone's started a chainsaw in my living room. I'm chilled to the bone and rub my hands over my bare arms. It does little to dispel the iciness invading every cell of my body.

Tom and Abi are involved?

Tom *loves* her?

My lungs seize and I drag in air so I don't pass out as realization hits.

I've been wasting my time all these years...

I've wanted Tom and he's been carrying on with Abi.

And she didn't tell me.

Does she have any idea what she's done?

In withholding the truth, she's prevented me from moving on with my life. The futility of biding my time, waiting for something that's never going to happen, guts me.

And once again, I'm second best.

Cal chose Abi over me and now Tom has too.

I can't take it anymore.

Fury surges through my body like molten lava and I'm burning from the inside out. I'm so livid I can barely see straight, so I do the one thing guaranteed to eradicate my pain.

I broach the short distance between us, press my body against Cal's, wrap my arms around his neck, and kiss him.

# TWENTY-SEVEN

## JO

THEN

I haven't been able to breathe for the last seven months since Abi told me she's expecting Callan's baby. I haven't eaten. I haven't slept. Every day is a repeat of the last, when debilitating pain makes the simplest of actions like getting out of bed impossible. I'm like the zombies I read about in my favorite paranormal novels, functioning on autopilot, my days shaded in gray.

My grades plummet. Mom's disapproving glares increase. And I don't care about anything anymore, I'm going through the motions. Kids at school snicker behind my back, calling me names for abandoning my best friend when she needs me most. They don't understand. All they see is me pretending Abi doesn't exist, and her looking sad whenever we pass in the hallways.

As for Callan, he swans through the school like he owns it, without a care in the world. He has rich parents like Abi, and they obviously haven't disowned him because he's here every day, still cocky, still charming, still gorgeous. I want to hate him but I can't. He didn't do anything wrong—Abi did. For all I know, he's had sex with heaps of girls. But Abi hasn't slept with anyone; until Callan, the one guy I want.

She's at school until her seventh month. Her mom buys a large school dress and she wears a letterman jacket over it, managing to look cool when most girls would be shunned and talked about if they showed up to school so obviously pregnant.

The weird thing is, when she leaves, I miss seeing her. As long as she was around, with her protruding baby bump, I had a focus for my hatred. When she's gone I'm lost, foundering, wondering what she's doing and if Callan is doing it with her.

They're not a couple officially, but classmates talk and they're all saying the same thing: that Callan's going to stick by Abi and raise the baby with her.

One big happy family.

When it should've been me.

Not that I want to be pregnant at seventeen—with my parents, I'd be disowned not supported—but to have something of Callan's, to share that bond with him forever, would be a dream come true.

I go through graduation in a haze. Walk up to the dais when my name is announced. Accept my diploma. Join my class. Throw our hats in the air. Lilydale High goes all out for their senior graduates and there's a fancy lunch served on the football field after the ceremony, where parents, students, and teachers mingle.

I can't eat let alone talk to anyone and I'm in the process of slinking away when Mandy and Lara waylay me. Just when I thought I'd finally escaped them.

"Where are you off to, Joelle?" Mandy tilts her head to the side, studying me like a bug under a microscope. "The party's only just starting."

Before I can respond, Lara chirps up. "Maybe she's going to the hospital?"

"Hospital?" I ask, like an idiot, because the second I say the word, I know what's happened.

Abi's gone into labor.

"That's where I'd be if my best friend was having a baby." Mandy snaps her fingers. "Oh wait, but you don't have a bestie anymore. Abigail finally came to her senses and dumped you."

"It was inevitable," Lara adds, her eyes wide and filled with retribution. "Abi wouldn't want someone like you trailing after her like a puppy."

Touché, considering I'd said the same thing to her. I want to curse at them, tell them to leave me the hell alone, but not saying anything is best. After today, I don't have to see their perfectly made-up faces again.

"Or maybe they're not friends anymore because someone's a wee bit jealous," Mandy drawls. "Maybe Red here has a thing for Callan and thought she actually had a chance with him?"

They burst out laughing and I feel incriminating heat creeping into my cheeks.

"As if someone like Cal would look twice at someone like you." Lara points to my hair, pulled tight in a French braid. "I mean, seriously? Abi's ten times more gorgeous than you."

"There's no comparison," Mandy sneers. "Ugly on the outside, ugly on the inside."

Hatred and rage fill me, and I'm on the verge of exploding when I see my folks approaching.

"Congrats, girls," Mom says, her smile wide, oblivious to the tension. But thankfully, Dad's more aware and says, "Time to go, Jo."

I walk away from Mandy and Lara without a backward glance, beyond relieved I'll never have to see them again. At home, Mom and Dad throw me a mini-celebration—Mom actually allows carbs to grace our table in the form of store-bought lasagna—before they rush off with Talia to a dance recital.

I'm at a loss, wandering through the house, absorbing the weirdness of finishing school but having no real plans, trying not to think about Callan at Abi's side while she's in labor, when there's a knock at the door. When I open it, Callan's on the other side and even after all the pain I've been through, my heart pounds so loudly at the sight of him I can hear it in my ears.

He's wearing jeans torn at the knees and a crumpled gray T-shirt, and hasn't shaved for days, yet still manages to look sexy. He hadn't been at the graduation ceremony for obvious reasons. Looks like Abi robbed me of that too. When will I see him again now? School's done, he'll be busy playing daddy, whereas I'll be... what? Trying to figure out what the hell to do with my life? Filled with regret I didn't make a move sooner? Still hating my best friend?

He must see something in my face that indicates my foul mood because his expression is wary. "Hey, got a minute?"

"Sure, come in," I say, opening the door wider but he doesn't move, shifting his weight from one foot to the other, the first time I've seen him uncomfortable.

"Abi's had the baby. It's a boy, Robert." His goofy grin makes my animosity drain away and I want to hug him. "She says he looks just like me."

"Congratulations." My heart breaks a little at the image of a baby looking like Callan.

"I'm here because Abi wants to see you."

I subdue my first instinct, to slam the door in his face, because no matter how much I hate Abi, Callan's here and I know deep down I'll do whatever he asks.

"Her exact words were, 'Tell Joelle Jackson I miss her and love her and I need her now more than ever.' Personally, I think your name's pretty but it's a bit of a mouthful, so I'm calling you JJ." He points to his car. "So, JJ, are you coming with me?"

I've never had a nickname before. Not a nice one, that is, and hearing Callan call me JJ with a teasing twinkle in his eyes, how can I say no?

"Congrats on graduating, by the way." He smiles and I swear my heart leaps out of my chest. "Can you believe we're done?"

I shake my head. "It's surreal. And congrats to you too."

"Thanks." He touches my arm and heat streaks from his fingertips all the way to my toes. "It's a shame we didn't get to know each other better this year."

I don't know what to say to that, so I manage a nod.

"You seem really nice. I hope Mandy laid off you after I spoke to her?"

I don't have the heart to tell him that whatever he told her in my defense expired a few hours ago, considering how awful she'd been to me. He'd been amazing in standing up for me and it makes me like him more.

"That's a bonus about finishing high school. No more mean girls." I dust my hands off and he laughs, the deep, rich sound that warms me from the inside out.

"Any idea what you'll do now?"

"None," I say, and shrug. "But I'll figure it out."

"Well, whatever happens, we should stay in touch, JJ."

I'm floating a foot off the floor when I say, "I'd like that."

This is why I like him—and every other girl in my class does too. Callan's a nice guy and treats everyone the same way. He doesn't play favorites, he's accepting of everybody, and to have him pay me attention let alone want to stay in touch makes me wish we got to spend more time together. He's one in a million and I'm so jealous of Abi, I'm green.

"Anyway, we better get to the hospital," he says, with a

smile that's so persuasive I would agree to anything just to be with him.

I don't remember what we talk about in the car. I'm tongue-tied because I'm *in Callan's car*, like I've dreamt a thousand times before. It's messy, with fast-food wrappers and soda cans on the floor, but the back is pristine, with a baby seat in the middle facing backward. It's incongruous, to think this eighteen-year-old kid has fathered a child, and that he'll be a family with Abi.

Thinking of seeing her again, speaking to her after all this time, puts a dampener on the thrill of sitting beside Callan and watching his long, strong fingers grip the steering wheel. What will I say to her? That if she really missed me, loved me, and needed me, she shouldn't have done what she did?

"So, JJ, how come you and Abi had a falling-out?"

I can't tell him the truth. *That she stole you from me*, no matter how accidental it was? That she took something that should've been mine?

"Why didn't you ask her?"

"I did and it just made her sad, so I'm asking you."

Now's my opportunity to tell him how I feel. How there's still a chance for us. He'd been so nice to me back at the house and he wants us to stay in touch. Surely he wouldn't ask me that if he didn't feel something too? But first, I need to find out how he feels about Abi.

"Friends have arguments sometimes and it takes a while to resolve." It's a vague answer to placate him before I ask the tough question, "What's going on with you and Abi? Are you just co-parenting?"

He takes his eyes off the road for a moment to shoot me a puzzled glance. "Abi's special and now we have Robert, we're moving in together. Her parents are retiring to Fort Chester and they've bought us a house there. Pretty generous, huh?"

I mumble an agreement when I swear my chest has just cracked open and my heart has splattered on the dash.

He thinks Abi's special.

They're moving in together.

They're leaving San Francisco.

Once again, I'll be alone, with no one in my corner.

This is all Abi's fault.

# TWENTY-EIGHT

## ABIGAIL

I'm not in a good mood this morning. I really wanted to chat with Jo last night, but she'd been vague and standoffish, like she couldn't wait to get off the phone. Noah had been out late, doing some research for his book, and there'd been another screw-up at work I needed to fix first thing today. At this rate, I'll be out of a job at the end of the week. Derek isn't a patient man and I think my boss is at breaking point with the constant costuming dramas. Considering he mentioned me being on my last chance when he first warned me, I'm surprised I'm still employed.

To make matters worse, Mandy or whoever's been vandalizing my place, has taken it one step further and I'm so shaken I start hyperventilating. I forgot to check the mail when I got home last night, so a moment ago when I opened my mailbox and saw a giant scorpion curled up on an envelope, I freaked. Usually, I don't even look first, I just reach in and grab whatever's there, but ever since the weird incidents around the house I'm extra careful.

I back away from the box and slam into something, which makes me scream again.

"Hey, are you okay?" Noah's arms wrap around me from behind, strong and comforting, and I allow myself the luxury of sinking into his embrace before straightening and pointing to the mailbox.

"There's a scorpion in there."

He spins me around to face him, his expression incredulous. "Are you sure?"

"Do I look like I'd mistake a scorpion for a grasshopper?"

He takes my snark in his stride. "Okay, let me search online for a local pest controller and call them."

"It's not a spider or termite infestation, it's a scorpion with a tail this big." I hold my arms apart by several feet, finally getting my heart rate under control and managing a tight smile when he laughs. "And I've got another problem at work so I can't stick around to handle it."

"Go. Leave it with me, I'll take care of it."

I could protest but what's the point? Here's a dependable guy taking care of a nasty problem for me. I should be thanking him rather than clinging to my independence like I've done since I had Rob. Cal may have been around for those first few years but he'd never been fully present, not in the way I needed him to be. Sure, he had said all the right things and done all the right things, but his heart hadn't been in it and I saw that every single day. It had almost been a relief when we'd officially called it quits, agreeing to remain friends while co-parenting Rob.

Our son hadn't known about our split. He accepted the fact his father had a job that took him away from us for long periods of time and whenever Cal returned, we resumed our family life, which stupidly included me welcoming him back into my bed. But the arrangement had suited us and I would've done anything for Rob.

Now here's a guy I can depend on, who's offered to take care of a problem, and I'm dithering? I must be nuts.

"Thanks, Noah. I appreciate it." I press a quick kiss to his lips. "Call me if you have any problems finding someone to take care of... that."

I shudder as I point to the box again. "And don't go near it. I don't know much about scorpions, but I know badass ones like that can be poisonous."

He holds up his hands. "You'll get no protest from me. I'll leave the rehousing of our unwelcome visitor to the experts."

I like the way he said "our." It implies we're a team. I like it a lot.

"Thanks again." I blow him a kiss this time and make a run for my car. I can't afford to be late to work, not today.

Thankfully, when I arrive at the studio, the mistake is easily rectified. An underling made a genuine mistake and I'm relieved it doesn't reek of sabotage like the other problems that have befallen me here lately. But my relief is short-lived when I return to my office to find Lara pacing it. She's not dressed for work today and it's the first time I've seen her without make-up and in black yoga pants and hoodie. She looks like she did in high school, rather plain and nondescript, apart from big blue eyes that dominate her face.

"Hey, Lara."

She stops pacing as I enter my office, her expression startled. "Hi, Abi. Sorry to barge in like this, but I needed to see you."

"What's up?"

She's jittery, like she's had one too many coffees, and her eyes are darting all over the place. "Can we go somewhere and talk?"

I have no idea what's going on but I don't want any part of it, especially if she's cozying up with Mandy. I wonder... is she going to confess to knowing Mandy's behind everything happening to me? Is she the one undermining me here at work and leaving nasty surprises at my house?

"I'm swamped and can't leave the office, but we can talk here if you like?"

She's hesitant, the tension in her neck muscles making them pop, so I close the door to ensure privacy. She relaxes a little but she's still nervous.

"Take a seat." I don't sit behind my desk. Instead, I take one of two seats in front of it, gesturing for her to take the other. "Are you okay?"

"Not really." She drags in a breath and blows it out slowly, her gaze drawn to my computer, my calendar, my pen holder, anywhere but me. "I have to tell you something, Abi. It's why I came to town."

"Is this about the vandalism?"

Confusion creases her brow. "No. What vandalism?"

She may appear perplexed but she can't meet my eye, which tells me I'm right not to trust her. But I'll play along for now, find out why she's here.

"Never mind. What do you want to tell me?"

She pauses and I can practically see her drawing on an inner reserve of strength as she slowly squares her shoulders. "Before I tell you, can I ask what's your relationship with Cal?"

I refrain from rolling my eyes, just. What is with these women and their obsession with Cal?

"He's the father of my child. We're friends. Why?"

"So you're not in a relationship?"

I hesitate, before shaking my head. "Not really."

"That's not a no."

"And this is none of your business but I'm humoring you regardless."

She winces but I don't feel sorry for her. I haven't got time for this. If she's going to admit to having some secret crush on Cal, I don't care. She's welcome to him. He's still in my bad books for not fronting to Rob's farewell.

"I just want to make sure this isn't going to affect you or your relationship with him, that's all."

"You're not making sense, Lara—"

"I'm pregnant."

Her hands flit protectively to her still-flat belly and I know what she's going to say before she opens her mouth.

"And Cal's the father."

# TWENTY-NINE

## JO

Cal's a heavy sleeper. I've been up for two hours and out to the bakery to pick up the chocolate croissants I know he loves for breakfast, and he's still asleep when I return. I want him to wake up so we can talk about us.

We made love twice last night and it wasn't fantastic. I know why. He's not to blame. Revenge sex isn't conducive to pleasure, and me sleeping with Cal in a warped way to get back at Abi and Tom had been a mistake. Even now, the next day after finding out about them, I'm spinning out.

I can't believe my best friend didn't confide in me about her relationship with Tom. She never mentioned it once over the years. As for her hinting that Tom and I should get together... what was she playing at?

Tom calling me recently when I'd been in San Francisco makes sense now. He hadn't wanted to see me. He'd wanted to get the lowdown on Abi and how she's coping without Robbie.

Their treachery makes me sick.

Once again, a guy has chosen Abi over me but this time, I'm not going to give in.

Abi still cares about Cal. I know she does. If she's been sleeping with him until recently, it means she's still invested emotionally.

What better way to get back at her than make a play for Cal?

I'm too old for games but hearing about her and Tom last night triggered something in me I can't ignore.

A lifetime of not being good enough.

My parents preferring Talia over me.

Kids in grade school bypassing me for everything from gym to lunchtime tag.

Mandy and Lara rubbing my face in my inadequacies in high school.

Abi sleeping with Cal when she knew how I felt.

And now Tom.

I'm done.

Besides, I was once crazy about Cal. And though that teen infatuation waned over the years, I enjoy being with him. After last night, it's not such a stretch to see the two of us together. I'm tired of being alone and if I can't have Tom, why not Cal?

The irony isn't lost on me, that I'm settling for second best. But nobody knows how devastated I am over losing Tom before I really had him, so why not have fun with Cal?

Besides, a small part of me has savored the illicit thrill of flirting with him all these years and I'd be lying to myself if I didn't admit to having several "what if" moments.

What if I allowed my old feelings for Cal to resurface?

What if our flirting could develop into something more?

What if deep down I want Cal more than Tom?

What if I've used my supposed feelings for Tom as an excuse to foster my relationship with the man I really want, Cal?

After I set out the croissants on my best china, pour freshly squeezed orange juice into crystal glasses, and switch on the coffee machine, I cast a final critical eye over the table to make sure it's perfect. With the sunny bunch of orange gerberas I'd picked up this morning and placed in the middle, the setting looks elegant and romantic—the exact vibe I'm going for, and in stark contrast to the breakfasts I often walked in on at Abi's place.

Abi isn't a morning person so over the years she'd be in a bleary-eyed rush trying to get Robbie ready for school. The table had been littered with mismatched crockery and several cereal boxes while she made his lunch and Cal made Robbie laugh with lame dad jokes. It had been chaos, but I'd envied it regardless because their familiarity with each other made for a special brand of warmth amid the madness.

Time to start creating new memories and that's what my breakfast table is about. Showing Cal how good it can be with us. A calm casualness that still evokes warmth without the mess. Peaceful, without drama.

I'm about to head to the bedroom to wake him—maybe breakfast can wait—when I hear footsteps coming down the hallway and he enters the kitchen fully dressed.

"Good morning," I say, crossing to the kitchen to kiss him, but as I wrap my arms around his waist, he ducks his head at the last minute to place a quick peck on the top of my head like I'm a damn kid.

"I can't stay, JJ. Work to do."

I take a step back from him and gesture at the table. "But I got your favorite croissants."

If he sees how much trouble I've gone to in setting the table, he doesn't show it. Instead, his gaze darts to the door, like he can't get away quick enough. "Thanks," he says, gulping down a juice and grabbing a croissant. "I might take this to go."

My chest is tight with disappointment, but I paste a smile on my face regardless. "How long are you in town for?"

"I'm not sure." His answer's as evasive as his weird kiss a moment ago.

"Well, you're welcome to stay here."

Abi will hate it, which is why I offer. I've imagined this scenario so many times, but with Tom taking the starring role in my fantasy. But that's not going to happen now so I need an alternate reality. One where Cal and I are a couple, so I can rub Abi's nose in it every chance I get.

"Stay as long as you like," I say, making it sound casual and ignoring my inner voice of reason that insists what I'm doing is the dumbest thing ever.

He hesitates, then shakes his head. "I don't think that's a good idea."

Neither do I, but I'm done being a doormat and what better way to demonstrate it?

"Why not? We're good together, Cal. Last night proved it."

"Last night was two people getting a flirtation out of their system," he says, and I subdue a flicker of guilt. I slept with him out of sheer, unadulterated fury at my best friend; I never would've taken our flirtation so far otherwise. I used Cal and he didn't deserve that. "I like you, JJ, but I haven't got time for complications."

Neither have I, but I can't leave this as a one-night-stand. That's not going to hurt Abi enough.

"Your life has been one giant complication, Cal. I'm willing to give you the opposite of that."

"Aww, you've always been too good for me, JJ."

This time when he embraces me there's genuine warmth and some of my resentment melts away. He smells great, a fruity soap he's used for years, and I hope it's branded on my sheets—a reminder that he's chosen me over Abi this time.

When he eases away, he flashes the lopsided grin that makes him irresistible. "I'll see you soon, okay?"

I nod and bite on my bottom lip to stop from crying. *I'll see you soon* could mean anything from later today to a month from now. It's typical Cal. Noncommittal. It shouldn't surprise me because I've watched him do this same dance with Abi for years but now I'm on the receiving end, it's not so good.

"You're the best," he murmurs, his lips melding to mine for a few seconds, before he waves his croissant and walks out the door.

I wait until I hear his car before collapsing onto a chair, brace my elbows on the kitchen table, and rest my head in my hands.

What am I doing?

This is all wrong.

We should be sharing an intimate breakfast for two. I should be happier than I've ever been. Instead, I'm numb; hollowed, like someone has scooped out my heart and left a gaping hole.

The kicker is, the one person I want to talk to and get her take on this crazy situation is the one person I can't tell. After what Cal told me last night, I can't trust Abi ever again.

Though I'm tempted to confront my best friend and ask why she's been lying to me about her involvement with Tom for years. But I need to tread carefully. Did Cal exaggerate their relationship to justify his involvement with me? The thought didn't cross my mind until this morning when I'd been out buying the croissants and if so, what I did by sleeping with him is much worse than what she's done.

Though there's still the issue of Tom choosing Abi over me and stringing me along all these years... though technically, apart from a few loaded moments, he hasn't led me on. I'm the one who's built up our relationship into something it's not. Maybe as an excuse to justify my behavior with Cal...

I'm also the one who slept with my best friend's ex, the father of her child, and I may lose her over it.

Abi's important to me and she'll always share an unbreakable bond with Cal. In my optimism, I see the four of us still hanging out as friends, but if I'm with Cal and Abi's with Tom... I'm a realist and it's not going to happen.

And what about Noah? She may not have known him long but where does he fit into her plans? If she's only toying with Tom because she likes the attention and has ruined my chance with him because of it...

I'll never forgive her.

# THIRTY

## JO

The last thing I feel like doing is visiting Abi and her baby in the hospital but when Callan's on my doorstep practically begging me to come back with him, what can I do?

I can never say no to him. And I'm glad I agreed because for the all-too-brief twenty-minute drive to the hospital, I can pretend it's just him and me against the world. He talks about baseball and football and I feign interest. For all I care he could be discussing the first man to cultivate strawberries on Saturn and I'd find it just as fascinating, that's how smitten I am with him. Interestingly, he doesn't mention Abi or the baby, and I wonder if he's self-centered or doesn't want to risk annoying me, not when I've come this far.

I wanted to tell him the truth when he asked about what caused my falling-out with Abi. I wanted to say how much he invades my every waking thought, and most sleeping ones too. I wanted to say we'd make a great couple. I wanted to tell him how damn furious I am that Abi slept with him when she knew how I felt.

But I don't say any of it because I'm smarter than that. A guy like Callan won't like being caught in the middle of my drama with Abi and if they're planning on playing happy families and moving away, he'll choose her every time. When I tell him how I feel, I want us—Abi and me—to be on an even playing field. And right now, he has a newborn son and Abi's way ahead of me in holding Callan's attention.

I can't believe they're moving away. I've never even heard of Fort Chester and I'm dying to look it up to see how far away it is from San Francisco. The thing is, if I don't forgive Abi, Callan will be out of my life for good. I'll have no excuse to visit them, no reason to keep in contact, and as much as it irks, I'll have to pretend like all's well when I see her shortly.

"You're quiet," Callan says, as he comes to a stop outside the hospital. "You really don't want to do this, do you?"

I shrug, like my being here means nothing when it's a huge step after living with the pain of Abi's betrayal for the last seven months. "You asked me, I'm here."

He's puzzled, his eyes slightly squinty. "Abi said she reached out to you at the start, when she found out she was pregnant, but you blocked her. Yet you're here now because I asked you? That makes no sense, we hardly know each other."

More's the pity. So I reach for another lie to prevent him from guessing the truth. It's too soon. We'll have our chance. Eventually.

"I've missed Abi, and if she sent you to get me, I guess it's time we moved on."

"Good. She's feeling a tad blue and I think seeing you will cheer her up."

Unlikely, but I force a smile and get out of the car. I hate hospitals: the cloying antiseptic smell, the packed waiting rooms, the devastated people who've just had bad news. I've only been twice, once when I landed awkwardly on my head during gymnastics in grade school and my teacher suspected I had a concussion, the other when I had an allergic reaction to soft shell crab. Both times I couldn't wait to get out of here.

But this time is different. I'm not led through the ER. Instead, the entrance to the maternity wing is quiet and smells of lavender and talc rather than antiseptic. I take a deep breath and for some inexplicable reason, it brings tears to my eyes. I certainly don't want a baby now—heck, I have no idea if I ever will—but the thought of all the cute bundles lying in cribs makes me emotional.

Callan casts a curious glance my way and I manage a wobbly smile. He probably mistakes my tears for concern about my upcoming reunion with Abi and I don't disillusion him.

"She's this way," he says, leading me down a long corridor and past a nurses' station. The entire place is bright, with purple elephants dancing along the cornices and lemon butter-flies fluttering across the walls. I glimpse a room filled with baby baths and a woman in a hideous green robe learning how to bathe her child, and another room stocked with bottles, formula, and diapers.

"Here we are," Callan says, as we stop outside a room with a blue stork above the number. "Thanks again for coming, JJ."

He touches my arm, the barest graze of his fingertips against my skin, and I swear I float into the room after him.

"Hey, Abi, look who's here." He steps aside and sweeps his arms wide, like he's giving her the best gift ever.

I want so desperately to hold onto my resentment but the second I see Abi propped up in bed, cradling a sleeping baby, my bitterness fades and I take a tentative step forward.

"I've missed you so much, Jo," she whispers, and when

Callan lays a hand in the small of my back to propel me gently, my feet practically fly across the room.

"Meet Robert James McFee," she whispers, and as I look down at the face of the cherub she's holding, something warm and wonderful unfurls in my heart.

I'm not maternal. I'm not like other girls who gush over babies. But in that moment, I fall in love.

"He's adorable," I murmur, reaching out to brush a finger down his cheek. It's like touching the softest velvet and I fall a little more.

"I'm glad you think so." She exchanges a glance with Callan I have no hope of interpreting. "Because we want you to be his godmother."

My mouth falls open in shock as my gaze swivels between them. They're beaming at me but the emotions overwhelming me are too much and I burst into tears.

To make matters worse—or better—Callan takes a step toward me, like he's going to give me a hug, but I don't think I can stand it. I'll cling to him and somehow he'll know how I feel, so I cover my face with my hands and take a few steadying breaths before lowering them to find Abi staring at me with concern.

"What do you say, Jo?"

I glance at Callan one last time and find myself nodding. "I'd be honored."

"Yay," Abi says, lifting the baby slowly toward me. "Do you want to hold your godson?"

I'd love to hold him but I'm slightly terrified too. "I do, but I've never held a baby before."

"Me either, until he popped out," Callan says, and I laugh.

"There was no popping out. Try ten hours of agony," Abi mutters, but she's looking at Callan with a serenity I haven't seen on her before.

They're a team now. Parents. Something I can never compete with.

So I have two choices. Remove myself from their cozy family of three, or embrace being a part of their world whole-heartedly and take my godmother duties seriously.

To do that, I'll have to move to Fort Chester too.


"Haven't seen you around much," Rex says, handing me a takeout coffee. "You avoiding me?"

"As if." I accept the coffee, take a sip, and sigh with pleasure. "Thanks for this. I really need it."

"At the risk of you dumping that cup all over me, you look tired."

"I've been busy."

"Job hunting?"

I nod, but what he doesn't know is I am looking for jobs but not in San Francisco. That's what catching up today is about but I want to break it to him gently because for the last seven months while my hatred for Abi has festered, Rex has been my rock.

He's listened to me malign her for hours, he's let me cry on his shoulder and he's sided with me on everything. I've played down my obsession with Callan though, because no guy wants to hear his best friend go on and on about some other guy. And through all this, we've been making plans about what to do this summer and beyond.

He's not going to college either—his savings are limited despite his part-time job at a local fast-food chicken joint the last few years and he never wastes money on anything—so we've been throwing around a lot of ideas, centered around the two of us renting a place.

I know my folks will support me if I want to move out of home and into a place of my own—they've spent enough money on Talia's dance career over the years it's the least they can do to share some of their wealth with me—but the problem with keeping my friendship with Rex a secret all these years is they won't welcome me having a male roommate I technically don't know.

Rex is looking forward to moving in with me and I hate to disappoint him. But Callan—and in turn his gorgeous son Robbie—come first and I'm intent on following them to Fort Chester.

"I've been looking at apartments for us," he says, almost jiggling the cup in his hand with excitement. "Nothing too fancy, but I've seen a nice two-bedroom by the beach that could be perfect for us."

He wiggles his eyebrows and I can't help but laugh. "Who knows, a few moonlit walks along the sand and you might even start to see me as more than a friend?"

I'm too shocked to respond and he laughs, filling the awkward silence. "Too much?"

"Rex, you're important to me and I do love you. As a friend," I clarify, and while he's still grinning, I see the flicker of hurt in his eyes. "I'd never want to mess with that."

He shrugs, like my rejection means little. "That's what you say now but wait until you see me strutting around our apartment in my boxers. Or if you're really lucky, with just a towel wrapped around my waist."

He's deadpan for a moment before he bursts out laughing and I join in, relieved we got past any potential awkwardness. I value his friendship and even when I move away I'll keep in touch. I never would've thought we'd still be this close and I feel guilty I've never shouted our steadfast friendship from the rooftops rather than hiding him away like a dirty secret.

"When do you want to come with me to the realtor to start inspecting a few places?"

I have to tell him but I'm not looking forward to extinguishing the excitement in his eyes, not one bit.

"Actually, that's what I want to talk to you about."

His face falls but his irrepressible sense of humor is hard to tame. "Let me guess. You're having second thoughts since I mentioned the boxers and the towel. If it makes you feel any better, I promise to be fully clothed at all times when I exit my bedroom or the bathroom."

I smile but my heart's not in it and he notices.

"Uh-oh. I'm not going to like this, am I?"

I shake my head. "As much as I've been looking forward to us being roommates, it's not going to happen."

He takes a step back like I've slapped him. "Why?"

"Because I'm leaving San Francisco."

His eyebrows shoot up. "You're going to college after all?"

"No. I'm moving to Fort Chester."

"Where the hell's that?"

"About three hours from here. Almost halfway between San Fran and LA."

He's confused and he asks, "Why?" for the second time in a minute.

"Because Abi asked me to be her baby's godmother yesterday and she's moving there."

"You've got to be kidding." His mouth opens, closes, before he stalks a few feet away and flings his coffee cup at a pylon, his burst of anger startling me. "She's treated you like crap, you've spent months raving on about how much you hate her, now you're running after her like a lapdog?"

He shakes his head, fury tightening his lips. "What's so damn special about her that you'd ditch me?"

I reach out to lay a placating hand on his arm but he shrugs me off, vibrating with anger. "It's not like that—"

"That's exactly what it's like!" He lowers his voice when several people strolling along the wharf a hundred feet away turn to look in our direction. "You're the one person in this world I thought I could depend on. You've never made me feel second best for being poor. You've stuck by me when most would've judged." He clamps his lips together and for a horrifying second I think he's going to cry. "You're my best friend, Jo. I don't want to lose you."

"You won't. Just because I'm moving doesn't mean I won't call or text every single day if you'll put up with me."

He shoots me a smile. "Every day is overkill. A few times a week is tolerable."

He opens his arms and I place my coffee in the sand before flying into them and hugging him tight. "What am I going to do with you not around?"

"We're friends for life. Nothing's going to change that." I hug him tight, hoping we can maintain our friendship and wondering if it's worth introducing him to Abi now we've finished school.

I'd like my two best friends to get along. But I can't shake my old insecurities that insist he might take one look at Abi and like her better than me. Everyone else does.

Compartmentalizing my life is much easier. Less room for complications.

# THIRTY-ONE

## ABIGAIL

I'm still reeling from Lara's baby news when I arrive home. Noah's car isn't here and I'm relieved. As much as I'm enjoying getting to know him, it's days like this I value my solitude. He texted me earlier to let me know the scorpion had been removed and he'd be over later tonight, but for now I want a glass of wine and a hot bath.

Lara is thirteen weeks along, which means Cal slept with her about a week after the last time we slept together. He's a jerk. Then again, I'd been telling the truth when I told Lara we're not in a relationship, but a small part of me is hurt regardless. For all I know, he's slept with women across the country during his assignments and I'm just the dummy who warms his bed whenever he deigns to come home.

I know Rob hasn't approved for a while. Whenever his father has visited the last two years, I've seen our son withdraw. Sure, he pretends everything is okay by watching football games on TV and sharing burgers or pizza with his dad, but I also see Rob eyeing me with disapproval, like I deserve better.

It makes me wonder what Rob will think about Noah.

He'll be home for Thanksgiving, so I guess they'll meet then. Noah hasn't put a time frame on how long he's sticking around but when we'd been cuddling last night he'd mentioned he'd happily do research in Fort Chester for a year if he had me.

I'm so busy mooning over Noah I'm almost at the door when I see Cal stand from the old rocking chair in the corner of the porch.

"Hey, Abi, long time no see."

He gives me his signature smile, the one that melts my heart a little, the same one he bestowed on me when Rob had been born, like I'd presented him with the greatest gift. Cal has never been the love of my life but we've made a good team for Rob over the years and a small part of me will always love him for that.

"I'd like to keep it that way," I mutter, shaking my head. "Why didn't you make it back for Rob's farewell?"

He grimaces and swipes a hand over his face. "I'd planned to, but I had to step up at the last minute to cover for a local photographer on a major shoot. Rob seems happy enough."

Cal always has an excuse but I'm mollified a tad by the fact he's reached out to his son. "You've spoken to him?"

"Yeah. Sounds like he's thriving at college."

I nod. "I'm so proud of him."

"Me too." To my surprise, the sheen of tears shimmers in Cal's eyes. "The young man he's turned out to be is all because of you, Abs. You're an amazing mom and if I haven't said it often enough over the years, thank you."

I'm choked up and manage a nod in response. This is the Cal I love. The one who can surprise me at every turn. Who can be insightful despite his devil-may-care attitude toward life.

"Maybe the two of us can head up to UCLA for a long weekend soon? Spend some time with Rob as a family?"

I clear my throat, his thoughtfulness impressing me. "I'd like that."

But his mention of family reminds me that he may soon have another child to consider, and my heart hardens.

"Have you seen Lara lately?"

I see the slightest flicker of guilt in his eyes. "Not for a while. We ran into each other a few months ago in Seattle."

"Must've been fun, catching up on old times." I snap my fingers. "Though wait a minute, you two weren't that close in high school, so I guess you thought you'd rectify that."

His jaw juts in stubbornness. "We're not a couple, Abi, we're co-parents. You have no right to tell me who I can and can't sleep with."

Disappointed that the glimmer of the Cal I love has vanished, only to be replaced with the selfish man I eventually realized I couldn't depend on, I say, "I agree with you, Cal, but the problem is, I shouldn't be involved in the complications that arise from your dalliances either."

Confusion creases his brow. "What are you talking about?"

"It's not my place to tell you."

But Cal's not stupid and by the slump of his shoulders, he knows. "She's pregnant?"

I slow clap. "And I have to say, it makes me feel like crap when I discover an old high school acquaintance who pops into town occasionally and I catch up with has probably been cozying up to me to get to you."

"That's not how it is."

"Should you warn me about any other old school friends you've screwed, so I know how many other half-siblings Rob has?"

He reddens and can't meet my eyes. "I'll talk to Lara."

"You do that, and while you're at it, perhaps she'll let you stay with her because you're not welcome here anymore."

His eyes widen in surprise. "But this is my home."

"No, this is *my* home. My parents bought it for me. You just happened to be the guy who played at being a part-time dad whenever it suited you."

He flinches as if slapped. "That's not fair, Abi. We made the best of it for a long time."

"And you kept sleeping with me until a few months ago." I tap my bottom lip, pretending to think. "Yet I remained faithful."

"That's not fair either. We made a mutual decision to split up years ago. I didn't ask you to wait around for me. We were single."

He's right and my anger deflates. I'm not sure why I'm so furious with him. This is Cal, the guy I pegged as bolting as soon as he found out about my pregnancy back in high school, but to his credit, he stuck around and tried his best. It's not his fault his best isn't good enough and I always wanted more.

"You're right," I say. "Just get your life sorted and leave me out of it."

He flashes his lopsided smile, the one that used to make my heart beat a little faster back in the early days. Pity it had the same effect on every girl in our senior year. "So does that mean I can stay here?"

He steps forward and envelops me in his arms before I can move. "You're still my number one, Abi, always will be."

I snort and tolerate his embrace for another moment before shoving him away. "You've got to step up and take responsibility for another child now, Cal, and that has nothing to do with me."

I turn away and let myself into the house, slamming the door on his "Abi, please..."

Cal's always been good at undermining my defenses. Every time he screwed up over the years, he'd make a grand gesture, like the time he bought me a five-foot teddy or when he filled the bath with jasmine-scented oil and rose petals after I'd had little sleep when Rob had been teething and he'd been absent yet again. But that's the thing about Cal. He thinks occasional thoughtfulness should equate with those around him doing whatever he says, and I'm over it. Our son has left for college and I don't need to pretend anymore.

Time for Cal to handle his life and let me live mine.

# THIRTY-TWO

## JO

I've been at a loose end all day, alternating between mentally replaying every second of last night with Cal and walking around in a daze.

To my surprise, last night has awakened my teen crush and I want more. Beyond making Abi jealous. Beyond rubbing her nose in it. I want the life Cal and I should've had if Abi hadn't interfered.

The more I think about it, the more the idea of Cal and me as a couple makes sense.

When I'd started seriously flirting with Cal, I never expected we'd end up here. I had no intention of having sex with him, but now that it's happened and I've accepted Tom and I will never be together, I'm cautiously optimistic that this could be the start of something wonderful for Cal and me.

It's killing me that the one person I want to talk to about this major development in my life is the one person I can't tell yet. But I do want to talk to Abi. I want to ask her why she lied to me about her involvement with Tom. Not that I'm stupid enough to blunder in and demand answers. I'll be subtle and use her burgeoning relationship with Noah as a way to ask what's happening with her and Tom.

Not that it's going to change anything but if she's lied to me about this, I wonder what else she's lied about...

I walk to her place. It's fifteen minutes at a leisurely pace but I make it in ten because I'm in a hurry to talk to her. I almost step onto her driveway when I see her with Cal. I freeze. From my vantage point, I can see most of his face but only half of hers in profile. They're getting into something unpleasant because their body language is tense. He's trying to reason with her and from this distance I can imagine he's using his best cajoling voice, something I've heard him use on her many times before, usually when he got home late for babysitting duties or had to leave town for work and missed Robbie's milestones.

I wonder what they're talking about and for a horrifying second, I hope it's not me.

But Cal's not an idiot. If what he said is true and they've been sleeping together until he left a few months ago, the last thing he'll do is tell her he slept with her best friend last night.

Not that there was much sleeping involved and the thought brings the heat scorching to my cheeks. I can't afford to get distracted though and I wish I was closer so I could hear what they're saying.

Then Cal steps forward and wraps his arms around Abi, and the blood that has been burning my cheeks a moment ago drains away, leaving me shivery. I wrap my arms around my middle, every cell in my body urging me to run to them and wrench them apart.

But I can't, so I stand there and watch the man I have newly reawakened feelings for... what? Try to rekindle his relationship with Abi? Or give the mother of his child a comforting hug?

Whatever the reason, Abi pushes him away and I'm

relieved. But it's short-lived when I see the expression on his face.

He still cares about Abi. A lot.

And as much as it hurts to admit, he's never looked at me like that.

I wait until he leaves, ducking behind a towering oak to make sure he doesn't see me, and give Abi a few minutes before knocking on her door. She looked upset when Cal left and if he's done the unthinkable and told her about us, I want to give her time to compose herself and not shift her anger at Cal onto me.

Surprisingly, the back door is locked, and I knock. When she answers, she looks relieved to see me rather than mad.

"What's with locking the door?"

"I had an unwelcome visitor," she says, screwing up her nose, but before I can ask an innocuous question about who—when I know it's Cal—she adds, "Someone put a scorpion in my mailbox this morning."

I grimace and shudder. "You sure it didn't just crawl in there?"

She shakes her head. "It was too big. Wouldn't have fit through the mail slot."

I don't argue with her, but I've seen bugs squeeze through tiny holes. "So you think whoever's behind your incidents and my vandalism has upped the ante?"

"I could've been bitten," she says. "I have no idea how poisonous that thing was, so it could've been bad. Thank goodness I had Noah around to take care of it."

"Lucky."

She must hear something in my voice because she pins me with a direct stare. "Why did you say it like that?"

"Like what?"

"Like you have reservations about Noah being here."

I hesitate, not wanting to antagonize her. Besides, I came here to ask why she lied to me about Tom and getting her offside isn't conducive to probing for answers. "He seems nice enough, Abi, but how well do you really know him?"

"What do you mean?"

"Did it ever occur to you that all the stuff going on around here started happening after you two got together?"

Her eyes narrow and I can see she's mad. "Why on earth would Noah want to pull a bunch of pranks here and vandalize your place? And he was with me the other night when I saw that intruder. Besides, a lot of the minor pranks around here happened before we started dating."

"Doesn't mean he wasn't in town."

She's staring at me like I'm nuts and I need to backtrack.

"I don't know, okay? I guess it's just the timing of it." I shrug and cross the distance between us to give her a quick hug. "Forget it. I'm just suspicious by nature."

Which is why I need to find out more about her and Tom.

She accepts my hug but she's stiff and unyielding, so I release her.

She's frowning. "And to make matters worse, Cal just lobbed on my doorstep."

At last, the opportunity I've been waiting for to lead into a conversation I need to have. "What's so bad about that? You two get along."

"He's always got one complication or another going on in his life." She rolls her eyes. "I'm over it."

"But are you over him?"

An eyebrow arches. "What do you mean?"

"Seems to me you wouldn't be this upset about his complications if there wasn't still something between you."

She hesitates, and I can see she's conflicted about how much to tell me. "As you know, technically Cal and I split up a long time ago, but every time he stays here we end up having a prolonged booty call for however long he's in town."

So it's true and it takes every ounce of self-control to hide my loathing.

"I asked you about that before. Why did you lie?"

"Because I'm embarrassed to admit it. It makes me look like a doormat, inviting my ex into my bed whenever he's around." She shakes her head. "But I'm done. That's not happening any more and I've told him he can't stay here, even when he tried to cajole me with some lame line about me being his number one."

"Good for you," I manage to say, but all I can think is Cal left my bed this morning, then came straight here to ask Abi, his *number one*, if he could stay. After I offered my place and he refused?

My anger is a slow burn, trickling through my veins like molten lava, scorching my resolution to stay cool in its path. How can he do this to me? We're too close for him to use me, we're good friends, but for him to reach out to Abi after he'd been with me and to call her his number one... I'm so mad, I can hardly see.

"What's wrong?"

"Nothing," I mutter, through gritted teeth, the tenuous grip on my anger slipping, making my hand shake as I reach for the doorknob. "I have to go."

Before she can say anything else, I wrench open the back door and make a run for it.

# THIRTY-THREE

## JO

THEN

"What do you think of our new place?" Abi flings her arms wide like an exuberant contestant on a home reno show.

"It's great."

And I'm a tad envious. Abi's parents may have given her this house to raise Robbie in, but she's turned it into a home. There's a warmth here amid the chaos of diaper bags and strollers, a place I instantly feel welcome.

It's nothing like the tiny cockroach-infested studio apartment I've had to rent in town due to my meager savings—I'm grateful my folks gave me ten grand to move but I know it's not going to last long so I need to be careful until I find a job—and a pang of envy for all Abi has means I need to force a smile.

Not many teen moms have the support she has. Sure, she must've been scared, knowing she'd be a mom at eighteen with her parents retiring to a town three hours away. But then they'd bought her this house and she'd moved without a second thought. And Cal had followed.

Cal's another surprise. It's one thing to want to stand by Abi during her pregnancy and beyond, but to leave San Francisco behind, give up his college dreams, and move to Fort Chester? It shows a maturity I didn't expect.

From my observations during our senior year, I pegged Cal as shallow. One of those bad boys who are good to look at—and perfect crush material—but without a lot of substance. Then again, he stood up for me against Mandy when he didn't have to, and he showed kindness toward me when he encouraged me to reunite with Abi after Robbie's birth, so there's more to him than I gave him credit for.

He's a good guy and the one burr in moving here. Not seeing him for a few months has helped my crush to dissipate, but it may take a while and I'll need to be careful around Abi and Cal so they don't realize I'm still pining a little.

Moving to Fort Chester is an adventure for me, with the bonus of re-establishing my friendship with Abi. I haven't forgiven her entirely yet, though I'm not stupid. I need to get over my crush and start seeing Callan for what he is— Abi's partner—or I'm in for a lifetime of misery. Being a part of their family means I'll be spending a lot of time with Cal and I can't keep hoping something will happen for us. It's wrong on so many levels and I won't do that to myself.

"I'm so glad you're here." Abi takes hold of my hands and starts dancing, like we used to last year whenever our favorite band would start live streaming. "I'll never be able to thank you enough for being here for me."

A lump of emotion in my throat makes responding difficult, so I swallow several times. "I take my godmother responsibilities very seriously, so you'll never get rid of me now."

We release hands and smile at each other, and the glimmer of tears in her eyes makes me glad I took a chance and moved here. Our friendship will repair with time and soon we'll be back to normal: Abi and Jo, the dynamic duo.

The back door swings open and Cal stomps in, catches sight of me, and lets out a yell: "JJ, you're here!"

He sweeps me into his arms and gives me a bear hug, while I struggle to clamp down on my euphoria at being held by him.

"Put me down," I say half-heartedly, hoping my cheeks aren't too flushed when he does.

Abi's laughing, still on a high that I've arrived in town, and when Cal releases me I see a guy entering the back door behind him.

"JJ, I'd like you to meet Tom," Cal says. "He's our new bestie; alongside you, of course." He waggles his finger at Tom. "Though only I call her JJ so she's Jo to you."

The guy steps forward and the kitchen fades away as I lock eyes with him.

He's gorgeous.

Tousled dark hair skimming his collar, striking hazel eyes, tall, lean, faded denim, navy polo, though it's more than his looks and what he's wearing.

There's just something about him that takes my breath away.

An inner strength, shadows in his eyes, like he's seen what the world has to offer and is still finding his place in it, like me.

He holds out his hand. "Pleased to meet you."

"Likewise." I shake his hand, hoping mine's not clammy.

He smiles and my chest feels like it's caving in on itself. "So you're new to town?"

Embarrassingly, I'm so tongue-tied by the sight of his perfect smile that all I can manage is a nod.

"Well, if you need the grand tour, let me know."

Before I can happily agree, Cal interjects. "Leave the girl

alone, Tom. She's only just arrived. Give her a minute to settle in."

Cal misses my glare as he's already turned toward Abi, and Tom is looking at her too, leaving me to process this momentous event.

I thought it would take me ages to get over Cal.

Turns out, not so much.

And as I stare at Tom's broad shoulders, wondering how old he is/what he does for a living/what his favorite color is/does he like redheads, I'm glad I took the chance and moved to Fort Chester.

## THIRTY-FOUR

I have no idea what Jo's so angry about so I run after her.

"Hey, Jo, wait up."

She's almost at the top of my drive and for a moment I think she'll keep going but she slows, stops, and turns back to face me.

"What on earth was all that about? Why are you so riled?"

She blows out a breath, another, before answering. "Do you really want to know?"

"Of course I do. It's like you're mad at me and I have no idea why."

None of this is making sense. First Jo implies Noah's responsible for all the crazy stuff happening around here lately, now she's angry because I didn't tell her about my ongoing hookups with Cal?

Unless... "Do you still have feelings for Cal?"

"Of course not," she snaps, her rebuttal fast and furious, but she can't look me in the eye and my heart sinks.

Surely she hasn't been harboring a crush for an unobtainable guy for the last eighteen years?

She's been a part of our family, privy to everything. She's

seen us at our worst, has comforted me when Cal let me down repeatedly—more precisely, let down his son. She's joked around with Cal like a buddy for years.

Has it all been a lie?

Is Cal the reason she stuck by me this long?

If so, I should be mad, but all I feel is soul-deep pity. I hope I'm wrong but she still can't meet my eyes and my heart breaks for her. Cal isn't worth her devotion and certainly not for almost two decades.

"Jo, it's okay, you can tell me—"

"I'm mad because you lied to me again, okay?" Her hands are clenched into fists and her back is ramrod straight. "The last time was the morning after you slept with Cal and it almost ruined us. And I thought for the last umpteen years since we've been here that we've been honest with each other. Then I find out that's not the case. How do you think I feel?"

I think she's overreacting, big time, but I wisely keep that to myself.

"As I said before, I didn't tell you because I was embarrassed." I hold my hands out to her, palms up, hiding nothing. "This isn't a big deal."

I've said the wrong thing as she flushes an angry puce.

"It is to me," she mutters, those fists clenched so tight her knuckles are popping. "We have to be able to trust each other."

"Trust works both ways."

She blanches and I continue, knowing I'm treading a fine line but needing to get to the bottom of this. I don't like to see my friend hurting. "Despite your denial, I think you do still have feelings for Cal. And maybe you're mad at the thought of me sleeping with him when I told you I wasn't, rather than the lie itself?"

"I don't want to discuss Cal with you." She's practically shaking with anger and my heart sinks. She wouldn't be this upset if I hadn't stumbled on the truth. "Besides, you being his booty call all these years is none of my business."

"So what's the problem?"

She can't quite meet my eyes, and when she does, I see her anger is still simmering. "How many other lies have you told me, Abi?"

I shake my head to clear it. "What are you talking about?"

"You and Tom?"

"What about me and Tom?"

"So you do have a relationship?" She's rocking on the balls of her feet, like she's spoiling for a fight. "How long has it been going on?"

My confusion intensifies. "Tom's a friend, like he's your friend. That's the only relationship we have."

The sincerity in my tone must get through to her a little because her shoulders sag a little. "I heard you were more."

"You heard wrong."

That's when I realize Jo must have real feelings for Tom and this visit and her bad mood has nothing to do with Cal and everything to do with Tom.

If so, she's been in pain for a long time, with the four of us playing happy families with Rob. What would that have been like for her? Having to hide her true feelings?

I've joked about her and Tom getting together over the years, but I thought she knew Tom's as irresponsible as Cal and can't be counted on for anything. But it's not my place to question her. All I can do is be supportive and try to steer her away from a guy guaranteed to break her heart.

"Do you have feelings for Tom?"

She hesitates, before nodding. "I have for a long time."

"Why didn't you say something? You know you can tell me anything."

She doesn't respond and the shimmer of tears in her eyes

makes me want to hug her even more. But she's still rigid and an embrace would be unwelcome at this point.

I have to get through to her, before she wastes any more time on a guy who's not good enough. "Tom is like Cal's twin separated at birth. They're the same when it comes to women. Not dependable."

To my surprise, defiance flashes in her eyes. "Seems to me like you're warning me off both guys so you can have them for yourself."

Shocked by her ludicrous outburst, I open my mouth to answer, but she continues, "If you and Cal are over, and Tom's not interested in me, you wouldn't mind if Cal and I started dating?"

I wouldn't wish Cal on my worst enemy let alone my best friend. I have no idea if she's speaking hypothetically or if it's her way of having a petty jibe, but Cal's interests lie elsewhere at the moment and Jo needs to know. I can't divulge Lara's news until Cal sorts out that complication, but I can warn my friend.

"Jo, you know Cal's not a keeper, so please be careful. And I'm not the one you have to worry about if you're seriously interested in him."

Her eyes widen as she eyeballs me. "What does that mean?"

I want to tell her, but I'm saved from divulging the truth when my cell rings and I slide it from my pocket and glance at the screen. "This is work, I have to take it."

Jo hesitates before raising her hand in a half-hearted wave. I want to tell her to stay but for the studio to call me now it can't be good and I can only deal with one crisis at a time.

"Chat later?" I ask and she nods before walking away, her shoulders slumped in dejection.

Dread settles like a lump in my stomach as I answer the call. "Abi speaking."

"It's Mandy."

I ease the cell away from my ear and stare at it in disbelief. How did she get my number? And why is she calling from the studio's main landline?

"Abigail? You there?"

"Yes."

"I know this is a lot to ask but do you think you could come into work tonight? I have an emergency."

No way in hell I'm going anywhere near this crazy woman if she's the one responsible for all the weird stuff going on, especially after hours. Though the studio is never fully empty, with some cast sticking around to rehearse late and crew prepping for the next day's shooting.

"What kind of emergency?"

Knowing Mandy, it's to try to get the lowdown on Cal's movements.

"Someone's shredded my clothes for my big scene tomorrow." I hear a hitch in her breathing, like she's trying to hold back tears. "I don't know what to do. I really need this job to go well so they'll hire me for other projects... Do you think you can help?"

She's desperate. It's more than the pleading, it's something akin to fear in her voice. Jo, me, and now Mandy have been targeted by some nutter. I can't see Lara slashing Mandy's clothes, unless... the thought that Mandy might be invested in Cal because they'd had some kind of relationship blows my mind and makes me feel sick to my stomach.

How many women I know has my ex slept with?

I'm exhausted after my long day and the last thing I feel like doing is heading back to the studio to help Mandy, but someone's sabotaging me and it looks like Mandy's inadvertently got caught in the crossfire. Unless she's really crazy and this is her way of getting me to the studio so she can stab me with my craft scissors.

"Abigail? You still there?"

I sigh. "Yes, I'll help you. Be there soon."

"Thanks, I appreciate it."

"See you in half an hour."

I head inside to grab a smoothie from the fridge and lock up. I wasn't kidding when I told Jo I intend on being more careful moving forward after the scorpion incident. What's next, a rattlesnake in my bed? I'd rather not find out. But I do want to discover who's behind all this madness, though I refuse to contemplate Jo's outlandish suggestion that Noah's involved. What would he gain by it? I can't help but think that Jo's jealousy is rearing its ugly head again and she's trying to undermine my relationship with Noah.

I accepted full responsibility for my drunken night with Cal that resulted in my pregnancy. I knew she'd be hurt when I told her the truth but to cut me from her life completely... I'd been devastated. She'd look straight through me at school like I'd turned invisible and ignored every overture I made. That's why I sent Cal to get her to come to the hospital after Rob had been born because I knew she wouldn't turn him down—and I'd been right. Cal and I had already discussed making her godmother because I wanted her back in my life and that's the only grand overture I could think of that might change her mind. Thankfully, it had, and when she followed us to Fort Chester to be near her godson and have a hand in raising him, it blew me away. We've been close ever since but I know she's possessive of our friendship and if she thinks Noah's encroaching...

I hate thinking badly of Jo so when I walk back into the studio, I'm in a bad mood. Mandy better watch out. Thankfully, she's surprisingly meek, sitting on the chair opposite my desk when I enter.

"This better not be a stunt," I mutter as a greeting and rather than jump down my throat, her expression is sheepish.

"Guess I deserve that for being bitchy toward you." She stands and extends her hand. "I'm sorry."

I'm wary of this newly contrite Mandy, at complete odds with our previous encounters, but I shake her hand regardless.

"It's been a long time since high school and we were never friends, but what's with the attitude since you got here?"

She glances away as color creeps into her cheeks. "I'm thirty-six, single, and scoring three minor acting roles a year if I'm lucky since I left school." She barks out a sarcastic laugh. "Nothing like good old inadequacy to transform into jealousy when I see someone who's got it all."

"You're *jealous* of me? But we hardly know each other."

"You got knocked up in senior year. Your life should've fallen apart. Instead, Lara tells me you have a smart, handsome son, you've been in a relationship with Callan all these years, and you have an amazing job. Plus a new hot man too."

"How did you know about Noah?"

"Lara mentioned it. Figures he'd have a cool name," she says softly, and of all the things she could've said I find this the most amusing.

I can't stifle a laugh and soon she's joining in. It's not that funny but we laugh so hard, tears stream from our eyes.

"I guess we needed that," she says, dabbing underneath her eyes with her pinkies. "So you think you can help sort out my wardrobe crisis?"

"I'll try."

When she leads me to the cubicle she's been assigned and I see what's left of her outfits for tomorrow's shoot, I'm stunned. Someone has taken a knife or sharp scissors to both dresses, leaving them shredded. Neither are particularly expensive but they're crucial to her character's scenes and I need to think fast to rectify the problem.

"Who could've done this?" I pick up the dresses and turn

them around, looking for some kind of clue and predictably finding nothing.

"I have no idea. I get along with everyone on the crew and cast." She reddens again. "You're the only one I had a problem with and I can't see you sabotaging your own work."

"There's been a lot of odd stuff happening lately." I eyeball her, wanting to see her reaction when I drop my bombshell. "It coincided with your arrival."

Her eyebrows draw together in a frown. "You think I did this?"

"I don't know what to think but no, you wouldn't do this. Sure, it makes my life hell but it messes with your job too." I hesitate, loathe to ask the next question but needing to if I have any hope of making sense of all this. "You and Lara seem chummy. And this may come from left field, but have you had any contact with Cal that you told her about?"

"By contact, you mean more than a catch-up cocktail?"

"Yes."

Once again, she has difficulty looking me in the eye. "Some of the old gang from school had an impromptu reunion about six months ago. Cal came. Said he was single. We had a lot to drink and..." She shrugs and I can fill in the blanks. "It was one night, meant nothing, but when Lara was asking me about him during lunch the other day, I told her. We had a good chuckle over it, talking about the popular guys from school and where they all are now, that kind of thing."

My mind's spinning with the implication. Lara's pregnant with Cal's baby. Is she obsessed with him to the point that learning about Mandy's involvement sent her loopy? It's outlandish, and I'm sure I'm missing a connection somewhere, but my head's aching at the end of a long day and I still need to fix these ruined dresses.

"You think Lara did this?" Mandy says, shaking her head. "But why? She's nice."

I can't betray Lara's confidence so I lift the dresses and scrutinize them again. "I have no idea who did this but I need to get started ASAP to fix them. Ready to help?"

Mandy nods and falls into step beside me as we head to the sewing room next to my office. She's quiet, eerily so, and I can't help but feel I'm missing something here.

I'm still stewing over Abi's cryptic comment an hour later.

*I'm not the one you have to worry about if you're seriously interested in Cal.*

What did she mean by that?

The only other women in town who know Cal and have asked after him are Mandy and Lara. I'm not a stalker but I know if I dwell on this I won't sleep tonight so it can't hurt to do some reconnaissance.

The easiest way to do a little spying is by process of elimination. I know what Cal's car looks like, I know Lara's probably staying at one of four motels in town, so it's fastest to cruise around and see if I can spot him. With Mandy working at the studio, she's probably staying at one of the cottages on the grounds where actors live in shared accommodation, but I'll start with Lara because I can't imagine Mandy getting cozy with Cal while living with other people. Though Cal has a car... the thought of the two of them going at it in the backseat turns my stomach.

It breaks my heart that the day after we shared such a

special night, Cal doesn't want to be with me. Unless he's taking care of complications? Maybe that's what his visit to Abi had been about? He couldn't tell her the truth about us but he wanted to make sure she knew they were over. And while I have no idea what sort of involvement he has with Lara or Mandy, perhaps he's setting the record straight with them too.

I'm relieved Abi didn't freak when I mentioned my possible interest in Cal. But she did warn me off him, so maybe that's her way of telling me to back off? Either way, I'm done trying to figure out if she's sincere or not. She appeared genuine when I asked about her relationship with Tom, but I can't believe her. Not when she's lied to me several times now.

Besides, what would Cal gain from lying about Tom and Abi? Nothing, so out of the two of them, I know who I believe. I need to have faith in him. He's been flirting with me for ages. He turned up on my doorstep last night wanting more. All these years Cal has been in the background, noticing how I've supported him, cared for him, and maybe he's realized I'm the woman he needs by his side. If that's what he wants, I'm all for it. We're good friends so it'll be easy to slide into a proper relationship, one that will need little to rekindle my old crush.

Damn Abi for sewing that seed of doubt.

Besides, who cares if Lara or Mandy have feelings for him? I'm the one he wants. Last night proves it. Though I'm not a complete idiot. We can't start flaunting our relationship. Abi may profess she's over him and is happy with her new man, but it's icky, me being involved with her ex.

Technically, he was mine first and her sleeping with him stole any chance I had, so maybe if I lay it out in those terms... uh-uh, I'm delusional. Abi won't like it no matter how I try and justify having a full-blown relationship with Cal.

There's Robbie to consider too. He's the one male in my life who loves me unconditionally. We share so many precious memories: lazy days spent picnicking in the park, picking him up from school when Abi couldn't and Cal was away, throwing him a surprise ninth birthday party with a gaming theme, taking him to the action movies Abi dislikes, dinners at my place. I never regretted moving to Fort Chester to be a part of his life and our bond is unbreakable.

But how will he feel when I start dating his dad?

Abi's a great mom and Robbie adores her, so if it came to a choice, he'll pick her every time. I can't lose him.

I strike out at the first motel, the second too, but as I cruise past the third, I see Cal's sedan parked outside a room. I can't exactly barge up to it and knock on the door, but it's dusk and darkness is descending fast, so I park a little way up the road and walk back. The motel is one of those cutesy "old Wild West" themed places, with a giant wagon wheel at the entrance and an old buggy perched on stumps outside the reception. There aren't many cars in the parking lot so occupancy must be low.

There's an old woman manning the check-in desk. She has her nose buried in a romance novel with a very saucy cover, a bare-chested man, all abs, and all I can see is her wiry gray hair perched in a messy topknot. I could wait until she goes on a toilet break but that could be forever so I risk sneaking past. Besides, I have an excuse worked out if she busts me. I've spotted my boyfriend's car parked here when he should be at home with me. Not that far from the truth, even if Cal and I haven't labeled what we are to each other yet.

But the book must be riveting because she doesn't glance up as I slink past, keeping to the shadows. I feel like an idiot creeping around like this but I know my obsessive personality— I won't rest tonight until I know what's going on with Lara and Cal.

Thankfully, my worst fears aren't realized as I reach the

room and see the blinds are open. If they'd been drawn, I would've gone nuts imagining what Lara and Cal could be getting up to in a motel room.

I can see them through the slats. They appear at ease with one another. She's sitting on the edge of a double bed, he's seated in a chair. She's talking and Cal's leaning forward, elbows braced on his knees, smiling and nodding.

They seem... cozy, and a stab of jealousy makes me draw in a sharp breath.

This level of comfort indicates they know each other. More than old high school acquaintances. And the thought he might've slept with her too makes me lean back against the wall, dragging in deep breaths to calm the rage slowly filtering through me.

I have no right to be this furious. It's not like he went from my bed to hers after last night and a single man can sleep with as many women as he likes. I'm being irrational and I need to calm down before I blow this.

Once my anger has faded and I'm not so lightheaded, I peek through the blinds again, in time to see Cal enfold Lara in his arms. He looks stunned and I wish I could hear what's being said in there.

If Lara has professed feelings for him, which would explain the shock on his face, it's too late. Now I know for sure Cal is single and Abi has no further claim to him, and after the night we shared, Cal is mine.

Time to let him know it.

# THIRTY-SIX

## JO

THEN

Moving to Fort Chester is the best thing I ever did.

I've become indispensable to Abi and Callan. I'm at their house almost every day—I have my own key, which shows how important I am to them—Robbie adores me, and I'm growing closer to Callan than I ever thought possible. I try not to let it affect me while I foster my crush on Tom, but he's a travel writer so he's away a lot. When he's in town he's always at the house and the four of us have a ball. Informal nights sitting on the floor sharing pizza, binge watching the newest thrillers, playing cards.

I'm confused, because while I'm struggling to get over my crush on Callan by supplanting him with Tom, Callan seems to be depending on me more. He's always reaching out to me.

Like tonight.

Abi's doing a part-time fashion design degree and is stuck in Valspo on an assignment, two hours away. I know, because I made sure of it. Turns out, it's not that difficult to create car trouble with a little help from the internet. Nothing dangerous, because I'd never wish harm on her, but a problem that manifests once she reaches her destination. Like a drained battery. Her car would've been slower to start than usual when leaving Fort Chester, but once she tried to start it in Valspo... well, let's just say she'd need a mechanic.

I know Callan will call me. He always does. Like that time Abi got food poisoning from the carrot cake I made especially for her because I know Callan and Robbie won't touch the vegetable. And the other time she badly sprained her ankle when I accidentally on purpose tripped and landed on her. And that time she got locked in overnight with the puppies at my first job, a giant pet warehouse, without her phone.

It's easy to stage incidents to disrupt Abi's picture-perfect life and she's too busy seeing the world from behind her rose-colored glasses to suspect anything. Besides, she thinks I've forgiven her. I'm here, aren't I? I babysit, I gush over Robbie, I pick up the slack when she can't.

But what my best friend doesn't know is, I may be able to try to forgive but I can't forget.

I know I'll get over my resentment eventually; become older and wiser. And I do feel bad for these silly sabotaging incidents. It's just at times I get overwhelmed, having my nose rubbed in the perfection of Abi's life, and I secretly lash out. But I've made a vow to myself that this car thing tonight is the last time. I need to stop dwelling on the wrongs of the past and move on.

As for my feelings for Callan, Tom's definitely helped in that regard. They're so alike that it's easy to transfer my affection. Not that either of them know how I feel. I don't want to ruin the easygoing friendship of our foursome. Besides, I know no matter how much I try to convince myself Tom's the guy for me, it's Callan I truly want. I know he's off-limits but the forbidden nature of our relationship is so tempting.

My cell rings and I smile when I see who it is. "Callan, hey. How are you?"

"Frantic. Swamped. Abi's stuck in Valspo, car trouble. Do you think you can come over and help with Rob?"

"Sure. I'll be there in half an hour."

"You're a lifesaver, JJ. What would I do without you?"

"Anytime, Cal. You know you can always count on me."

"You're the best. See you soon."

He hangs up and I'm so smug I do a pirouette—probably better than any I executed during those excruciating dance classes Mom forced me to attend. I haven't seen my parents or Talia in the three years since I moved here. They issue the obligatory Thanksgiving and Christmas invitations, but I always say Abi needs me so I can't come. They don't seem particularly upset. Talia's dreams of being an elite dancer are almost fulfilled and Mom accompanies her around the world. Their flawless photos on social media make me sick.

Rex is the only person I miss from my old life and I travel to San Francisco every few months to catch up. Thankfully, he let go of his resentment when I first told him I was moving and we're closer than ever. He's doing handyman work for a carpenter at the moment and he's living in a share house with four other guys. It's messy and noisy and I hated it on sight, but he's proud of his achievements and I'd never tear him down: he means too much to me.

Besides, he loathes Abi for taking me away from him, a gem he let slip the last time we caught up after he got rip-roaring drunk, and it's nice to have someone else who doesn't think Abi is Little Miss Perfect.

I glance in the mirror on my way out, pleased with how I look. My hair's pulled back in a slick ponytail, my freckles are covered by a light foundation, and the turquoise singlet brings out the blue of my eyes nicely. Teamed with jeans and flip-flops,

I'm casual yet cute—the exact look I know Callan likes because he once complimented Abi for wearing something similar.

My pulse speeds up as I park outside his house, and I swipe my sweaty palms down the side of my jeans as I stroll around the back. I like that I'm family to them and don't use the front door. I'm barely on the porch before the back door swings open and there he is, taking my breath away. I may have my crush under control but it's times like this, when he's wearing a white T-shirt, faded denim that hugs his long legs like a second skin, bare feet, and his eyes fixed on me like I'm the best thing he's ever seen, that I have a hard time remembering I need to move on.

"Robbie won't eat his dinner and I'm going nuts," he says, pulling me in for a swift hug as I reach the door. "Thanks for coming."

I don't answer. Instead, I savor the illicit thrill of being pressed against his chest, breathing in the scent of him. He releases me all too soon and leads me into the kitchen, where Robbie's sitting at the table, arms folded, turned away, ignoring the chips and chicken nuggets on his plate.

"Rob, look who's here." Callan places a hand in the small of my back and nudges me forward, his simple touch making me melt.

Robbie glances over his shoulder and his face lights up when he sees me. "JoJo," he yells and holds his arms out to me. I swear my heart cracks wide open every time I see this kid.

Abi had wanted him to call me Aunty Jo but I vetoed it because of my age. Technically, she'd made me an "aunt" at eighteen and now, at twenty-one, I'm glad I stood my ground.

"Hey, Robbie." I bend down and give him a hug before sitting next to him. "Wow, your dinner looks delicious. Mind if I share?"

"Sure." He pushes his plate over and mimics me when I pop

a French fry into my mouth, then a nugget. I chew slowly, ensuring he's almost cleared the plate by the time I reach for another fry.

When he's finished, he reaches for his juice, then stops. "Dad, JoJo doesn't have juice."

"She does, buddy, but hers comes in a bottle." He hands me a beer with a wink. "Do you want to watch some TV before bed, champ?"

"Can I have your phone instead?"

Robbie's a smart kid and knows his father will give in to letting him play games online with Abi not around and me to back him up.

Callan doesn't hesitate to hand over his cell, obviously relieved Robbie's eaten. "Here you go, kiddo. But only for fifteen minutes."

"Thanks, Dad," Robbie says, but he's already staring at the screen, his thumbs tapping on some game featuring animals on a farm.

Callan points to the living room and I follow him, glad to have some alone time. I treasure these moments with Callan, just the two of us, with Robbie being a good boy in the other room. But I can't keep orchestrating more "emergencies" requiring Abi to stay away because they'll get suspicious so I'm going to make the most of tonight before I listen to my conscience and grow the hell up.

"Cheers, JJ." He clinks his beer bottle to mine before taking a seat on the sofa, where I'm already sitting. I take that as a good sign—he wants to be close to me rather than choosing one of two armchairs. "You're a marvel with that kid."

"It's easier when you're not the parent. I just get to be the fun one who pops in and hangs out."

"Fun." He snorts and a tiny crease appears between his

eyebrows. "Can't remember what that's like or the last time I had any."

He sounds so forlorn, I clamp down on the urge to hug him. "You've got Tom, you guys go out."

"I'm a father at twenty-one when I thought I'd be attending keg parties at college." There's a hint of rancor in his tone and he washes it away with a slug of beer.

"Do you resent Abi?"

The question pops out before I can censor it and his eyes widen. "Abi's great and she didn't pressure me to stick around when she told me she was pregnant, but it was the right thing to do. It just wouldn't have been my first choice, you know?"

I nod and place a comforting hand on his knee. "You're an amazing dad."

"You think?" He gestures at the kitchen. "I can't even get my kid to eat his dinner."

"You're here and Robbie loves you. That's all that matters."

His gratitude is palpable as he places his hand over mine, sending heat streaking up my arm. "What would I do without you, JJ?"

"You'll never have to find out," I say, maintaining eye contact before lowering my gaze to stare at where our hands are joined.

I want to tell him everything.

That while I'm technically over him, it's times like this I don't want to be.

That if he wasn't with Abi, I'd still welcome him into my arms, my life.

How I feel when it's just him and me, like there's the slightest possibility we could be more than friends.

But I'm determined not to be this person anymore, secretly fantasizing about a future I can't have—I'm smarter than that.

I have to be.

# THIRTY-SEVEN

## ABIGAIL

I'm exhausted after fixing the damage done to Mandy's wardrobe for the shoot tomorrow and would like nothing better than to head home, but she offered to buy me a drink as a thank you and I said yes.

"This town has some cool bars," Mandy says, raising her Mojito. "And some nice people. To you, Abi, for coming to my rescue when you didn't have to, considering how much of a bitch I was in high school."

"To me," I say, clinking my cocktail glass against hers, and she laughs.

It's not forced and for the first time I see a glimmer of what it would've been like if we'd been friends back then. We were both popular, but for different reasons. Mandy was the quintessential cheerleader who wore her status as a beautiful girl like a badge of honor, whereas I liked talking to everybody. I never discriminated against anybody and never lauded my popularity over classmates like Mandy did. It's a shame.

"At the risk of alienating you and ruining our newly formed truce, why were you such a bitch back then?"

She grimaces and takes a sip of her Mojito before answering. "Usual teen angst. The youngest of five at home, single mom who worked two jobs and didn't have enough left over to pay attention to her kids, let alone the youngest. School was the only place I was noticed so I played up to it." She shrugs, remorse written all over her face as she gnaws on her bottom lip. "I took it too far. I wasn't a very nice person."

To her credit, she eyeballs me. "I'm really sorry, Abi."

"Apology accepted, though I think it's Jo you should be apologizing to."

She screws up her face. "I was awful to her. And to a lot of the quieter girls." She shakes her head. "I believe in karma, considering I'm still single and can't score a major role no matter how hard I try."

"Have you come close to being married?"

"Not really. Was too focused on getting a foothold in the industry to foster relationships." She holds her hands up and shrugs. "Now I'm thirty-six and wondering where the years went and if I've done the right thing."

"It's normal to have regrets," I say, feeling sorry for her. "We all do."

She raises an eyebrow. "Even you?"

"Don't get me wrong, I adore my son and have loved every minute of raising him, but I do wonder how different my life would've been if I'd gone to college and hadn't been a teen mom."

"I was so jealous of you back then. Lara was too." She gives a self-deprecating laugh. "Every girl in our senior class would've happily had Cal's baby, that's how much we all wanted him."

I bite back my first response, "You can have him", because disparaging him isn't my style, especially considering Lara's now carrying his baby.

"I can't remember you and Lara being close back then?"

"We were paired up in biology for a major assignment and it grew from there. She's great. We've been friends ever since."

Odd, that Lara never mentioned her friendship with Mandy the few times we've caught up over the years. Then again, not many people outside of her group liked Mandy so that may be why.

If they're close, I wonder if Lara has mentioned her pregnancy to Mandy? Doubtful, considering that's a big deal and Mandy would've said something. Unless she doesn't want to get me offside because Cal's the father and she's afraid of how I'll react?

"Though it's weird, her being in Fort Chester the same time I am, and she didn't mention it last time we chatted on the phone a few weeks ago." Mandy sips at her drink and her brow furrows. "And she's been acting a little off."

Pregnancy will do that to you, but it's obvious Mandy doesn't know and it's not my place to gossip.

"Maybe all of us can have a girls' night out? You, me, Lara and Jo?"

Mandy looks so excited by the prospect that I don't have it in me to burst her bubble. Jo hated Mandy and I doubt she'll want to be buddy-buddy with her now. Then again, I never expected to be sitting here with her, having a drink and enjoying our conversation. It's a long time since high school and I'm glad we're adult enough to move on, even though I can't completely dismiss the chance she may be behind some of the incidents that have befallen me lately.

When I realize she's staring at me expectantly, waiting for an answer, I say, "That sounds fun," resulting in her launching into her current taste in music and her favorite wines.

I'm glad we've set aside the animosity of the past, but I can't help but wonder if I'm being too trusting and is she lulling me into a false sense of security?

. . .

I finally make it home at eleven thirty. I'm glad I averted the crisis and Mandy has her outfits ready for filming tomorrow. Considering the way we bonded over drinks afterward, it seems impossible she would've slashed those clothes to get me in trouble, especially when she reached out to me to help fix them.

So that means someone else is messing with me and I have no idea who or why.

I step from the car and roll my shoulders. When I look up, I notice two things: Noah's room above the garage is in darkness, meaning he's either out or in bed earlier than usual.

Secondly, someone has egged the front of my house.

I stare in disbelief at the mess all over my front door and windows, bits of shell clinging to yolk, stuck in clumps. Of all the stupid, childish pranks... I know Jo had been mad earlier but surely she wouldn't be this juvenile?

I instantly feel bad for thinking it. Jo's a grown woman and wouldn't resort to this if she had a beef with me. I know because we've had our arguments over the years. Nothing major, but she's a strong-willed woman and my easy-going nature annoys her sometimes. She never holds back in letting her feelings be known and throwing eggs at my house is beneath her.

I've been with Mandy the last few hours, so it's not her. And Lara's come clean to me about her pregnancy so what's she got to be angry about? It doesn't make sense and I'm over it.

A car pulls up. What now? But it's only Noah and I'm ashamed by my sudden urge to blubber.

"What the hell happened?" He stares at the house in disbelief, before slinging a protective arm across my shoulders. "Are you okay?"

"Yeah, I just got home after dealing with a work emergency and having drinks with a friend. Then I find this."

His eyebrows rise. "Local kids?"

"No idea, but I've lived here for almost eighteen years and haven't had an incident."

"Weird." He wraps his other arm around me and I rest my face against his chest, grateful for the support. "You must be exhausted if you've just got home. I'll clean it up."

I'm tired to my bones and his intuitiveness is impressive. How many times had I arrived home late from my course when Rob had been young to find Cal sitting in front of the TV, with dishes stacked in the sink, the kitchen a mess, and toys strewn across the living room floor? He'd been oblivious to my fatigue most nights and had resented me when I didn't want to go out with him and party. On the few occasions I'd given in and Jo or Tom had babysat for us, I'd watch Cal flirt with women in the bar, wishing all the while I could be back home, tucked up in bed.

I'd put up with a lot for Rob's sake, wanting him to have a father. But as Noah's arms tighten around me, strong and supportive, I wonder if I did myself a disservice? Sacrificed my happiness for the sake of my son's?

"I can help," I say, the words muffled against his chest, and he eases me away to smile at me.

"I think you almost fell asleep for a moment, so why don't you head on up to bed and I'll take care of this?"

"Thanks." I brush my knuckles across his cheek. "I knew I asked you to move in for a reason."

He gets this goofy look on his face that makes my heart flip. "I'm glad I met you, Abi Smith."

"Right back at you, Noah Powell."

He kisses me and the stresses of my day fade away.

"Now go." He pats me on the butt.

"You'll find cleaning stuff in the garage," I say. "Come in when you're done for a treat."

"Hot chocolate?"

"That too." I wink and he grins.

"I'll make this the fastest clean up on record."

"You do that."

I let myself into the house and head for the bathroom, eager to shower off my day. Though Noah will need a shower once he's done and it might be fun to do together...

I've never felt this alive with a man. Then again, considering I've only ever been with Cal, I don't have a lot to compare him to. It reminds me of that weird accusation Jo made, about me being involved with Tom. I have no idea where she got that idea but I know how jealousy can trigger her possessiveness and I hope this won't cause a rift between us again.

As for my intense attraction to Noah, I could've dated over the last few years after Cal and I officially called it quits, but I didn't have the inclination. Rob had been a good teenager but I was so tired at the end of a day I preferred to curl up with a book than a man.

I'd dreaded being an empty nester but turns out, being thirty-six and single again isn't so bad if Noah's the quality of man I attract. I can't wait to see how our relationship unfolds.

# THIRTY-EIGHT

## JO

I need to know what's going on between Cal and Lara, but I know him. He won't react well to being bailed up and questioned. He used to hate it when Abi interrogated him every time he got home after a late night. He'd get this look on his face—narrowed eyes, compressed lips—stubborn as they come.

I need to be smarter so I invite him over for his favorite dinner.

I don't know where he stayed last night. It galls me that he could've been with Lara the night after he slept with me. Or worse, he went crawling back to Abi and she let him stay despite telling me she wouldn't. I've stewed over it all day and my furry clients suffered. A poodle nipped at me after I cut a nail too close, and a golden retriever growled when I combed too vigorously. I'd been more careful after that, but all I could think about was Cal.

I don't cook often. Making meals for one is a chore so I usually exist on salads, tuna from a can mixed with brown rice and avocado, or takeout. Abi invites me over for a lot of family meals too, but with Robbie gone, I'm guessing those won't be happening so much; especially now she has Noah.

She called me this morning, wanting to clear the air between us, and I apologized for my erratic behavior last night. We can never stay mad at each other for long—discounting those seven months of her pregnancy when I wanted to kill her —and she told me that someone had egged her house. These pranks are getting ridiculous. She was with Mandy at work last night, and I can't imagine Lara doing it, so that leaves my first assumption: Noah. But I didn't make the mistake of bringing his name up again as a possible culprit; she hadn't liked it so much the first time around.

Maybe he's doing it to her to scare her into keeping him around? That's my first supposition. But why spray-paint messages for me? No way would he know about my obsession with Tom and the recent developments with Cal so asking me to leave "him" alone is ludicrous.

I don't have time to dwell as I carefully carve the pot roast, layering slices on a platter alongside roast potatoes and honeyed squash. It smells delicious, and as I add a bowl of green beans sautéed in garlic next to the platter in the middle of the table, I'm salivating.

I hope Cal's appreciative of the effort I've gone to. I made this meal for him and Robbie a few years ago when Abi had been out of town and Cal had gushed. He'd been so appreciative that night... when Cal looks at me like he really *sees* me, I can't help but wish I hadn't given up on my crush and he'd chosen me.

I uncork a bottle of Shiraz and choose an easy-listening playlist, keeping the music low so we can have a proper discussion: I want answers tonight.

There's a knock on the door and I smooth the front of my

simple black dress once before heading up the hallway and opening it.

"Hey, JJ. Something smells good." He presses a kiss to my forehead like I'm a kid and I instantly bristle. He's been inside me and that's the best he can muster by way of a greeting?

"It's pot roast."

He follows me into the dining room and when he catches sight of the table, he wolf whistles. "Wow. What are you having?"

I laugh as he intended and gesture for him to take a seat. "I've opened a bottle of red but I have beer too?"

"Red's fine."

He sits and I quell my disappointment he didn't pull out my chair first. It's silly, because he's not the kind of guy who's big on old-fashioned manners but I'm probably wrapped up in some fanciful fantasy scenario in my head that I wish for a little romance.

"What have you been up to?" I ask, as he pours wine into our glasses.

"Doing my usual photographing update I do every time I return to town, looking around, taking snaps of whatever grabs my attention. I swear something new pops up in a few months." He gestures to the platter. "Can I start?"

I nod, biting back my disappointment once again that he didn't offer to serve me first.

I want to ask where he stayed last night so badly, but I'll lead into it gently. "I thought you might pop in yesterday?"

"Was busy catching up with a few people." He shovels meat, roast vegetables, and beans onto his plate like he hasn't eaten in a month. "Crashed at Tom's place last night. He's still out of town."

I take a big gulp of wine to prevent myself yelling a loud "Woo hoo" that he hadn't been with Lara.

"How is he? I haven't spoken to him since we caught up recently in San Fran."

"The same. Give him a beer or two and you can't shut the guy up. He's infatuated with some surfer chick in Malibu at the moment."

I hate hearing that the guy I've waited years for is hooking up with random women. Then again, it's better than the alternative: his obsession with Abi, according to Cal.

I know that side of Tom, and Cal's the same. Whenever he has a few drinks, he becomes overly garrulous. It used to embarrass Abi, especially at gatherings with parents from Rob's school. Most of those parents were older than Abi and Cal, and even I could see they looked down on my friends. To Abi and Cal's credit, they never let it bother them and continued to attend bake sales, school fairs, and trivia nights because their love for Rob was absolute. I admired them for that, because no way could I pretend with a bunch of phonies like those judgmental parents.

"You didn't have to stay there, you know. You could've stayed here."

"It was nice of you to offer, JJ, but it's too complicated. Even with things finally over between me and Abi, it's too soon."

I latch onto those last three words.

*It's too soon.*

Meaning there will come a time for us in the future and he sees it too. But I need to know what's going on with Lara, or if there's anyone else he's involved with before I throw myself wholeheartedly into a relationship.

"You travel a lot. Are you seeing anyone?"

His fork pauses halfway to his mouth before he quickly stuffs pot roast into it and studies the vegetables on his plate with great interest. "No."

He took too long to answer and I know he's lying. There's

definitely something going on between him and Lara, but I don't want to push too hard. I know he felt trapped by Abi early in their relationship and I don't want to make the same mistake.

I need to play this smarter. Cal's a guy that hates being hedged in. He likes to come to conclusions in his own time. I need to remember that.

# THIRTY-NINE

## JO

THEN

It's been the perfect day. Robbie wanted a low-key fourteenth birthday so he invited a few school friends around and Cal's grilling in the backyard. The burgers and hot dogs are being demolished as soon as he cooks them and Abi's keeping the coolers stocked with sodas. I'm in charge of desserts and have gone all out with my ice cream station. Vanilla, chocolate, and strawberry on offer, with an array of toppings: sprinkles, nuts, marshmallows, candy, choc chips, licorice, and crushed cookies. Turns out, teen boys have bottomless stomachs and can squeeze in waffle cones loaded with ice cream and toppings after demolishing hot dogs and hamburgers.

We've been on food duty for an hour when there's a lull and the kids are crowded around Robbie as he shows off the drone I gifted him. It's an extravagant gift Abi had frowned upon, but Robbie loves it and that's all that matters. He's the center of attention but rather than boasting, Robbie is passing it around, letting all the kids have a look—he's the best.

"I need to duck out and grab some more soda." Abi touches me on the arm. "Do you need anything?"

"All good, thanks. Can you believe how much these kids can eat and drink?"

"I can, considering my grocery bill lately has gone through the roof courtesy of my growing boy's voracious appetite."

I chuckle. "It's good to see him surrounded by friends."

"He's the best kid. I'm so blessed."

She is, but I don't like how she says "I". What about Cal? He's part of their family too, but I've noticed he's not around as much lately, always hitting the road for work. Being a photographer is the coolest job and I love hearing his tales when he returns after a trip. Though the increasing frequency of his absences makes me wonder if they're on the verge of breaking up. There's no real affection between them. Cal's always touchy-feely with Abi but she seems distant recently.

"Anyway, I'll be back soon." She smiles at me. "Thanks for helping out today, Jo."

"My pleasure."

And it is because any time spent with Cal and Robbie brightens my day. I wait until I hear Abi's car start up before approaching Cal. He's leaning against a table near the grill, chugging a beer, looking at Robbie with adoration. It's wonderful to see how much he loves his son.

"Hey, chef, good job on the grill today."

"Thanks, ice cream queen."

When he smiles at me, I swear my internal body temp ratchets up. I thought I'd be over my physical reactions to him by now. I've dealt with my crush, I've moved on. But it's times like this I remember what it felt like when I had all the feels for Cal.

I shouldn't, but I can't help myself. My three-year relationship with Dave ended months ago and Tom's still treating me like a friend despite the occasional loaded moment between us. It's nice to have a guy pay me attention and Cal's guaranteed to do that. I know it's nothing unusual for him, he flirts with every woman, but with Abi out, there's nothing wrong with basking in his attention for a little while.

"Today's been fun." I gesture at the kids. "They've had a ball."

"Yeah." He appears uncertain for a moment. "Rob said he wanted to keep his birthday low-key so I thought firing up the grill would be best."

I'm surprised this was his idea, not Abi's. "What did Abi want to do?"

He rolls his eyes. "Make the kids' parents drive an hour to that new paintball arena that's just opened up on the highway."

"This is much better. How long are you staying in town this time?"

He shrugs. "No idea. When a job comes up, I take it. The money's good and I can't afford to knock it back. Photography is competitive and it pays to stay current."

His eyes glow when he talks about his passion and I can't help but wonder what it would be like to have him look at me that way one day.

"Everything okay with you and Abi?"

He hesitates, before nodding. "Why do you ask? Has she said something?"

"No. Just seems you two aren't so close lately."

"We're cool," he says, but I'm doubtful.

"Well, if you ever want to talk, I'm here." I lean in close so our arms are pressed against each other. "You know I'm always here for you and anything we discuss is confidential."

"You're sweet, JJ." He rests his cheek on top of my head and I wish I could capture this moment with one of his cameras, a treasured memory to pull out whenever I need to.

When he doesn't move, prolonging the contact, I'm emboldened to say, "Text or call any time you're on the road. I'd love to hear from you."

"Maybe I'll video call so I can see your gorgeous face?"

I'm beaming and that's the moment I look up and see Abi watching us, a crate of soda in her arms.

# FORTY

## ABIGAIL

For the first time in what feels like weeks, I arrive home from work upbeat rather than exhausted. I had a hassle-free day and my house is still intact, so I take that as a win. Maybe I should kick-start every morning with a leisurely wake-up call from a gorgeous guy?

Noah had been particularly attentive in bed last night; after our scorching interlude in the shower, that is. Several people at work remarked about my glow today and while Noah's skill in the bedroom had something to do with it, it's the intimacy that's making me feel more alive than I have in a long time.

I've never had a guy hold me, caress me, kiss me, and stare into my eyes like he does. When I'm with him, his focus is absolute, and he makes me feel like I'm the only woman in the world. Heady stuff compared to the quickies with Cal that were more about satisfying a physical urge than anything else.

It makes me realize I've been short-changing myself all these years. Being a single parent for much of Robbie's life has been rewarding, but I've missed out if dating someone who genuinely cares about me could've made me feel this good before now.

I glance at the room over the garage, wondering if it's too needy to knock on Noah's door for the simple fact I can't wait to see him, when he opens the door and waves.

"How was your day?"

"Good." My smile is coy. "Must've been the great start."

"Are you talking about my legendary scrambled eggs?"

"No."

We grin at each other and as he approaches me, I subdue the urge to run to him like some starry-eyed heroine in a romcom.

"Want to go out tonight? Have a drink, maybe share a plate of nachos and some buffalo wings?"

"That sounds great." I wrap my arms around his neck. "Give me fifteen minutes to have a quick shower."

"We could make it thirty if I joined you?"

I blush at the memory of what we got up to in the shower last night. "We'll never leave if we do that, which is fine by me."

"Me too, but I want to take you out, spoil you a little." He slants a soft kiss across my lips. "I'll go distract myself with work and meet you back here in quarter of an hour."

"Deal."

I make it back to him in ten and I'm glad I cut my shower short to take extra care with my make-up when he lets out a whistle.

"You're gorgeous."

"You're just saying that so I'll invite you in later."

"Never entered my mind," he deadpans, and I laugh. "But if I am to come in, I need sustenance, so let's go."

He takes me to one of the smaller bars in town. It channels an intimate saloon, with plush crimson velvet chairs around ornate mahogany tables, the walls covered in beveled mirrors, with strategically placed sconces casting a warm glow over everything. The cocktail list is impressive and as Noah heads to the bar to place our order, I glance toward the door.

In time to see Cal and Jo enter.

They've been friends forever. Jo's a part of our family. But there's something about the way he's standing close to her and the way she's looking up at him that makes me think there's more going on between them.

My chest twangs with a momentary flare of pain that has more to do with Jo not confiding in me than jealousy. I'm done with Cal and have been for a long time but Jo can do so much better than him. I've tried to warn her but she won't listen. He'll end up hurting her. And if he hasn't told her about Lara... the whole thing can blow up in Jo's face.

I stare a tad too long and end up catching Cal's eye as it roves over the bar like he's checking everyone out. I raise my hand in a half-hearted wave and his face lights up. Great, just want I need: my ex and my best friend crashing my date with Noah.

Cal leans down to say something to Jo and her gaze zeroes in on me.

She's not happy.

But Cal's already half dragging her toward my table and I brace. If they are dating, this has the potential to be awkward. Cal has no filter and no clue when it comes to social niceties.

"Hey, Abi, here alone?" Cal bends to kiss my cheek and Jo manages a tight smile.

"No. My date's at the bar."

"Date? Good for you. Though Rob's barely flown the nest and you're already out there?"

Indignation makes my fingers curl into my palms. Who the hell is he to lecture me on getting "out there" when he's done his fair share of that even while we were together?

Noah's arrival prevents me from saying something I'll regret. "Hi, Jo," he says, and sticks out his hand to Cal. "Noah Powell."

Cal sizes him up and he's not impressed. Cal likes being the most noticeable guy in a room and Noah has him beat. If Noah's a ten, Cal's an eight; one of those guys who's a standout in high school but deteriorates with age. Or maybe I'm just in a catty mood and still fuming over his smart-ass comment.

"Cal McFee, Rob's father."

I roll my eyes. "Noah knows who you are, Cal. Now, if you'll excuse us?"

Cal looks like he wants to stick around but Jo threads her arm through his. "Enjoy your evening."

I stare at where their arms are joined. It's a possessive gesture, like Jo's laying claim, and when I raise my eyes to meet hers, I glimpse a smirk before she wipes it. I want to say "He's not a keeper, Jo, he'll end up breaking your heart" but if she didn't listen to me the other day, she certainly won't want to hear it now when she's practically clinging to him.

When they head toward the bar, Noah lays a hand on my back. "You okay? I know he's your ex but that guy's a jerk for making that comment."

I lean into him, more grateful by the minute for having Noah in my life. "How do you do that? Know exactly the right thing to say?"

"It's a gift." He swoops in for a kiss. "The food and drinks should be here any moment so let's take a seat and unwind."

I don't have to be asked twice but as I glance at the bar I see Jo watching me with the oddest expression on her face.

Jealousy.

# FORTY-ONE

## JO

Cal doesn't like Noah. And I've had to sit here at the bar for the last ten minutes and listen to him whine about how Abi could do so much better—Abi-this and Abi-that.

I'm ready to slug him.

When we finished dinner and Cal suggested we go out for a drink, I'd taken it as a good sign. He wanted to be seen in public with me. An official declaration of sorts. I'd leapt at the chance. Now, with him mooning over Abi, I wish we'd never left my place. He'd been a different person there, at ease, his usual jovial self, and not this brooding, sulky man-child.

"Do you want to go somewhere else?" I ask, despite the fact we've ordered drinks. I'll happily ditch my Cosmopolitan if it means I don't have to listen to him whinge about Noah looking like a Zac Efron wannabe. Personally, I think Zac's hot, like most of the females on this planet, but I keep that gem to myself.

"No," he snaps, and when I recoil, he's instantly contrite. "Sorry, JJ."

"What's up with you? Are you jealous?"

"Of course not."

But his rebuttal sounds hollow and my heart sinks. If he still has feelings for Abi, there's no hope for us. I don't want to come second to her. Not again.

"Are you concerned she might wonder what we're doing here together?"

"No." Once again, his short, sharp response hurts. "We're friends. Abi knows we're friends. What's wrong with two buddies hanging out?"

*Friend. Buddy.* Each label driving a knife into my bruised heart.

I want to let this go and not push him, but I need clarity. "I think we moved beyond being just friends the other night."

He tears his gaze from Abi to look at me and I don't like what I see. Indecision. Wariness. Regret.

"What do you want from me, JJ?"

Everything.

But it's too much too soon, and before I can answer he says, "I'm not in a good place right now. I've got a lot of stuff going on so if you're looking for a relationship, I'm not that guy."

In that moment, I see the next few months so clearly. Abi's kicked him out, of her bed and the house, so whenever he's in town, he'll lob on my doorstep. I'll be Abi's substitute. Second best, yet again.

No way in hell I'll be anyone's sloppy seconds.

"Can I ask you something?"

He nods but he's eyeing me with skepticism.

"If Abi wasn't around, would things be different?"

He's confused, so I clarify. "If she moved away. Or we did. Would that make a difference to the 'stuff' you have going on?"

"Not really."

But he's back staring at her and I know he's wrong. As long as Abi's in our faces, in our lives, we don't stand a chance.

I need to rectify that.

# FORTY-TWO

## JO

THEN

The day after Robbie's birthday party, I'm back at Abi and Callan's on the pretext of helping clean up. In reality, I hope to see Callan again and make sure I hadn't imagined that spark between us yesterday.

I could've screamed when Abi arrived home with the soda and interrupted our moment. He'd been resting his cheek on my head while we stood side by side, so close I could smell his delicious woodsy scent over fried onions and grilled burgers. I thought I'd pushed my luck when I suggested he text or call next time he was on the road, but he'd upped the ante by saying he'll video call to see my gorgeous face.

He'd called me gorgeous. Me. The redhead no guy notices.

But Callan had finally noticed and if Abi didn't have such bad timing, who knows how far our flirting would've gone? Not in a physical sense, but wordplay is powerful and he's never been that overt with me before. I can't wait to see what happens next.

Not that I'll take it too far, but every time Tom and I have had a "moment", it's been after he's observed Cal flirting with me. So, if I up the ante with Cal, will that finally jolt Tom into making a move? I've lusted after Tom for years, and it's about time I get the happiness I deserve. Not that I'm foolish enough to think it'll happen overnight but Cal and Tom tell each other everything, so if Cal and I start texting, Tom will know about it.

About time he sees me the way I want to be seen.

I've waited long enough.

But first, I need to allay Abi's suspicions. She'd been cool when she returned with those sodas and saw me cozying up to Callan. I need to smooth things over between us because the last thing I need is her distancing herself from me, and in turn, I won't get to see Callan and Tom as much.

As I enter the backyard, I see her collecting soda cans from the back of the garden.

"Need some help?" I call out and she beckons me over.

"Hey," she says, and hands me a large trash bag. "You didn't have to stop by, you did enough yesterday."

There's an odd lilt to her voice and I scan her face, trying to get a read. Is she referring to me manning the ice-cream stand or what happened with Callan?

"Not a problem. Robbie and his friends had a great time and that's all that matters."

"Yeah. And those ice-cream concoctions were a big hit."

"Teens and sugar, the perfect combo."

We share a laugh but there's tension in the air and I know she'll say something about Callan and me. Abi's always upfront to the point of bluntness. Except when it counted, like the night she slept with Callan in the first place.

An awkward silence stretches between us, punctuated by the clang of soda cans as we fill the trash bags. Hers is full and when she ties it off, she turns to face me.

"Jo, we've been friends for a long time, so don't take this the wrong way, but do you have feelings for Cal?"

My chest constricts with apprehension she's seen right through me and I force a laugh. "Of course I do. He's my best friend alongside you. We spend all our time together. Honestly? I don't know why you two haven't got sick of me long before now."

She won't let me hedge and pins me with a knowing stare. "You know what I mean."

I could be obtuse and make her spell it out, but we're above that. Besides, she knows me better than I know myself and lying now will only prolong the awkwardness between us. If I'm flippant and make light of it, she'll be appeased and leave me alone. Because the last thing I need is Abi discovering how I plan on using Cal to make Tom jealous.

"You know I've had a crush on Tom forever." I smile and roll my eyes, playing it down. "Not that he seems to notice, the moron. We've been a foursome for fourteen years and he still has no clue. But Cal and me? Not a chance in hell."

She's staring at me so intently I resist the urge to squirm. I know what she's doing. Trying to see if there's more behind my glib response. So I maintain eye contact when every instinct is insisting I look away before she sees the truth I'm hiding: that I like Cal's attention and even if it doesn't encourage Tom to finally make a move, I'm going to enjoy it while it lasts. Because ultimately, it's always been Cal for me.

She gnaws on her bottom lip, as if questioning the wisdom of saying more. "What I saw yesterday... the expression on your face, it looks like you were buying into Cal's crap. And you know he flirts with every woman that way, and I'd hate for you to get the wrong idea."

I want to yell at her, "Don't you think I know that?" Does my friend think I'm that stupid?

"No wrong idea here." I draw my shoulders back and stare her down. "I know what Cal's like. Besides, already told you, my interest lies elsewhere." I lay a reassuring hand on her shoulder and give a little squeeze. "Not that I'd ever go near him. He's yours, Abi. You have nothing to worry about."

I see the conflicting emotions play out over her face. She wants to believe me but she's unsure.

"Look, if it makes you feel any better, do you want me to stay away for a while?"

It's the last thing I want and I'm pushing my luck because if she takes me up on my offer, I'm screwed. Though deep down I know she'll refuse because Robbie adores me and she won't want to upset him.

"Of course not." She rests her hand on top of mine and pats it. "I'm just concerned about you and I don't want you wasting your life hanging around us all the time when you could be living it. Or worse, waiting for Tom to make a move when that could take forever."

My anger is swift and it takes every ounce of willpower not to show it. Who the hell is she to tell me how to live my life? But I damp it down. It's too early to fracture our friendship. Yesterday with Callan was only the start. I need to stay close to the family, even if that means pretending in front of Abi.

For someone so ready to give relationship advice, she should take a look at her own. Callan and Abi never married and she tolerates his over-the-top flirting. Doesn't she have any self-respect? They don't love each other, not in the way a couple should. They're little more than co-parents at this stage, sharing a house for the sake of their son. Housemates and little else. But Robbie's growing up and there'll come a time soon when Callan won't feel obliged to stick around anymore. What will Abi do then?

She has no right to judge me when her relationship is less than solid. I know what I'm doing. Does she?

# FORTY-THREE

## ABIGAIL

Noah and I are halfway through our buffalo wings when I see Jo head for the bathroom. It's the opportunity I've been waiting for.

"Be back in a sec." I press a kiss to Noah's lips, the hint of honey, hot sauce, and spice from the wings lingering.

"You taste yummy," he murmurs, and I laugh.

"I was just thinking the same thing."

"Maybe we should takeout an extra serve to eat in bed later?" He wiggles his eyebrows suggestively and I waggle my finger at him.

"Messy." I lean closer to whisper in his ear. "But doable if I get to eat off you."

His groan is strangled. "Go. Before I get them to pack these leftovers and we leave now."

I smile and pat his cheek, eternally grateful I met this amazing guy. I'd much rather stay and flirt with Noah but I'm worried about Jo and it's my duty as her friend to warn her.

She won't like it.

She didn't appreciate it when I warned her about unrequited feelings for Cal after Rob's fourteenth birthday and she won't now. She'd deflected then, dismissed her feelings as a crush on Tom, but I'd seen the way she looked at Cal, had seen it for a while. Nothing overt, just a general perkiness whenever Cal was around. Back then, I hadn't been worried because our friendship was strong and I know she had a thing for Tom too, and I hoped they'd get together. Besides, Jo adored Rob and I knew she wouldn't do anything to be kept away from him, and that would've happened if she'd interfered in my relationship with Cal.

But I'd watch her when she didn't know it and I saw a lot: her surreptitious glances at Cal, the way she laughed longest and loudest at his lame jokes, how she'd smile at him. Her entire face would light up in a way I rarely saw otherwise. Cal being Cal lapped up the attention. He fed off Jo's open adoration, but not in a malicious way. Cal thought every woman worshipped him, so he never noticed the effect he had on Jo. But I did and I didn't like it. Not because of envy, but the fear I'd lose Jo if Cal overstepped and ruined our friendship.

It makes me worry about her now. Can't she see Cal's using her? I wouldn't let him stay with me so he's moved onto the next easy target. I wouldn't put it past him to know about her crush all these years and he's taking advantage of it. If so, he's a bigger jerk than I give him credit for. I'm protective of Jo. She's lonely. Not that she'd ever admit it but beneath her tough exterior, I know she wants the family she never had.

It kills me that she can't have kids because I see the way she is with Rob. She lavishes him with so much love and has done since the moment he was born. Heck, if it wasn't for her infatuation with Rob, I doubt our friendship would've been resurrected. She'd fallen for him on sight, like Cal and I had, and had uprooted her life and moved to Fort Chester to be close to him. And while she never talks about the endometriosis that ruined her chances to conceive, I see the way she looks at mothers with strollers: wistful, yearning, like she's missing out.

I think Jo's had to become an excellent actress over the years to hide her pain. I feel sorry for her. Not that I'd ever tell her that. Who knows, maybe she told me the truth that day after Rob's fourteenth and she doesn't have feelings for Cal, but if there's the slightest chance she's been pining for him and hidden it well, I need to warn her. Seeing them together now, I want to make sure she's not getting in too deep when it could be a simple case of Cal reaching out to a friend for a place to stay.

Thankfully, when I enter the bathroom, we're the only ones here. She's at the basin washing her hands and our eyes meet in the mirror.

"Having a good time, Abi?" She sounds friendly enough but there's a hint of recalcitrance in her tone, like she doesn't want to talk to me.

I nod. "Noah's great. You?"

"Cal's always fun to hang out with."

She lowers her gaze so I can't get a read on her. Her noncommittal answer doesn't reassure me. When they entered the bar, they looked a lot closer than just friends.

"Yeah, as we both know, Cal's the life of the party. Everywhere, apparently."

Damn, I hadn't meant to say that last bit. I desperately want to tell her about Lara's baby, but I don't want to get caught in the middle of this. It's not my news to tell. If Cal's remotely toying with Jo, he needs to tell her, and I'll make sure I ram that point home when I next see him alone.

"What's that supposed to mean?" Defensive, her back is rigid as she dries her hands and I need to backtrack, fast.

"He travels a lot, Jo. Do you think he's been faithful to me all these years?"

Her anger fades as she realizes the truth behind my question.

"But you two haven't been a couple for years. Or so you told me."

She's point-scoring, reminding me I lied to her when she asked me if Cal and I still sleep together when he comes home.

"I just don't want to see you hurt, Jo. Cal's unreliable and he'll break your heart if you let him."

She rolls her eyes and by the stubborn set of her mouth I'm not getting through to her at all. "Haven't we had this conversation before? Like four years ago?"

"And I thought you listened."

I see the glint of anger in her glare. "You're my best friend, Abi, and I love you, but when it comes to Cal, I'd appreciate it if you butt out."

Sincerity underlines her harshness and I sigh, wishing I could protect her from what's to come. If she gives Cal her heart, he'll break it, and I'll be the one left to pick up the pieces. Not that I begrudge her leaning on me, but she may resent me even more, thinking I'll remind her with "I told you so". I'd never do that but if she is left shattered when Cal lets her down, I can see it being potentially difficult for all of us.

Rob's the glue that holds us together and if Cal hurts Jo, she'll want to stay away from family functions and holidays, and my son will suffer. He openly adores Jo and if she indulges in a fling with Cal, it's going to get messy.

If I can prevent her heartache, I have to try and get through to her. "Jo, please listen to me—"

"No, Abi, you've said enough." She holds up her hand, the other resting on the door handle. "I don't know if you're jealous or resentful or just want to control my life, but this conversation is over. I'm going back out there to be with Cal because he makes me feel good."

She opens the door. "You of all people should understand I've waited long enough."

Dread makes me grip the basin to steady myself.

Does Jo's last comment refer to the way she reacted to him at Rob's party four years ago or does she mean she's waited eighteen years to be with Cal? That she's guarded her secret crush for almost two decades?

If so, I'm even more worried.

If Cal breaks her heart like I expect, who knows what she'll do?

# FORTY-FOUR

## JO

I stew over Abi's warning all the way home. Cal's drunk one beer too many and is babbling about some photography exhibition coming up in Arizona that he can't miss, but I'm only half-listening.

Once again, Abi hinted at Cal being a player and I don't like it. I think she's jealous and is trying to throw me off. It makes me wonder... are they still involved? Wouldn't be the first time she's denied it. But I watched her with Noah tonight and she's completely smitten. Unless it's an act and she wants to make Cal jealous? After all, he'd chosen that bar tonight. He'd insisted we go after dinner... did he know she'd be there? Had she told him so he'd witness her fawning over Noah in the hope they'll reunite?

The thought alone makes me sheer off the road a little and I scrape the curb.

"Hey," Cal says, jolted from his ramblings and I quickly correct the steering.

"Sorry. Guess I'm more tired than I thought."

"That's a shame, because I plan on keeping you up all night."

His tone is laced with innuendo and when I glance across at him, he winks. Usually, his overt flirting would send a thrill through me but I'm too wound up, worrying about his ongoing relationship with Abi.

"I need to ask you something."

My sharp tone doesn't register as he leers at me, the lopsided smile that usually sets my heart racing having minimal effect.

"Shoot."

"I bumped into Abi in the bathroom at the bar. She warned me off you. Which makes me wonder why. Are you two still involved?"

"Hell no." He laughs, a harsh sound that raises my hackles as I pull into my drive. "You need to forget about Abi."

"That's difficult, considering she's my best friend."

I get out of the car and slam the door, stalking toward my house, not caring if he's following or not. Though that's a lie. I do care, more than is good for me, and I'm relieved when I unlock the door and he follows me in, pressing up against me from behind.

"Come on, JJ, you're the one person who never gives me a hard time. We have fun together. Let's not ruin it by talking about my ex."

He presses a kiss to the side of my neck and I lean back, resting my head against his chest. I want to believe him so badly but I can't dismiss Abi's warning. She doesn't suspect a thing at this stage—about how I've been flirting with Cal the last few years, how I secretly enjoy Cal's attention, how I've already slept with him—so that means she reached out as a concerned friend. I'd be a fool to dismiss her lightly. Besides, I saw him with my own eyes in that motel room with Lara and I need to know what I'm dealing with before I give him my heart completely.

Cal wraps his arms around my waist, pulling me flush against him, and I feel the evidence of where tonight is heading. I want him too. I want the connection, the closeness, that comes with intimacy.

But for my peace of mind, I need to ask one last time.

I spin in the circle of his arms so I can see his face. "If there's anything you want to tell me, Cal, now's the time to come clean. I won't judge you, I won't blame you. I need to know if you're involved with anyone else. I just want to know the truth."

"The truth is, Tom's an idiot for not seeing what's right in front of his face all these years, but I'm not that stupid." His fingers strum the base of my spine, sending a wave of pleasure outward. "I know you've had a thing for him forever, JJ. So why me? Why now?"

I'm surprised by the serious turn our conversation has taken, impressed by this deeper side of Cal I rarely see. But I can't tell him the truth, that I've been using him to make Tom jealous but deep down it's him I've always wanted, so I settle for, "I could ask you the same question, Cal. Why me, now? We've known each other forever and I never thought..."

His fingers skim my butt and I have a hard time focusing on anything.

"You're beautiful, JJ. And you get me in a way nobody else does. You're sweet and uncomplicated and I feel good when I'm around you. I'd never mess with that." His hands splay on my butt and haul me closer, and I'm suitably distracted when he kisses me, coaxing my lips apart, his tongue tracing my bottom lip.

He hasn't given me a straight answer but like a foolish woman giving in to a long-subdued crush, I push my concerns aside and get swept away in the moment.

# FORTY-FIVE

## JO

THEN

Robbie leaves for college in three months.

I can't believe it.

He's an amazing kid—outgoing, clever, and charming, just like his dad—and as much as I want to see him thrive at college, I'll miss him terribly. These last few years of high school have been busy but he squeezes in time for me amid his hectic schedule and I treasure our movie nights, bowling, or mini golf outings, no matter how corny.

Abi will be a wreck when the time comes. She's already lamenting how fast the years have flown by and mentions empty nest syndrome every time we catch up. It's getting on my nerves. She'll be thirty-six when Robbie heads off to college, plenty of time to start a new life. Heck, she can even have more kids if she wants.

Though her relationship with Cal is officially over and has been for a while. He rarely makes it back to Fort Chester these days and while he stays in the family home when he does, Abi says they're platonic co-parents and nothing else.

It makes me feel less guilty for ramping up the flirtation between Cal and me.

We've exchanged texts over the last few years when he's been on the road. Mine are long because I usually dictate them and he seems to appreciate the contact because he's started reaching out on his own, making the first move with increasing frequency. We talk about anything and everything, from the fast-food joints he visits to my latest rambunctious clients, pampered pooches who receive better care than their elderly owners. Emojis pepper our chats and he makes me laugh so often the face with tears coming out of its eyes is permanently at the top of my frequently used.

But it's our exchanges over the last week that have given me hope. His last text, late last night, said he wants to chat face-to-face today.

Because he misses me. With an accompanying flame emoji, indicating I'm hot. Followed by a long diatribe about how he'd told Tom about our conversations and his friend had gone berserk, acting like a possessive boyfriend. Cal thinks it's hilarious. I've been floating all day, grinning like an idiot at the pooches I've been grooming. Luckily, dogs don't judge, and I sped through my regulars to head home and get ready. Quick shower. Subtle make-up. A peacock blue top I'd worn once that he'd complimented because it made my eyes pop.

It's silly to be this excited over a video call but I've waited a long time for Tom, and if Cal notices me as a woman and continues to tell him, I'm not going to blow my chances.

When the call comes through, my hands are shaking. Cal's face appears on the screen and for an insane moment I'm tempted to bring the computer toward me and kiss it, I'm that excited.

"Now there's a friendly face," he says, his smile wide. "JJ, you're a sight for sore eyes."

"How are you? Still in New Mexico?"

"I've moved on to Seattle and I'm great." He pauses. "Now."

"It's nice to chat like this." I wave my hand between us.

"Much better than texting." His gaze dips to my cleavage and I'm glad I wore the top. "Did you wear that for me?"

"Maybe." I'm not good at flirting but I remember why I'm doing this—to give Tom the kick in the butt he needs to take our relationship to the next level—and I try.

He grins. "I like this side of you, JJ. Wish I'd seen it sooner."

I refrain from answering that would've been awkward, considering he was living with my best friend. "I've always been here, Cal."

He nods, thoughtful. "Yeah, but sometimes we don't see what's right in front of us."

My breath hitches. Is he saying he has feelings for me? If so, it's a complication I hadn't counted on. And how do I feel about it? It took me ages to get over Cal and I'd done it by shifting my affection onto Tom. But what if that's a mistake? What if there's a chance for Cal and me now he's finished with Abi?

It's something I've never contemplated. In these last few years while we've been flirting remotely, I never took it to mean anything, justifying it as a way for me to gain Tom's attention. But maybe I'm delusional and this thing between Cal and me has been developing into something more?

If so, what does that mean for all of us?

Damn it, I'm in over my head and have no idea what to do.

"Can I ask you something?"

I nod.

"When Abi got pregnant and you two had that major falling-out, was that over me?"

A lot of time has passed and I'm sure he can't remember I fobbed him off on the day Robbie had been born when he first asked me why we'd fought.

"Because you said it wasn't when I asked you all those years ago, but with how things are developing between us now, I'm just wondering."

So he does remember. I could lie again but what's the point? I've been flirting as much as he has during our texts the last few months and he'll think I'm an idiot.

"Surely you knew every girl in our senior year had a crush on you?"

His bashful shrug is endearing. "So that included you?"

"Yeah."

"And you still like me?"

"A little."

He laughs at my offhand response. "JJ, I've always had my eye on you, but I've been loyal to Abi because you and me could get messy."

"I don't mind mess."

I eyeball him as a test. To see how far he wants to take this.

"Feisty. I like that." He grins and my stupid impressionable heart flip-flops. "You're too good for me, JJ, but it's going to be a hell of a lot of fun corrupting you."

There's a noise, like a creaky door opening, off-camera, and I glimpse a momentary flare of panic before he says, "I have to go, JJ. I'll call again soon."

He disconnects quickly and I know why. Looks like Cal has company and I'm surprised by the jealousy that makes me clench my fists. Then again, he's single, why shouldn't he?

All in all, our call tonight has solidified what I already know.

Cal's ready to take this to the next level. And if Tom doesn't make his move, maybe I should let this thing between Cal and me play out to its expected conclusion.

The two of us, together. A happy couple.

Which means I need to formulate a plan.

# FORTY-SIX

## ABIGAIL

The last few days have lulled me into a false sense of security. I know I should be relieved there haven't been any more pranks, but I feel like I'm on a weird hyper alert, expecting the worst when I shouldn't.

The filming on Mandy's show is winding down so she'll be leaving town soon. She's been fine with me since the night I fixed her costuming disaster and we caught up for a drink, and has mentioned meeting up for dinner when I'm next in San Francisco. I'm glad we've healed our rift from our toxic interactions in high school.

I haven't seen or heard from Lara. She's probably mad I told Cal about the baby. But he had to know, and I hope Cal's standing by her or figuring out how he'll support her child. It's weird, thinking Rob will have a half-sibling after all this time. My amazing son will take it in his stride but I fear it'll be one more nail in the paternity coffin for Cal. The older Rob gets, the more cynical he is of his father, and while I've never maligned Cal to him, Rob's an astute kid and can see what's right in front of him: that Cal isn't father material.

With Mandy leaving and Lara traversing the co-parenting rules with Cal, it's Jo I'm worried about. She's avoided my calls —I've tried twice from work—and has answered my texts with brief responses. She's citing a surge in new clients but I'm not buying it. She's avoiding me after I warned her off Cal at the bar. If she doesn't answer my latest voice message, I'll lob on her doorstep tomorrow. The last time we went this long without talking was when she froze me out during my pregnancy and I don't like it. We're more like sisters than friends and I miss her.

But for tonight, I shelve my worries about my best friend because Noah has a surprise for me.

"Where are you taking me?"

We parked near the river and have been walking for a few minutes, his hands loosely covering my eyes.

"Just a little further," he murmurs in my ear, and a shiver of excitement runs through me.

"You better not be throwing me in the river."

"Do I look like the kind of guy who'd do that?"

"No."

With every passing day, he looks like the kind of guy I've been waiting for my entire life. The kind of guy to make me feel safe and loved and adored. The kind of guy I should've had from the beginning if I hadn't screwed up, got drunk, and had sex with Cal. But then I wouldn't have Rob and I can't regret that one night no matter how much I wish it didn't happen.

"We're here." He stops and lowers his hands. "Surprise."

I gape at the fold-out table perched on a flat rock jutting over the river. The table is covered in an ivory tablecloth, with two place settings: crimson linen napkins, silver cutlery, and white china plates. The flames of five tealights flicker and the sound of the rushing river is better than any music.

"This is... beautiful." Surprisingly, I'm choked up. I'm too practical to be sentimental but seeing the trouble Noah has gone to is making me sniffle.

"I'm glad you like it." He snags my hand, lifts it to his mouth, and kisses it, before lowering it and tugging. "Come on, I've got champagne waiting."

"If I ever get married, this is how I'd like to be proposed to," I say, feeling like I've stepped into a romantic movie, instantly wishing I could take it back when he looks at me funny. Great, way to go with scaring off a guy I haven't been dating long. "Don't mind me, I'm addicted to romcoms."

Noah smiles. "You've never been married?"

He pops the cork on an expensive bottle of champagne, produces two flutes from a cooler, and fills them before handing me one.

"No. I guess it never entered my head with Cal because we fell into a relationship for the sake of Rob rather than any grand passion. And though it's not something I think about often, I occasionally wonder what it'd be like."

"In that case, will you marry me?"

He's grinning as he gets down on one knee and I laugh. "You're cute, but I want better than an offhand proposal like that."

I pull him to his feet and he swoops in for a kiss. "Do you think that's something you'd consider one day? You and me getting hitched?"

It's crazy. I barely know him but I know enough. I know he's kind and considerate and always puts me first. I know he's respectful and helpful. I know that when he holds me in his arms, I've never felt so safe. And when I imagine him leaving, whenever that may be, I feel bereft.

I try not to think about when Noah leaves, because I see a quiet house and lonely evenings in my future. With Rob gone, and Noah making me fall for him then leaving, all my empty-nester fears return, and I contemplate a scenario where Noah and I get married and live happily ever after.

"Wow. I've shocked you into silence. Guess I have my answer."

He pretends it doesn't bother him but I can see a glimmer of hurt in his eyes, like I've rejected him even if the proposal wasn't real.

"Hey, give a girl some time to think about it," I say, picking up my flute and raising it. "To a future filled with possibilities."

"To our future," he says, and when he clinks his glass against mine I can almost see it: Noah and me, together, forever.

Our evening is perfect. He serves me pea and mint dip with labne, an artichoke tart with salsa verde, curried chicken pie, and lemon tart for dessert. We stroll hand in hand along the river. We make out under the stars. And we can't wait to get home.

But as we sprint from his car to my back door, I see something on the porch, and as the newly installed sensor light clicks on, I let out a scream.

"Don't look," Noah says, instantly enveloping me in his arms and turning me away.

It's too late. I can't get the image of all that blood and gore out of my mind. "What is it?"

"Some kind of disemboweled animal." I'm trembling as he leads me to the front of the house. "Should we call the police?"

I contemplate it for a second, but what are they going to do apart from ask a bunch of questions I have no hope of answering? Besides, I'll have to tell them about all the other vandalism stuff, they'll ask if I have enemies or if there's anyone new in my life, and I don't want to give them the only names I can think of: Mandy—who I've pretty much disregarded as a suspect; Lara—who's pregnant, not crazy; Jo—my best friend, who has no reason to target me; and Noah.

Out of all the possibilities, he's the most likely suspect the police will focus on and I can't stand the thought of him being under suspicion. Is my judgment that off? Have I been so blinded by lust and a need for genuine affection that I've missed any red flags? I don't think so, but the police will drag him through unnecessary interrogations regardless. Besides, he's been with me tonight, so this has to be the work of a twisted mind.

"No, let's leave the police out of it. Probably some new kids in the neighborhood." Neither of us believe it and I rest my head against his chest. "Who's doing this?"

"I have no idea, but maybe it's time to install security cameras?"

"Yeah. You're right."

I want to know the crazy person who's targeting me but a small part of me doesn't, because I don't think these incidents are random.

And that means it's personal.

# FORTY-SEVEN

## JO

My friendly neighborhood psycho has been at it overnight as I open the back door the next morning to discover a spray-painted HANDS OFF HIM on one of the porch posts. The lettering is crude, like it's been done in a hurry, though when I touch it, the paint's dry.

Cal's still asleep and I don't want him seeing this and asking a bunch of questions I'd rather not answer so I get the solvent from the laundry and go to work. My knuckles are almost raw by the time I finish scrubbing but at least the words are unintelligible now.

I'm over this.

It's not the work of idle kids. These warnings are directed at me because of my involvement with Cal and I need to get to the bottom of it.

I'm not a complete idiot. While last night with Cal had been wonderful once we made it to the bedroom, I know he'd used sex as a distraction technique. Rather than answering my question about being involved with anyone, he'd kissed me, and I'd let him.

Maybe I don't want to know?

But I do so that's a cop out. He's evasive whenever I bring up Abi and if they've been involved all these years despite officially breaking up, who knows what's going on? I've already asked her and she's denied it, but I'm determined to try one last time. She'll be at work already and my first dog wash isn't until ten thirty, so plenty of time to pop in. With the added bonus if I ask her at work, she can't yell at me for being a persistent pain in the ass.

After leaving a scribbled note for Cal—waffles in the oven, freshly squeezed orange juice in the fridge, see him this afternoon—I head to the studio. It's a gloomy day with low-hanging clouds, matching my mood as I park. I should be enjoying my time with Cal, not dreading another confrontation with his ex. Abi's been a good friend once I got over the pregnancy betrayal and I know my badgering is going to annoy her.

I'm also going to tell her about Cal and me. Last night solidified what I already know: I want us to be a couple who shouts their love from the rooftops rather than hides it because we may offend. Abi will understand. She'll be happy for me, I hope.

As for her warnings about Cal breaking my heart, I anticipate that when she sees us together as an official couple, she won't worry about me so much. I know her concerns come from a good place; she doesn't want Cal hurting me. But I can't help but wonder if that stems from a general concern for my wellbeing or does she know something I don't, like he still wants her and is just using me to make her jealous?

After all, I've been doing the same for years, using Cal in the futile hope of making Tom want me. It seems so pointless and immature now, especially with how Cal makes me feel. If I'd stopped playing games earlier, would Cal and I have had more time together to nurture our obvious connection?

Cal using me to make Abi jealous is something I hadn't

considered until she warned me in the bathroom at the bar, throwing in that offhand comment about Cal being the life of the party everywhere. It's not the first time she's implied he's sleeping around, and I want to ask her about it. If she truly cares about me, she won't give vague platitudes, she'll have to spell it out so I know what I'm dealing with.

A small part of me hopes her comments are indicative of *her* jealousy, that she doesn't want to see me with Cal because she has residual feelings, rather than an uglier truth: that even if Cal and I do get together officially, he's the type of guy who'll sleep around regardless.

Abi's in her office, her head in her hands, staring at photos of clothes strewn across her desk. She looks dejected and nothing like my vivacious friend. Maybe work's getting her down but by her disconsolate expression, there's more going on.

When I knock on the door, she looks up and her eyebrows rise.

"What are you doing here?"

I smile, but she doesn't return it. "Can't I visit my best friend on a whim?"

"Of course." She gestures me in and I close the door behind me.

Abi's not herself. She's wearing a plain black jacket and skirt, with a hint of white camisole poking through. She's always in vibrant colors so to see her in neutrals is a surprise. And no matter how much concealer she's used, she can't hide the dark smudges under her eyes.

"Are you okay?" I sit opposite her desk. "You don't look so good."

"Didn't sleep well after someone left a nasty surprise on my doorstep." She screws up her nose. "It was horrific."

"Heck, not you, too."

Her eyes widen, accentuating the dark circles ringing them. "What happened at your place?"

"I got another spray-painted message this morning, more of the same drivel about keeping away from 'him'."

"Mine's worse. A disemboweled animal." She pales and I glimpse fear in her eyes. "Noah took care of it for me but the blood has stained my porch."

"That's awful." I reach across the desk and squeeze her hand. "This is getting crazy."

"I know. I'm going to install security cameras."

"Good idea. I might do that too."

I can't decipher the look she shoots me, but she's on edge. She sits back in her chair and folds her arms. "So how are you?"

"Good. Great, in fact." The last time we spoke at the bar, she warned me off Cal. Time to set the record straight. "Cal's staying at my place."

There's a flash of something I can't identify in her eyes before she shakes her head. "I'm guessing he's not in the guest bedroom."

"No." I lift my chin, defiant, and stare her down.

The pity I see in her eyes infuriates me but I won't let her spoil this for me. Not this time.

"I know how charming he can be, Jo, but I'm afraid he may be using you."

I try to damp down my anger but my hands are shaking and I rest them in my lap so she can't see how much her opinion rattles me. "So he can't be interested in me for anything more than sex, you mean?"

"That's not it..." She unfolds her arms, before re-crossing them again. "I know you, Jo. You have real feelings for him, probably always have, and if that's the case, you're amazing. You've stood by us all these years, you're a part of our family, and you haven't let those feelings affect how we interact. But don't you think it's rather timely, Cal coming onto you because I won't let him stay with me?"

"Get over yourself," I snap. "We've been flirting for years."

Damn, I hadn't meant to let that slip and she shakes her head. "All the more reason to be wary of him, considering the last time we slept together was only three months ago."

My anger morphs into fury. Is she deliberately taunting me? Implying that he only turned to me because she doesn't want him anymore? That I'm so pathetic I'll gladly accept her cast-offs?

"Look me in the eye and tell me there's nothing between you and Cal anymore."

"Apart from sharing a son, you mean?"

Her droll response riles me further. "We're together, Abi, and I wanted you to hear it from me. We've been friends for so long, you deserve that courtesy."

Her stoic mask crumples a little. Damn, is she really hurt over me being with Cal? Maybe they're not over and I'm a fool blinded to his faults, willing to look the other way because I've been lonely for so long?

"Jo, please, you have to listen to me." She's on the verge of tears and the sick feeling in my gut intensifies. There's more going on between Cal and Abi than they're telling me. If so, she's right: I'm headed for heartbreak. "I'm telling you this for your own good. Cal isn't the guy for you."

The nausea in my gut congeals into a hard ball of anger. She may be my friend with my best interests at heart, but she has no right to tell me Cal isn't the guy for me. If she gave me something concrete to be worried about rather than these vague warnings I might take heed, but I think she's just messing with me now.

I never thought Abi was the type of woman to be jealous of me. It's been the other way around for so long. But maybe her consistent warnings stem from a place of envy rather than caring and my resolve hardens.

Nobody tells me what to do, least of all a woman who's had everything her entire life, a woman who's popular and loved by everyone, a woman used to getting all the attention.

A woman who stole what was mine over eighteen years ago and is still hanging onto Cal when she shouldn't be, ridiculously determined I shouldn't have him.

Time to set the record straight.

"Abi, I'm not going to back down over this. Honestly, I didn't think I had feelings for him beyond a teen crush all those years ago, but lately something's changed between us and it could be real—"

"There's something you need to know," she says so softly I have to lean forward to hear. "You're right. We've been friends a long time and I owe you the truth."

A chill sweeps over me as a dull roar fills my ears. I've been in this position before, when she told me she was pregnant, and by her distraught expression, this news is just as bad.

When she doesn't speak, I yell, "Tell me."

She jumps and the pity in her eyes morphs into sympathy. "Lara's pregnant, and Cal's the father."

# FORTY-EIGHT

## JO

THEN

"Rex, I need your help."

The only friend who's never let me down stares at me, his beer raised halfway to his mouth. "Are you okay?"

"Yeah. But it's complicated."

"It always is with you." He clinks his bottle against mine. "What is it this time? One of your pooches need de-worming and you thought of me? Want me to pick fleas off a litter with tweezers? A kennel's worth of poop needs to be cleaned up?"

I laugh as only Rex can make me. I'm lighter around him. He's the only person in my life who doesn't make me feel inadequate; with him, I'm enough.

"Have I ever asked you to do anything so torturous?"

He pretends to ponder. "Yeah, when you made me read that nine-hundred-page fantasy novel packed with steamy romance."

"As I recall, we spent a week discussing the main character's arc and how much she grew by the end of the book."

He rolls his eyes. "You know I prefer the vampires, were-wolves, and zombies to go to war by the end of it, not fall in love." He mimes barfing. "Gross."

We smile at each other, and I wonder if he remembers how many afternoons we spent down by the wharves, debating the merits of various books. He'd tease me about my literary choices but he'd read them anyway, just so we could talk about them. No genre was off limits, and I can't believe how tolerant he was when I deliberately chose romance-heavy paranormal or sci-fi when I knew he preferred his stories all-action, less-smooches.

"What are you reading at the moment?"

He takes a sip of beer before answering. "Nonfiction, mostly American history."

"Why?"

"I have a few ideas jobwise, and research pays."

It does. Which is why I've spent an inordinate time over the last week brainstorming ways to get what I want.

"So why do you need my help?"

"It's Abi."

His lips thin and a frown appears between his brow as it always does at the mention of her name. His intense dislike of her borders on hatred and that's what I'm counting on.

I need Rex for my plan to work.

And a little subtle feeding of his resentment will guarantee he comes through for me.

"What's she done this time?"

I feign nonchalance and shrug. "Just the usual. Being self-ish. Taking me for granted. Doing a hundred and one things to annoy me."

Anger smolders in his eyes. "Why do you put up with her crap?"

"Well, that's the thing. I'm not going to anymore."

I can't mention why I'm doing this. Rex's opinion of Cal is

only a rung higher than his low opinion of Abi, so I need to be careful.

"That's where you come in."

One of his eyebrow's arches. "What do you want me to do?"

I tell him in intricate detail.

He listens carefully, asking questions, trying to poke holes in my plan. But it's foolproof. At least, I hope it is, otherwise everything I'm working toward will tumble down around my ears and my life will be in tatters.

I don't tell him everything, of course.

He wouldn't approve of how far I'm willing to go in order to get what I want.

But this will be worth it.

Finally, *finally*, after all this time, I'll get what I deserve.

And so will Abi.

# FORTY-NINE

## ABIGAIL

My hands are shaking when I pick up my cell to call Lara.

I have to warn her.

After I told Jo about Lara's pregnancy, Jo lost it. Completely. And I'm staring at the aftermath, with my entire desk swept clean and strewn all over the floor, including my shattered PC screen.

I've never seen Jo like that. It terrified me.

I tried to calm her down but she wouldn't listen. She didn't utter a word either. But with her face flushed crimson and her eyes demonic, she systematically demolished my desk. Snapping pens in two, tearing documents in half, flinging the phone against the wall, before the grand finale of picking up my PC screen and smashing it to the ground, before stomping on it.

She ran out of here as my co-workers filtered in, looking equally shocked as me, but I've herded them out of here so I can speak with Lara in private.

If Jo's capable of this destruction, I'm genuinely fearful for Lara's safety.

Thankfully, Lara picks up on the fourth ring. "Hey, Abi, how—"

"Lara, where are you?"

"On the road, actually."

"In Fort Chester?"

"No. I'm leaving LA to head down to San Diego for a meeting with a client. Why? Are you okay? You sound a little weird."

I don't want to worry her unnecessarily, especially if she's nowhere near Fort Chester, thank goodness. But I need to tell her regardless in case Jo's really nuts and tracks her down. Or Lara comes back into town and is caught unawares.

I've known Jo a long time and don't think my friend's capable of hurting anyone, but I never would've thought she'd be capable of the kind of destruction I'd just witnessed either so better to be safe than sorry.

"I'm okay, but you need to listen. Jo's got a thing for Cal—"

"Tell me something I don't know. Seriously, the way she looked at you after you got pregnant to him, I'm surprised you didn't spontaneously combust on the spot. She hated you. Which is a credit to you both, how far you've come in resurrecting your friendship."

The few times we've caught up, Lara's always like this. Garrulous and verbose. But I need to make her listen.

"Lara, they've slept together, and I think Jo's taking it to mean more than it is. Anyway, I didn't want her getting in too deep with Cal as he'll probably end up hurting her, so I told her about your pregnancy."

There's silence for a moment, before Lara responds, "That's okay, it's not a secret. Cal and I talked it through and he's going to support me financially if I need it, which I don't, but he's not keen to be a hands-on father, says he's been there, done that, and I'm okay with that too." She chuckles. "Personally, I think

Cal's a flake. Pretty to look at and good for a bit of fun, but you deserve a medal for sustaining a relationship with him for as long as you did."

I'm glad Lara's smart enough to get an accurate read on Cal, but I'm not appeased by her blasé attitude. She doesn't understand how unstable Jo is and from what I've just witnessed, I don't want her anywhere near Lara and her baby.

"Lara, when I told Jo about your pregnancy, she trashed my office."

"What do you mean?" Her tone is more cautious now, less offhand.

"She went berserk. Swept my desk clean, including my computer, throwing things everywhere. It's like a bomb site in here and I've never seen her like that. It's why I called because I think you need to be careful."

There's a heavy sigh on the other end of the phone. "You think she'll come after me?"

"Honestly? No. I've known Jo for twenty-three years and I don't think she's capable of harming a fly. But she's narrow-minded when it comes to Cal and if she thinks you and your baby stand in the way of her happiness... I just want you to be careful, okay? Stay clear of Fort Chester for a while, until Cal has a chance to talk to her and it all blows over."

"Okay. Thanks for letting me know, Abi."

She sounds shaken and I'm relieved I finally got through to her.

But my relief is short-lived, because if Lara's not around to bear the brunt of Jo's fury, is Cal next in line?

# FIFTY

## JO

I have no idea how I make it from Abi's office to my car to home. I'm blinded by rage, red spots and squiggles shimmering in front of my eyes the entire way.

Lara can't be pregnant with Cal's baby.

It's history repeating itself.

I'm so close to being happy with him, only to have it snatched away by another selfish cow who's entrapped him.

But I'd asked Cal if he had anything to tell me, if he was involved with anyone else... and he hadn't denied it. He'd distracted me and I'd been a fool to fall for it.

Now, I need the truth once and for all.

I push the back door open so hard it slams against the counter and Cal, who's eating a sandwich at the table, jumps.

"Hey, babe, what's up?"

I struggle to get my temper under control, dragging in deep breaths, blowing them out, until my vision clears.

He must see how angry I am because his gaze darts nervously to my face and then, ridiculously, to the knife block a few feet away. What does he think, that I'll stab him? I'd never hurt him. As for *her*...

"JJ?" He stands and starts approaching cautiously, but I hold my hand to ward him off.

Having him close, being able to smell his signature woodsy goodness, will only confuse me.

"Is Lara pregnant with your child?"

He laughs, not the reaction I expect, and he looks me in the eye. "Of course not. Where did you hear that?"

"Abi."

"And you believed her?" He shakes his head. "Abi's probably jealous of what we have, JJ, and is trying to get you to alienate me."

I'm not easily convinced, looking for the slightest sign he's lying, but he's not even breaking a sweat. "Why would she do that?"

He shrugs. "Rob's left. I'm with you. Tom's not around to trail after her. She's dealing with her first boyfriend ever. Do the math."

"Technically, you're her first boyfriend."

"I was never her boyfriend. I was the dumb idiot who used an old condom and got stuck with the responsibility of standing by her."

I hate to admit it, but I like his response. It proves he never had any feelings for her and only stuck around out of obligation. Which means if I'd made my move all those years ago, the morning after the party like I intended, we could've been together.

Abi stole that from me.

Because she lied then, just like she's lying now.

I'm done with her BS.

Time to do what I set out to do when I instigated my plan.

I spin on my heel and Cal calls out, "Where are you going?"

"To see a friend. Back soon."

I've been ranting against Abi for the last ten minutes and I know what Rex is going to say before he opens his mouth.

"Jo, you've got to calm down." He takes hold of my upper arms so I stop pacing. "You're talking like a crazy person."

I stiffen and he knows he's said the wrong thing. "I am not crazy, I'm a woman pushed to her limits by another selfish woman who can't deal with the fact I may be happy for once in my life."

He shakes his head and I wrench free of his grip. "Abi's gone too far this time, lying about the paternity of Lara's baby."

"Just listen to me for a minute. Have you stopped to think that Cal's lying and Abi's telling the truth?"

I bark out a laugh. "Since when do you take her side?"

I've never seen him so somber, and I don't like the way he's looking at me. Like I'm stupid. Or gullible. It hurts because Rex always believes me; believes *in* me. It's why I know I can trust him. He wouldn't be here otherwise, helping me bring my plan to fruition. I hope he's in it with me to the end because I'm done waiting.

His gaze is concerned. "I'm just saying, I think you should consider all possibilities rather than jumping to conclusions. Besides, what does Abi gain by lying to you?"

"She's always lied to me, it's what she does." I fling my arms in the air. "Who knows why? But I'm done trying to figure it out. I've had enough."

He must see a hint of the darkness invading my mind on my face, because he says, "What are you going to do?"

"What I've wanted to do from the start."

Either he misunderstands or he doesn't want to know. "But your plan's in place? It's working too."

I hesitate, wondering if I can trust him with the truth. The whole truth.

I wanted to tell him everything from the start, but he may not have helped me, and I've needed him to get Abi off-kilter. But the endgame is in sight now and if he's caught in the cross-fire, I'll never forgive myself: Rex deserves better than that.

"I may have withheld some vital information when I told you about my plan at the start."

A deep frown grooves his brow. "What do you mean?"

I take a deep breath. Here goes nothing.

"I don't just want to ruin Abi's life, I want to take it."

His eyes widen and I glimpse genuine fear. "What are you saying?"

"I'm saying I'm reclaiming the life that should've been mine."

His horrified expression means he understands. "Jo, you can't do this."

He reaches for me but I back away.

"Yeah? Watch me."

# FIFTY-ONE

## ABIGAIL

THEN

A week after Rob leaves for college, I'm missing him terribly.

Sure, meeting Noah has been a nice distraction and Jo's been supportive, but I know I'll feel better if I see Rob, check out his dorm, make sure he's okay. Otherwise, the insomnia that plagued me when he was little will kick in and I can't afford that, not when work is manic at the moment.

I haven't told anyone I'm driving to LA, not even Jo. Though I have a ready excuse if she asks or hears about it from Rob: I'm sourcing some new costumes for work. Easy. It feels weird to come up with a lie, but I know what she'll say if I tell her: give your son some space or why didn't you take me, so it's easier to avoid the questions all round.

Besides, no one will notice I'm gone. It's a three-hour trip each way and I'm not planning on hanging around, just long enough to give my son a big hug and grab a quick bite to eat.

I leave early, before dawn, and I'm at UCLA by nine. I feel ancient as I stroll around the campus, surrounded by bright, perky students milling the paved walkways. Some are deep in discussion, some are joking and sharing a laugh, some are hunched over laptops debating, all appear happy and like they belong. I can't help but feel a momentary pang of regret that I never got to do this.

How different would my life have been if I'd gone to college as planned. Would I have met a guy, a creative type, who understands my love of fashion? Would I have honed my love of sketching new designs and actually done something with my talent beyond dressing actors on a film set? Would I be more fulfilled now?

Probably yes to all those questions but no use contemplating the past and what I can't change. Besides, would I want to? Having Rob at eighteen was terrifying and a steep learning curve, but it was also amazing and wonderful and so right.

As if thoughts of my son conjure him up, I see him walking toward me. He's trying to act cool and temper his pace, but the closer we get he breaks into a half-jog and I'm fighting tears when he reaches me.

"Hey, Mom." He envelops me in a bear hug and I blink rapidly to stave off those tears. I can't blubber in the middle of UCLA and embarrass him.

"Surely you haven't grown in a week?" I say as we ease apart, desperate to keep things light so I don't beg him to come home with me because I miss him so much.

He rolls his eyes. "Mom, I stopped growing at seventeen."

"That's not what my grocery bills from the last year imply." He smiles and I add, "How have you been?"

Though I don't have to ask. My baby is all grown up. I see it in the way he holds himself: shoulders back, posture straight, like he's found his place in the world. He's always had a quiet inner confidence and been surrounded by people who care about him, so it didn't surprise me when he chose to major in psychology. My son has a genuine empathy for others and will thrive in the right conditions. Looks like being a student at UCLA suits him and I'm happy. Missing him terribly, but happy he's making his mark.

"I'm great, Mom. Come see for yourself."

We make small talk as we head to his dorm, about his classes mostly, and new friends he's made. He's leading a full social life, going out every night, and I'm glad. He'd never been a loner as a kid, but I always worried being an only child might make him more introverted. Then again, with Cal's DNA, he was never in danger of that—Cal could charm anybody.

When we reach Rob's dorm, his roommate, a pre-med kid from Ohio, is at breakfast, so he shows me their room—two single beds, two desks, tidier than I anticipated—then he takes me to the nearest café for a coffee. The place is packed and noisy, but I like it, the feeling of being immersed in a place of learning, the infectious excitement of the students. It's the perfect place for me to tell him about Noah, the other reason I wanted to see him today.

I haven't dated at all and I want to tell my son face to face I'm seeing someone, so he won't think the minute he left home I was on the prowl. Or worse, think he's been holding me back all these years. He asked me once if he was the reason I didn't date, and although I reassured him that wasn't the case, I could tell he didn't believe me. It's hard to explain to a kid I had no interest in dating because my life was enough. Raising him was fulfilling in a way I never anticipated and forging my own path career-wise has been a focus. And I had Cal for the physical stuff, sex without complications, so dating seemed unnecessary.

Noah changed all that and I can't believe that in seven days I've let down my guard so quickly. He's a great guy and I hope Rob thinks so too.

"What's on your mind, Mom?"

I pull a face. "Is it that obvious?"

"I know you miss me, but to drive here after I've been gone a week? Yeah, you want to tell me something."

"You know me too well." I ruffle his hair like I used to when he was little and he doesn't swat my hand away, which is sweet. "I know it's early days and probably way too soon to be telling you this, but I'd feel weird if I didn't, and I know in my gut this is special—"

"Mom, you're rambling."

I take a deep breath and blow it out. "I've met someone."

He wolf whistles. "Go, Mom. Is he good enough for you?"

"I think so. He's in town for research while working on a book."

Rob's eyebrows rise a little. "Not a poor and starving artist type, I hope?"

His protectiveness is endearing. "I hope not. But I'm getting to know him, and I'm having fun."

"That's great, Mom. I'm happy for you." He slips his cell out of his pocket. "Now, what's his name so I can cyberstalk him online?"

I laugh. "Noah Powell. But he's not on social media, I checked."

My adorable son frowns. "That's a red flag in itself. Got a pic? I can do a reverse photo search."

My smile is bashful. "Done that too, but nothing came up." With a few taps on my cell screen, I bring up the selfie I snapped the night of our first date. "I'm kind of glad, because he's so good-looking there'd be a bunch of crazy women trolling him if he was online."

I flip my cell so Rob can see and the flicker of recognition in his eyes surprises me.

"I know this guy, I've seen him somewhere before..."

As Rob takes the cell from my hand and squints at it closer, my heart sinks. If he has seen him, it'll probably be online, and I'm hoping not on some forum where women reveal horror stories about being scammed by gorgeous men. Cautionary tales about women being catfished are prominent in the media. Heck, even the studio's shooting a drama about it next month. I always pitied those women and judged them a little. Surely there'd been signs along the way they'd ignored, signs that the men they gave their hearts to weren't authentic?

It will be beyond embarrassing if Noah's a con-artist and I've fallen prey to him. Not that he's scammed me yet. Emotionally, that's another story, as he's the first guy I've trusted since Cal and I'll be devastated if he's not who he says he is.

Rob's face is scrunched up as he thinks and I'm inadvertently holding my breath when he snaps his fingers. "I know where I've seen him."

"Where?"

"On Jo's computer."

I freeze as ice trickles through my veins. "What?"

"Yeah, about six years ago. I was hanging out at her place while you were at a work function and she popped out to grab us dinner. She said I could play games on her PC, but I poked around a little too." His expression is guarded as he hands me back my phone. "She had a bunch of pics with this guy, though his name wasn't Noah."

His face screws up as he thinks, just like it always has since he was a kid trying to solve a problem. "I can't remember the labels on those photos, but I know damn sure the guy's name wasn't Noah."

"That's weird."

I force a laugh, because I don't want my son to worry about how seriously freaked out I am. I think back to the night I met Noah at the bar, how I introduced him to Jo, how they sat together at my dinner table when I wanted her to get to know my new man, how they've seen each other since.

No recognition between them.

Which means they're faking it.

Why?

If Jo wanted to set me up with a friend of hers, she could've said so. I wouldn't have been offended. But to lie... and what's Noah's endgame? Why is he pretending not to know my best friend?

The sadness I've been duped is quickly replaced by anger. Is Noah—or whoever he is—behind everything? The vandalism at home, the incidents at work?

And if so, why?

Rob is looking at me with obvious concern and he reaches out to squeeze my hand. "You need to speak to Jo and find out what the hell's going on, Mom, because this isn't cool."

Injecting false perkiness into my voice, I say, "You're right, sweetie. I'll ask her as soon as I get back."

But I won't.

I have a plan.

There are other ways to discover what's going on with Noah and my best friend.

# FIFTY-TWO

## ABIGAIL

When I get home from work, Noah's waiting for me. He's sitting on my front porch and leaps up from the rocking chair in the corner when he sees me pull up, and I've barely killed the engine before he's at the driver's door, opening it.

"Everything okay?"

"Not really," he says, and his expression chills me to the bone.

Fear.

"Can we talk?"

I nod and accept the hand he holds out to me. It's clammy and I swear it's trembling a little. "You're scaring me."

"Let's talk in the backyard," he says, glancing over his shoulder like he thinks we're being followed. After Jo's ballistic reaction at work, Noah's weirdness is rounding out my day nicely.

He waits until we're seated side by side on the loveseat in the garden to speak. "I have to tell you something. I'm not proud of this and it's going to hurt you, which I wouldn't have cared about at the start but now, I genuinely like you and..." He drops his head into his hands and mutters a curse.

I let him stew because I know what he's going to say.

He's going to confess.

"You're responsible for all the vandalism around here, aren't you?"

His head snaps up. "No. Why would you think that?"

"Because it started after I met you. And I know you're connected with Jo and hiding it from me."

His mouth drops open. "How—"

"I've known since the first week we started dating. My son recognized you from a photo."

He stares at me with wide-eyed confusion before pressing his fingers to his temples. Yeah, like that will resolve this convoluted scenario. Though I've wanted to know what's going on and now, I may finally get some answers.

"Why didn't you say anything?"

I shrug. "Because I wanted to see what game you and Jo are playing."

"This is a mess." He shakes his head, guilt all over his face. "That's what I wanted to tell you just now. You're right, Jo and I are friends. Best friends. She approached me about three months ago to help her undermine you."

"Undermine me?" Anger makes my voice squeak a tad and I swallow. "Why would she do that?"

As I ask the question, I know.

Cal.

She's never forgiven me for that one night I slept with him.

She's bided her time.

And now with Rob grown up and off at college, she wants to make a move.

"It's Cal, isn't it? She's had a thing for him forever."

Noah looks like I've said a nasty word. Interesting, so he's not a fan of Cal's. "I didn't know her motivation at the start but I suspect it has more to do with her fear of losing you rather than your ex. She thinks you'll move on now that your son has left home and you won't need her anymore."

Stunned, I shake my head, trying to make sense of this. "But that's crazy. We've been best friends forever. And why the hell would you say yes to whatever plan she had in mind?"

He grimaces and reaches for my hand but I swat him away. "Because I hated you for taking Jo away from me. I had plans too... I've been poor my entire life. Below the poverty line. Jo was my neighbor and even when we were kids she saw past my crappy clothes and skinny frame because I hadn't eaten in days. She became everything to me and when we finished school, I wanted to make a move on her because I liked her and because I wanted an easier life her money could provide. We were going to move in together as roommates at first, but I could've convinced her to become more."

Realization dawns. "And I took that away from you when she moved to Fort Chester."

"Yeah." Shame-faced, he swipes a hand over his eyes. "She's vented about you to me for years, and I provided a sympathetic shoulder, fueling her frustration in the hope she'd come back. But I guess she took my support as hatred for you and that I'd fall in line with whatever she wanted." He shakes his head. "She orchestrated our first meeting at the bar. The thing is, I expected to despise you, but when I met you I realized how I've misjudged you all these years and I've been an idiot, letting Jo disparage you so I'd fall in line with her plans."

He reaches out to me and I shrink away, the sorrow in his eyes doing little to subdue my simmering indignation. "It sounds so idiotic when I say it out loud, but poverty has made me do some stupid things over the years and I'm ashamed I let it get this far with you. I'm truly sorry."

"Your apology is moot considering I knew you were up to something and how far I let you go to prove I returned your interest." Nausea churns in my gut as I recall the romantic dates we've shared, the cozy mornings in bed, the incredible sex... "All this time you've been faking it? Trying to get close to me, for what?"

"Money. The plan was to win you over, then scam you. Get you to give me money for some cause you couldn't resist, then ghost you. You'd be so ashamed of being duped you'd need her even more. You'd depend on her and she could sweep in and be your hero." Regret twists his mouth. "But the closer we grew, I knew I couldn't do it. I like you, Abi—"

"Save it for someone who cares." I hold up my hand, relieved it doesn't shake. I refuse to give him the satisfaction of seeing how much he's hurt me. I have genuine feelings for Noah despite knowing all along he's had a link to Jo.

I thought I'd been so clever at the start, stringing him along —Jo too—in an attempt to discover their endgame. I'd played up to him, deliberately reeling him in, in the hope he'd reveal his intentions. But stupidly, somewhere along the line, I'd developed real feelings for him. I don't believe anyone can fake it all the time and that night down by the river when he'd pretend proposed...

"When you asked me to marry you, was that part of your plan? Taking it all the way and scamming me for everything I have?" My voice is quaking with anger and I have my answer before he opens his lying mouth.

"It never would've got that far, but yeah, I was testing the waters that night, seeing how committed you were to me. Moving into your house from the garage would've been the next step, maybe getting engaged..." He trails off, shame-faced, and he can't look me in the eye. "I'm not proud of this, Abi. It's a despicable thing to do. But I never counted on developing feel-ings for you."

"I don't want to hear any more of your lies." I glare at him to stop his sentimental drivel when I know he's played me all along. "What's changed? Why are you telling me all this now before your big payday?"

"Because Jo's irrational. I don't think our catfish scheme is enough for her anymore."

I remember her behavior in my office and suppress a shud-der. "What do you mean?"

He eyeballs me and I glimpse genuine fear.

"She wants to take your life."

# FIFTY-THREE

## JO

Being a dog groomer, I get asked all sorts of questions from pet owners. I'm no vet but I picked up a lot of knowledge as a vet's assistant and made it a point early in my career when I branched out on my own to be as knowledgeable as possible to ensure I got return business from clients. And by far the most commonly asked question is "What should I avoid in order not to accidentally kill my dog?"

Everyone knows the common dangers to stay clear of, like rat poison, slug bait, chocolate, and caffeine, but I've warned clients about mosquito repellent, yeast dough, nicotine patches, alcohol, and weed. Even everyday things like macadamia nuts, grapes, raisins, onions, and xylitol, found in sugar-free gum, can be toxic.

As for plants, the list is endless: azaleas, hydrangeas, clematis, cherry tree, daphne, devil's ivy, hemlock, holly... I could go on for days because I've carefully researched each and every plant so I can recognize them in a client's garden and advise them to keep their dogs away.

Learning the toxicity of plants fascinated me and I delved deep. It's how I know oleander, which grows prolifically in Southern California and is extremely toxic. Ingesting a small amount can be fatal. Such a pretty bloom in white, pink, red or yellow, with a lovely fragrance, that contains several toxic elements including saponins, digitoxigenin, nerioside, and cardiac glycosides, to name a few.

It's weird to think something so sweet can cause catastrophic results.

That's what I'm counting on.

I didn't want it to come to this but I can see Rex has fallen for Abi, just like everyone else in her perfect freaking life. I thought he had better taste than that. I thought he hated her as much as I do. I thought he was loyal to me.

Yet again, I'm wrong.

Abi is a magician who twists everyone she meets around her little finger, and now I know that my plan to control the narrative by introducing Rex to her won't work. He won't catfish her. She won't lose everything and be despised. She won't look like a stupid fool. She won't turn to me because she can't stand the humiliation. She won't depend on me like I want her to.

If her greatest fear had been becoming an empty nester, mine had been losing my best friend. I may have been envious of her perfect life all these years but I've been a part of it, and with Rob gone, it's only a matter of time until she meets someone new and I'm ostracized completely.

So I wanted to ensure that didn't happen. Frighten her so she turned to me. Make sure she didn't discard me like so many others in my life. Who knows, maybe even ask me to move in so I can really become indispensable?

At first, I'd wanted to disarm her. To see how she'd react to living alone and having her privacy invaded. With a little luck, decapitating her gnomes, pulling up her rose bush, messing with her precious veggie garden, egging her house, and placing dog poop on her lawn would've had the desired effect. Though she loves her flash new job and feels secure there, so I started sabotaging her at work too. Mandy's appearance at the studio had been timely, a ready stooge to take the fall. It had been too easy. I made sure to be extra-friendly with the security guards at the studio whenever I visited Abi over the last few months since she started working there—amazing what a few freshly baked brownies can do—so they never questioned me when I regularly dropped by to visit my best friend. I moved around the studio with ease, messing with Abi's costume orders, ripping Mandy's outfits—that prank had been particularly satisfying—causing general havoc.

But I hadn't counted on Abi inviting Rex to move in. That had thrown me. So I'd upped the ante and gone ahead with the scorpion—on a morning Rex had met me for a catch up so he wouldn't be in danger of opening that mailbox—and the disemboweled fox, a gift courtesy of a fierce Rottweiler, who'd dumped it on his owner's doorstep and that owner had been only too happy for me to take care of it.

With each incident, I'd seen how freaked out Abi had been; she'd been ripe for Rex to catfish her. My plan had merit. But then she had to go and lie to me about Lara carrying Cal's baby... it's pushed me over the edge.

I'm tired of waiting. Abi will never depend on me. Having her broke and mortified isn't enough anymore. She's too resilient and what's worse, she seems determined to undermine my new relationship with Cal and I won't stand for it.

I'm done with being second best.

It's why I've had to shake things up. Add a plot twist so I get the happily ever after I deserve in this story.

Removing Abi will ensure I get what I want.

Cal.

And to be a mother.

Being transformed from godmother to mother will make Cal see me in an entire new light and I'll finally have the perfect family I've always dreamed of. Mine were a huge disappointment and not being able to have kids means I've always wanted what my best friend has: the perfect son.

That's the kicker in all this and what makes me hate Abi so much; she fell pregnant so easily as a teen and I can't have a baby because of my useless uterus.

I resent her so much...

It didn't have to be like this. I've hidden my antipathy well over the years. Keeping her close. Being the perfect friend. And while she seemed to care for me too, all has been well. But having her undermine my relationship with Cal, having her lie, has tipped me over the edge. She doesn't need me the same way I need her. She's using me. And for the one person in this world I thought I could depend on to treat me as second best... I can't stand it. I won't.

My plan is foolproof. She's always trying new herbal concoctions in teas and salads. I've seen co-workers laugh at her lunches when she says she plucked a few things from her garden and poured dressing over it. So even when the toxicology results come back from a screen following her unexpected death, it can be explained away by her accidentally ingesting oleander in her garden foraging exploits.

I have to make sure of it, because I can't have Rex or Cal copping any heat from the police. Rex has always stood by my side and doesn't deserve it, and Cal can finally be mine.

It's a win-win.

Cal's allergic to cilantro and I know Rex won't touch anything with the herb in it, so I sprinkle it liberally over the salad, adding more to what she's already used, ensuring Abi's the only one who eats it.

With the amount of oleander in the leafy mix, the results will be swift.

And fatal.

# FIFTY-FOUR

## ABIGAIL

I can't look at Noah as he heads to the studio over the garage to pack.

I don't know who's the bigger fool: him, for agreeing to Jo's scheme to catfish me in the first place, or me for letting this play out when I knew they were up to something all along.

Though I'm not stupid. Deep down, I can admit why I let this unfold like a bad drama on a streaming service.

Because I had to see if my best friend truly loves me or resents me.

Since I discovered Noah's identity, I kept hoping Jo would come clean. That she'd admit she'd gone too far. Instead, her other best friend, Noah, is so worried about her mental state he's warned me to be on guard.

Not that I'm worried Jo will hurt me. What's she going to do, sic a dog on me? That'll make her look bad in Cal's eyes and she won't want that. Because ultimately, this is what her ridiculous plan is all about, to diminish me in his eyes so she can have him all for herself.

I wish she listened to me. My warnings about getting

involved with Cal came from a genuine caring for my friend, not some warped jealousy. And with Lara pregnant, surely Jo can see I'm not lying, that I only want what's best for her?

It's all I've ever wanted for her. I know how hard it's been for her to be around us, seeing Cal, Rob, and me a happy family when she never had one. As teens, she'd berated Dolly, Talia, and her father at length for being self-absorbed and uncaring, and I'd sympathized. It's why she spent so much time at my house and why we hung out together after school and weekends, because I felt sorry for her.

I never expected her to move to Fort Chester when I did but I'd been glad, because it showed she'd forgiven me for sleeping with Cal and she wanted us to resume our friendship. And she's been my biggest supporter since. So it's unfathomable to contemplate if Noah's lying about not being responsible for the vandalism—and that disemboweled animal I can't get out of my head—it means Jo is behind it all, and that points to one sick mind.

I can't keep rehashing everything in my head, trying to figure it out.

There's one way to resolve this: confront Jo.

But I'm not silly enough to do it on my own. I'll make sure Cal's with me, because I know she won't do anything rash while he's around.

It's astounding to think she's gone to these lengths for him. He's not worth it. Surely she knows that after all the years I've lamented entering into a relationship with him for the sake of Rob? I've confided in her about so much: Cal's lack of insight into what makes a relationship work, his selfishness in letting Rob down repeatedly, his uselessness around the house. She always sided with me, comforted me, but now I'm wondering if it was all an act. Had she been secretly counting down the days until Cal could be hers?

The thing is, I wouldn't have cared. If she'd admitted her residual feelings for him, I would've warned her off him more than I already have—because of who Cal is rather than jealousy —and wished her well.

But she's gone about this all wrong and I can't see any other outcome than a major bust-up ending our friendship. It saddens me, because it means I'll lose Rob and my best friend within the space of a few months. And Noah, who I genuinely care for.

I'll be all alone.

I reach the back door and slide my keys from my pocket, but I hear a crash from inside and turn the knob to find the door unlocked. As I enter the kitchen, I see Cal staggering around, arms outstretched, like he's trying to grab onto anything.

"Cal?"

He turns and I see a weird rash all over his face and he's blinking rapidly.

"Abi? I can't see. Everything's blurry and I'm really dizzy." He clutches his stomach. "I don't feel so good."

I've never seen him so sick and try to quell my rising panic as I guide him to a kitchen chair. "How long have you been feeling like this?"

He's pale as his head lowers to the table, like he can't hold it upright anymore, and he groans. "Fine when I got here an hour ago. Let myself in. Watched some TV. Got hungry. So desperate I ate some of your salad."

My gaze focuses on the half-eaten salad in the middle of the table. It's one I pre-prepared last night because I planned on having it as a side dish with grilled salmon tonight.

"But you hate salad," I say, picking it up and sniffing it. Smells fine and I doubt salmonella would have such drastic effects so fast.

"Already told you. I was starving..." He trails off and to my horror, he slumps forward so hard his head clunks the table. He's lost consciousness.

"Cal!" I yell, shaking him.

It has zero effect and I grab my cell to call 911. The operator answers quickly and I describe his symptoms while continuing to shake him gently, like he's asleep and will wake up with a little encouragement.

The operator tells me the ambulance is dispatched and to check his pulse.

But when I press my fingertips against his neck, I feel nothing.

Same at his wrist.

That's when I scream.

# FIFTY-FIVE

## JO

After Rex's call that something's wrong at Abi's place, I break the land speed record to get to her house. That's what concerned friends do. I'll be helpful and sympathetic and make myself indispensable. No one will miss her more than me.

When I pull up, there's an ambulance in the drive and an M.E.'s van behind. A medical examiner isn't called unless there's a death and I struggle to hide my glee.

Yes, I'm a bad person. I know it. But I've waited a long time for this.

To get what's mine.

I forage in my glove compartment for the pungent shampoo I used once and never again because it made tears stream from my eyes for an hour, long after the poodle I'd washed had returned to its owner's lap. I need tears now. Tears will make me look devastated and shattered, two things essential in a grieving best friend.

I unscrew the cap and inhale deeply, the burn in my eyes almost instantaneous. After another whiff, I recap the bottle and exit the car, picking up the pace as I round the back of the house like a concerned friend would upon seeing an ambulance and M.E. van at her bestie's house.

The back door is open but before I can peek in, Rex comes out. He's pale, his eyes wide, shock rendering his mouth slack.

I was right: he's grown to care for Abi.

All the better to reclaim him as my best friend too.

"You don't look so good," I say, stepping onto the porch as he holds up his hand.

"Don't go in there, Jo..." His voice cracks on my name and I reach out to touch him, but he evades me.

"What have you done?" he whispers, glancing over his shoulder, panic-stricken.

"Nothing." My face is blank. I've become good at doing that over the years, hiding my antipathy, my loathing, my resentment.

He opens his mouth to speak, closes it again, shaking his head.

"I need to go in there," I say, pushing past him, and this time he doesn't stop me.

The kitchen is crowded, but I zero in on one thing.

A body bag on a gurney.

I burst into noisy tears, and everyone turns to look at me. One of the paramedics steps toward me and that's when I see something so terrible, so shocking, my legs give way and I crumple to the ground.

Sitting on a chair, staring at me in triumph, is Abi.

# FIFTY-SIX

## ABIGAIL

Jo faints when she sees me. Her eyes roll back in her head and she slumps to one side. Lucky she already collapsed on the floor or she could've done some serious damage. Then again, perhaps a good hard head-knock is what she needs to give her a wake-up call.

I knew the instant she laid eyes on me and had such a dramatic reaction that she'd meant to kill me.

However she doctored the salad, whatever she put in it, had been meant for me.

While a paramedic revives her, the police arrive. I told the medical examiner about my suspicions, and he'd instantly called it in. Now, when Jo wakes up, she'll have an audience to her lunacy. For I have little doubt her psyche will snap like a brittle twig when I push the right buttons.

As if on cue, her eyes open, focusing unsteadily on Cal in the body bag before searching me out.

When she eyeballs me, I smile, and she lets out a god-awful groan that raises the hairs on my arms.

"Who's in the bag?" she yells, and we all jump.

The paramedic looks concerned as he helps her into a standing position. "Miss, I think a sedative will help—"

"Who is it?" She's ignoring everyone, her wild-eyed gaze fixed on me.

"It's Cal," I say, seeing the exact moment her world implodes.

Her face collapses in on itself and she staggers to the nearest chair and falls onto it. Tears are streaming down her face, but it looks like she'd already been crying before she came in. Crocodile tears for me, the friend she thought she'd eliminated.

With everyone staring at her, she regains some composure as I knew she would. Consummate actresses are good like that.

"Did he have an allergic reaction to the cilantro?" she asks, and the medical examiner looks at me and gives a brief nod. He knows Jo has just incriminated herself.

She's too distraught to realize and one of the policemen draws up a chair next to her. "How did you know he ate salad with cilantro in it, miss?"

Jo freezes and for a moment I almost feel sorry for her. Her face flushes that incriminating red it always does when she's flustered and her eyes are darting around like a trapped animal, knowing whatever she does is futile.

"Well, Cal's allergic to cilantro and he's dead, so it makes sense—"

"He's not allergic," I say. "He only said that because he hated your curries."

"That's not true!" She leaps to her feet, startling everyone. "He loved everything I cooked. He loved me! Me, not you. And now you've ruined my life again... I hate you."

She takes a step toward me, but the policeman lays a hand on her shoulder to restrain her.

"You killed him." She's gesticulating wildly at me, her arm

swinging in the air like a pitcher winding up. "You're always putting weird crap in your salads."

She's trying to shift the blame onto me and it's almost laughable, so I reach for a little white lie I know will set her off.

"Aren't you going to ask why Cal was here, Jo, if he's so in love with you?" I pause for dramatic effect. "He was begging to move back in. Said he couldn't stand being at your place, how clingy you are, how pathetic you are in the way you keep throwing yourself at him, how you fawning over him has been going on for years and he's tired of it—"

"It was supposed to be you in that body bag!" she screams. "I should be Robbie's mother, not you. You're ungrateful and undeserving and you stole my life." She thumps her chest. "Cal should've been mine in high school. Robbie should've been my baby. We would've been happy without you around and that's what I thought would happen once I got rid of you..."

She trails off as the police snap handcuffs on her wrists and read her rights.

It's over.

# EPILOGUE

## ABIGAIL

You can get anything on the internet these days.

Including spy cameras so small, nobody can ever spot them.

After I discovered Noah's connection to Jo, I ordered several cameras online. They were easy to install, and I set them up around the house and one on my front and back porch.

So I watched the feed when Jo defaced my garden, egged my house, and placed that dead animal on my doorstep.

I watched Jo pluck leaves from my oleander plant in the backyard, enter my kitchen with the key she's had forever, and dice them finely before adding to my salad.

I watched Cal enter my house despite not being welcome.

But I didn't see him eat the salad as I'd been on a conference call. Cal hates salad and wouldn't touch the stuff usually, so it had been sheer bad luck he'd been so hungry he'd eaten it. If I'd seen him, I would've called and warned him. Instead, Cal had consumed the bowl of death meant for me. Ironic, that if Jo hadn't hated me so much, she wouldn't have murdered the only person in this world she truly loves.

"You okay, Mom?" Rob slides an arm around my shoulder

as we walk back to the car alongside other mourners after the funeral.

"Yeah, thanks, sweetie." I look up at him. "You?"

My tall, handsome son is stoic, but I glimpse the sadness in his eyes. "Dad was a great guy, but we haven't exactly been close the last few years. You'll miss him more than me."

I nod, knowing that in a weird way, I will. Cal may have let me down more times than not over the years, but he stood up when it counted and raised Rob with me. For that, I will always be grateful. "Your father was certainly one of a kind."

I see Mandy comforting Lara by a red sedan. They paid their condolences to me earlier and I reassured Lara her baby would be taken care of, regardless of what's in Cal's will. He would've wanted that, because despite my ex being flakey, he took responsibility for his actions and would've done right by Lara.

Tom's alone in the parking lot, looking lost. He spent hours with Rob and me last night, making sure we ate something, trying to rehash all the good times with Cal. I know how he feels about me. I've known for a while. But I've never encouraged him in any way. I never wanted to complicate our makeshift family but now, with Cal gone and Jo out of my life for good, who knows what may happen? I'm alone and having Tom around will be nice. I need to feel safe again and having an old friend to depend on will provide the stability I need in my topsy-turvy world.

The only person not at the funeral is Jo. She's locked up, awaiting sentencing. No need for a trial when you confess to murder in front of the police.

I'd been astounded when she'd unraveled in my kitchen. I may have deliberately baited her but a small part of me had hoped I'd been wrong, that she wouldn't go to such lengths to get rid of me. So to witness the extent of her hatred, to hear her vitriol... I'll never get over it.

Noah toying with me had hurt, but it had nothing on Jo's disloyalty, her willingness to kill to get what she wanted. It'll haunt me for the rest of my life.

I haven't visited her yet. Not because I'm caught up in grieving Cal, but because I want to let her stew. It's petty of me, I know, but if I hadn't installed those cameras, I'd be the one lying in the ground right now and Rob wouldn't have a mother. I would've eaten the salad and I wouldn't have had proof for the police. I know now that Jo wouldn't have stopped—she would've continued her vendetta against me and wouldn't have quit until she got what she wanted.

My life.

We stop at the car and I snuggle into my son. "Sweetheart, can you do me a favor?"

"Anything, Mom."

"The wake doesn't start for half an hour, but if I'm a few minutes late, just make sure everyone's glasses are filled and all the food from the fridge is on the table, okay?"

"Sure. Where are you going?"

"Just something I have to do." I touch his cheek, before enveloping him in a hug. "Love you, Rob."

"Love you too, Mom." He presses a kiss to the top of my head and squeezes me tight.

We hold each other for a while because I know by the fierceness of his hug my son needs it. He may be tough on the outside, but I know he's hurting. Cal may have been an absentee father for most of Rob's teen years but he'd been around in the younger years when it counted and I love him for that.

I'll miss Cal. He stood by me when not many guys would've and he tried his best, even if it wasn't good enough. He certainly didn't deserve to die. It's a nice touch that Rob wants to honor his father by auctioning off Cal's most sought-after photographs and donating the proceeds to women's mental health. Losing his dad has been tough but it's Jo he's really grieving for. I heard him crying in his room last night and when I peeked in, he'd been staring at a picture of him and Jo taken at a fair. It had sat on his bedside table for years and I know he'd been torn about taking it to college, not wanting to appear too sentimental to his roommate by having personal pics around.

When I'd gone in to comfort him, he'd flung the photo away and the edge of the wooden frame had chipped. I'd hugged him and asked if he wanted to talk about it, but he didn't, and later, I saw him pick up that photo and throw it in the trash.

I know we'll discuss Jo eventually and because he loves her, I won't speak too badly of her. Besides, what can I say? She's obviously nuts and her actions speak louder than words.

When Rob releases me, I ask, "Do you want me to drop you home?"

He shakes his head. "I'd rather walk. See you later."

I watch my son lope away, looking way too mature in a black suit. He's staying for a few days before heading back to college and I intend on making the most of our time together. It'll be weird when he heads back this time, as I'll be more alone than ever.

No Noah, who, despite his initial intentions to catfish me, actually had a conscience. He didn't have to confess the truth to me and while I'm not sure if I'm being gullible in believing he had real feelings for me, I choose to accept his version of the truth. He's promised to leave me alone, because I threatened to tell the police about his involvement in Jo's catfishing scheme if he doesn't, and I hate to admit that I miss him.

And I won't have Jo in my life anymore.

Despite everything that's happened, I'll miss her most of all.

She's been by my side for many years, and if she hates me as much as she's demonstrated lately, that must've killed her.

I have to confront her. For closure.

When I reach the police station I go through a rigmarole before being taken through to her holding cell. I requested a room but apparently crime is high in Fort Chester at the moment and they don't have one available, so I have to see my best friend behind bars. It's where she belongs but it doesn't stop my chest aching when I see her, slouched on an iron bench attached to the wall, her gray jumpsuit making her look pale and washed out. Her hair is lank, her shoulders slumped, but when she catches sight of me, she leaps to her feet, her eyes blazing hatred.

"What are you doing here?" she hisses, baring her teeth like a feral cat.

"We've been friends a long time, Jo. Do you think I'd leave you in here to rot?"

My genuine answer catches her off guard. "After what I've done, yes."

"We all make mistakes." I shrug. "I thought you'd forgiven me for mine. Turns out, not so much. How long have you hated me?"

"Since the day you told me you slept with Cal." There's no hesitation and her eyes have turned mean again. "The one person I thought I could trust. I thought I could never forgive you but then Robbie came along and you asked me to be godmother and I loved being a part of his life. So I pretended to care about you but it hurt, seeing you with Cal, so I did small stuff at first. Gave you food poisoning. Tinkered with your car. But I couldn't risk Cal finding out so I backed off."

I'm shocked. I remember those incidents. She's been undermining me that long?

"Then I grew a conscience and really tried to move on. I

deluded myself into thinking I wanted Tom, but deep down it's Cal." She shrugs. "It's always been Cal."

"So you've been... what? Biding your time? Ingratiating your way into our lives, pretending to love Rob, while plotting my downfall like some ridiculous villain?"

"Robbie means the world to me, I didn't have to pretend. He should've been mine, and would've been, if you hadn't lied yet again." She flushes an ugly puce. "You told me Cal was allergic to cilantro. I never would've doctored that salad if there'd been any kind of risk to anybody else."

"That's the least of my lies." I feign indifference, watching her squirm with how badly she wants to ask what I'm talking about. "I know you were behind all the vandalism at my place because I installed cameras. Did you spray-paint those threats at your place so I wouldn't be suspicious?"

She slow claps. "Well done. Now what did you mean about more lies?"

I ignore her question. It's childish, making her wait, but when I leave, I want her to ruminate at length about what I've said.

"Lara sends her regards, by the way. It's pretty cool that Rob's going to have a half-brother or sister, don't you think?"

For a moment I think she's going to faint again but then I realize she's so furious it appears like her eyes are rolling back in her head. "She's lying, Cal told me."

"Cal would say anything to make his life easier and lately, that's been so he could stay with you. He lied about Tom and me being involved, perhaps because he knew how you felt about him and thought it would drive a wedge between us. And he lied about Lara, because she's definitely pregnant and Cal knew." I snap my fingers. "Wake up, Jo. He used you. He never loved you, no matter how delusional you are in believing that. Why do you think he was at my place when he ate that salad? He was waiting for another chance to beg me to take him back."

She flies at the bars fast and slams against them so hard, I jump back. "You're lying."

"According to you, that's all I do, but think about it. What's the point now? He's gone."

She breaks down then, tears leaking from her eyes and trickling down her face, her head drooping. I pity her, but not enough to stop.

"That night I slept with Cal at his party, I knew what I was doing."

Her head snaps up. "What do you mean? You told me you were drunk and had no recollection."

"I lied." I shrug and walk a few steps before spinning back to face her. "When you left the party, I started talking with Lara. She told me how you fibbed about me not wanting her in our friendship group, how you ostracized her. I was mad. So I deliberately targeted Cal."

She's rigid, her hands clenched into fists, her back ramrod straight. "You went after him, knowing how I felt?"

I nod. "Yeah. My bad."

She grips the bars so tight her knuckles pop, her furious face pressing against the steel. "I hate you."

"Now, now, is that any way for best friends to talk to one another?" I tsk-tsk. "And for the record, I knew about Noah a week after you pushed us together and, in the end, he chose me over you too."

I know she'll hate my gloating smile as much as my next words. "It must hurt, Jo, having the two guys closest to you choose me over you every time. And Tom's wanted me for ages too, the only reason nothing's happened yet is because I have a conscience, unlike you. I guess it looks like you screwed up there also."

Taunting her isn't making me feel better but I can't get over how much she must hate me to want me dead, so I hit her where it hurts most, playing on her biggest insecurity.

"How does it feel, knowing every guy you've ever loved has chosen me over you?"

She screams and lunges for me, her arms flailing through the bars. I raise my hand in a wave as a guard comes rushing in. The last glimpse of my best friend I have is of her banging her head against the bars so hard her eyebrow splits and blood pours down her face as she screams profanities about what she'd like to do to me.

Maybe Jo's right and I'm a bad person, because I do lie.

I never targeted Cal the night of his party. I did talk to Lara and was appalled by Jo's possessiveness, but that had little to do with me getting together with Cal. We were just two kids with the hots for each other that got drunk and hooked up.

But the other version will torture Jo a lot more and after what she's put me through, she deserves it.

# A LETTER FROM NICOLA

Dear reader,

I want to say a huge thank you for choosing to read *The Ex Between Us*. If you enjoyed it, and want to keep up to date with my latest releases, just sign up at the following link. Your email address will never be shared and you can unsubscribe at any time.

*www.bookouture.com/nicola-marsh*

I appreciate you taking the time to read my book. As an avid reader myself who enjoys getting whisked away in imaginary scenarios, I'm incredibly humbled to be able to provide that same escapism experience to others. Like my other domestic suspense novels, this one flew from my fingertips in a crazy eighteen days. I absolutely love taking the glimmer of an idea and turning it into a convoluted plot. Fun!

I hope you loved *The Ex Between Us* and, if you did, I'd be very grateful if you could write a review. I'd love to hear what you think, and it makes such a difference helping new readers to discover my books for the first time. I love hearing from my readers—you can get in touch on my Facebook page, Instagram, TikTok, Twitter, Goodreads, and my website.

Thanks,
Nicola

# KEEP IN TOUCH WITH NICOLA

www.nicolamarsh.com

facebook.com/NicolaMarshAuthor

twitter.com/NicolaMarsh

instagram.com/nicolamarshauthor

# ACKNOWLEDGMENTS

Writing is such a solitary profession, and it takes a team to bring a book to life. Many thanks to the following who made this happen:

Laura Deacon, my fabulous editor who brainstormed ideas with me, then told me to run with the one that spoke to me the most. It's incredibly exciting to work with someone who has the same vision and can see the story unfold. It's been a blast working with you on this book, Laura.

Noelle Holton, my publicist, who champions every book tirelessly.

Jane Eastgate, for her keen copyediting eye.

Jane Donovan, for proof editing.

The entire Bookouture team, for publishing my domestic thrillers and working to ensure every book gets into as many hands as possible.

Peggy Burn, a reader in Your Book Escape on Facebook (where I'm a founding author.) When I put the call out for ways to "accidentally on purpose" dispose of someone, I had so many great ideas provided by enthusiastic readers, but I ran with Peggy's. It fitted my plot perfectly!

My oldest friend, Jen Maciel, who I've known since Prep. I'm very thankful we don't have an ex between us (LOL!) and your thoughtfulness in dropping over gourmet charcuterie products while I was hunkered down is truly appreciated.

My darling boys, everything's for you, as always.

Martin, for making me laugh every day (especially when you try to come up with plots!).

Soraya Lane and Natalie Anderson, my rocks in this topsy-turvy industry and beyond.

Mum and Dad, who love me unconditionally.

For the librarians, bloggers, reviewers, bookstores, bookstagrammers, and booktokers who take the time to read my books and spread the love.

And to my loyal readers who buy my books. I appreciate you all, as every book you purchase enables me to keep writing more books. Thank you!

Printed in Great Britain
by Amazon

40167308R00179